The Transcendence of Marcianna

THIEF OF DESTINY DUOLOGY BOOK 2

ISABELLE MARKUS

First edition: ISBN 978-1-7372699-3-9 (Paperback)

978-1-7372699-2-2 (Ebook)

Cover design by L1graphics

Published by Labyrinth Moon Press LLC

"Do not feel lonely, the entire universe is inside you." ~ Rumi

This book is dedicated to my family. And to all those brave enough to love fiercely and unconditionally, with the entirety of their heart . . . and include themselves in that love.

I own you! You are my slave, and you do what I command. Now, take Sarah and go!

Fighting back tears, I watched the man in possession of my whole heart sail away. My hurtful words, demanding his obedience, throwing his servitude in his face, had been my parting gift.

I was trapped once again in this memory from over two thousand years ago, reliving my last day of life as Razma. The people from this memory—from this lifetime of mine—were long dead, yet the pain was forever etched within my spirit.

Taking in a deep breath, I fumbled with errant strands of my bright red hair, shoving them within the tightly bound plaits as viciously as I tried to shove the terrible last moments with Kynan out of my mind.

A heavy hand descended on my shoulder as my second in command, Mordos, a mountain of a man, grunted. "They'll be upon us soon. What do you need us to do?"

I couldn't think; though it had been hours since I'd sent my lover away, my mind still begged, *Kynan, Kynan, my love, don't leave me.*

Begging, even though I forced him away. But protecting Sarah was more important than my heart. It was my responsibility to guide this critical moment of destiny forward as decreed by the One Spirit.

Destiny writes our book, and we cannot, will not, veer from the story, I reminded myself.

I couldn't let my warriors see me distracted, not with them looking to me for instruction. I needed my mind clear. Focused.

I was still vulnerable, transitioning to my awakened state two moon cycles ago, only recently summoning my sisters to help me locate Sarah, the keeper of humanity's destiny. When we'd cleared Roman-occupied lands, I'd sent one sister with Sarah and Kynan in hopes her fledgling powers could help guide the rickety vessel across the sea. The other sister now stood by my side, light brown eyes unwavering from my face, her silent plea for direction mirroring that of my men.

Squaring my shoulders, I glanced at our surroundings, looking for advantages in our fight. If I could just stop feeling sorry for myself, I could focus on strategy. At least my mind was now free of the constant fear for Kynan's safety.

I'd known there'd be no clean death for the one who'd orchestrated the Roman's humiliation, freeing a group of people to be slaughtered in the Colosseum in broad daylight and in plain view of the Romans. I'd convinced my brother, the ruler of the Roxalani tribe of Sarmatia, that this bold attack would further our strategy to destabilize Rome.

Yet it was Kynan that took the blame.

My people had fought hard against the encroaching Roman empire, rallying together tribes threatened by this plague of conquerors. We provided our skill in strategic combat to strengthen our allies' forces, but some of these foreign tribes weren't used to seeing a woman leading men. They'd sneered at my small size, calling me weak, saying I should return to tend my child. It had been easier for Kynan to appear as the leader of our warriors rather than to continuously fight through the same male stubbornness and pride.

A smile haunted my lips as I remembered how furious Kynan had been at any rejection of me—trying to force these men to see me as a worthy warrior—convincing them of my talent in battle strategy. In the end, he'd given in, playing the role I requested of him, saying my commands as if they'd come from him.

But it was this charade that had put him in danger after we'd freed Sarah and her mother from the Colosseum. For his own good, and the sake of destiny, I had to send him away.

And I'd likely never see him again.

The thought of Kynan brought tears to my eyes. I'd never wanted to cling to a mortal life as much as I did to this one. The need to fight my way back to him ripped at my heart but protecting Sarah and her mother took precedence over my desires.

Glancing at my sister, her straw-colored hair whipping around her face in the strong breeze, I tested my newfound powers, pushing a question into her mind. She abruptly turned in my direction, eyes wide in surprise.

"I don't know what we should do," she replied out loud. "Why do I not have powers as strong as yours if we are sisters?"

I shrugged, which only seemed to aggravate her, her hands fisting by her sides.

"My powers are so weak compared to yours. I feel useless here. Helpless," she said, kicking a stone in my direction.

I should've kept the sweet, supportive sister with me, and sent this one seeped in vinegar on the boat with Kynan, my mind quipped.

I pushed the thought away, guilt tightening my chest at my cruel jest.

In truth, I should've sent them both away to guide the boat to shore and watch over Sarah as she and the others made their homes in a foreign land. My sisters' powers usually manifested much stronger by now. But both had difficulty in their awakenings in this life, and with their limited powers, they didn't belong in the fight against the Romans.

Motioning to Mordos, I pointed out some areas ideal to conceal a simple snare. "Let's set up some traps. Hopefully, that'll give us the advantage in the fight."

He grunted his response and collected the few men left in our party to scour for materials.

Turning back to my sister, I steeled myself against

her anger, noting how her eyes had narrowed as she chewed on her lower lip.

"You go hide," I said.

She shook her head. "I want to help, not hide."

"You can help by hiding, staying safe, and then checking in on us once the fighting is done. Report to my brother what happened in case we fail and are taken as prisoners. Or—"

I didn't finish the sentence. The words "or take my body back home" never leaving my lips. There was no need to terrify her at this moment, any more than she already was.

She didn't move. Putting her hands on her hips, she raised her chin, daring me to make her.

With a drawn-out sigh, I walked over to her and grabbed her arm, dragging her deeper into the woods until I found a small cave. She'd fought me with each step, but despite her height advantage, I was stronger and more determined.

Her eyes darted to the narrow, dark entrance, and she opened her mouth as if to protest, but I gave her a firm shove. "Go in and stay silent. Do not come out until you're sure the Roman threat is gone."

Grunting in satisfaction when she finally obeyed me, I headed back to the camp, anxiety making my palms sweat. We didn't have much time. Soon our enemy would be upon us, and we'd narrowly escaped our last encounter.

I choked back bile as I remembered that moment, for it was there I saw the leader of the Roman forces.

Tarquin, my husband, the father of my son, who

I'd thought long dead, who hated Rome with passion, was now a Centurion. His eyes under his iron helmet had been unnaturally cruel as he confronted me. In that moment, I'd known he was lost to me, taken by demons, transformed into one of them.

I shuddered at the memory, biting my lip to force back the scream of rage as guilt gnawed at me over the injustice befalling Tarquin. Had I done something to signal my identity to the demons even before my awakening? Is this why they targeted Tarquin?

Quickening my pace to get back to my men, my toe caught on a tree root, and I stumbled hard, skidding onto my stomach. All the pain buried deep within me suddenly ripped out from my control and I slammed my fists into the ground, beating it as if the fault of my predicament lay with the dirt and leaves: Tarquin taken from his son and transformed into a monster, my sisters awakened but weak in their power, and the love I've yearned for finally within my grasp and I had to let it go.

It wasn't fair . . . none of it was fair.

My energy spent, I rested my forehead on the cool earth, tears stinging the cuts on my hands as I covered my face.

The stillness of the forest caught my ear, the strangeness of it unsettling—not one bird chirped, not one animal rustled in the underbrush. A blanket of thick silence engulfed the forest, as if the creatures feared to make a sound.

Scrambling to my feet, I ran as fast as I could back to our small encampment, pushing my muscles to their limits. As it came into view, my nostrils flared, catching the metallic scent of blood. I froze in my tracks.

My men were dead. All of them. Even Mordos.

Roman soldiers lay next to my fallen warriors, their red woolen tunics mixing with the blood and guts of my beloved people. I was grateful to my warriors. They had not run away or surrendered but fought hard to the end, taking out many soldiers before falling.

There amongst the dead and dying stood Tarquin. I couldn't stop the strangled scream escaping at the sight of him. Covering my mouth with my hand, I watched his eyes focus on me like a predator, his strides long as he stepped over the mangled bodies, closing the gap between us.

My breath came in frantic gulps. I focused, using my power to watch the demon within him swirling, its smoky darkness wrapping around the remaining light of Tarquin. Though faceless, the creature taunted me, emitting growls of satisfaction at the agony radiating from me.

"Call *him* now, she's here," the thing controlling Tarquin hissed to a Roman soldier by his side, the emphasis on the word "him" sending my blood racing through my veins. I stared at his companion, the demonic darkness inside the soldier returning my gaze.

Him. Panic overwhelmed me at the word. A spark of recognition flashed deep within my spirit, a mix of fear and anticipation. I didn't know for sure who they spoke of, but I had to get away. I couldn't be here when whoever they called came for me.

My power burst through my fingertips, catching the soldier off guard and knocking him down. Grappling with the demon within him, I prayed to the One Spirit it had not yet managed to summon its master.

Out of the corner of my eye, I saw Tarquin charge at me. I held out my hand, diverting any spare energy through it as I tried to repel him, while still fighting for control over the demon inside the soldier.

I couldn't keep this up. My current body was untrained for the amount of power I'd unleashed. I trembled with exhaustion. At least the remaining human Roman soldiers had fled, screaming, and praying to their gods as they ran.

Cold sweat beaded on my forehead, and I bit the inside of my cheek, using the pain to help me focus on targeting my energy and pulling out the demon.

I dragged the creature out, its tentacles of smoke snatching at its human body. I yanked harder, and the body slid from its reach, its frantic screeching echoing throughout the forest. This demon was still young, and I easily ripped it apart with my light, obliterating it from existence.

Before I could celebrate, Tarquin grabbed me by the throat, slamming me into a tree. He held me there, snarling in my face. I wanted to scream; his eyes were black as night, the pupils dilated to the point of eclipsing the green of his eyes.

I focused on summoning my power once more, my exhausted body shaking, my energy churning within me.

And then I heard him begging—*my* Tarquin, the

father of my child was begging for me to stop him, to stop this creature from destroying me. My hands on his chest sensed his spirit within, his love for me valiantly battling the ancient being controlling him.

I couldn't fight against it. I couldn't destroy the demon inside. Even though I was newly awakened, I recognized the way the darkness had wrapped itself around the remainder of Tarquin's light. It was not repairable. If I pulled out the demon, I'd kill him—kill a man who'd only ever shown me kindness and respect, who had loved me and trusted me above all else even if I couldn't return the love in a manner he craved.

An idea came to me, born from desperation and love. Perhaps I could free him, transform him with my own essence so he'd not die. My mind raced. He had the strength to fight the demon when most would've been destroyed by now. Above all else, he was noble— by nature, a protector. Even with his waning light, I sensed the battle he fought to stay within his body, as if his soul's presence would shield others from this monster.

He deserved to live, and I needed someone to protect me, to keep me safe the next time I'm summoned to preserve destiny. Again, I'd be weak, vulnerable, and so very human. It would be good to have him guide me until I was fully awakened and able to fight.

Not thinking further about the consequences of my decision, I reached my energy into Tarquin's body, entwining it around the darkness, and pulled, my other hand pushing my essence into him.

Tarquin screamed, his sword slicing through my stomach and pinning me to the tree, but I did not stop. His teeth clamped down on my neck, the demon within him now howling, throwing itself desperately into the fight as I laughed with hysteria, blood seeping out my broken body.

Find me again. I pushed that final thought into Tarquin's mind before the demon within him and I vanished.

CHAPTER TWO

I jerked awake, my heart pounding against my ribs, the sound echoing in my ears. For a moment I didn't know where I was. Ray wrenched up next to me, his body tense and ready to fight before realizing we were alone.

"Are you okay?" he asked, peering into my sweat-drenched face.

I was in the cabin, the familiar angles of the bedroom taking shape in the early morning light, not in a forest battling Romans.

Was I okay? Physically I was safe in bed with my husband. But mentally, I wasn't sure. The memories, Razma's memories, were becoming more vivid, forcing their way to the surface through my dreams.

Pushing my tangled auburn hair away from my eyes, I drew in a calming breath, tucking my trembling hands within the folds of my nightshirt.

"Yeah. Just a nightmare," I said, my voice shaky.

Ray wrapped his arms around me, pulling my

body into his and rubbing my back in a calming, circular motion. "What was it about?"

I shrugged my shoulders, burrowing deeper into his chest. Being in Razma's memories was intense, her jumble of emotions—love, fear, duty and regret—still flowing through me.

I didn't want to go into details and relive the dream again, especially not before getting properly caffeinated. Nor did I want to remind Ray of the past hurt I'd dealt him when he was Kynan—I'm sure deep down his soul must remember, but I wasn't sure if for humans these memories ever surfaced. Besides, Ray would not be overly thrilled having to listen about my dreams of Tarquin, murderous or not.

No point dredging any of this up. Not right now anyway, my mind assured me.

The silence stretched on. Ray didn't pressure me to respond, and after a minute, he kissed my forehead and got out of bed.

"Coffee?" he asked, and I nodded enthusiastically.

While he was in the kitchen, I rifled through the clothes someone had packed for me when we'd made our escape from our home. They were thoughtfully picked, and despite my disgust at having a hand in making my immortal companions, I was grateful for them—for Tarquin and James, and even Astrid.

It felt as if we'd been hiding in this cabin for ages. But it was only a week since the demons had found me and my family and we had to flee.

Holding up a sweater Cece had given me for my birthday last year, my thoughts darkened, my inner voice reminding me bitterly that it was also only a week since I'd killed my best friend and hid my family in a new reality to keep them safe.

The thought of Cece triggered my tears, images of her lifeless body invading my mind.

This was my whole week in a nutshell—one minute I'd be selecting an outfit and the next I'd dissolve with anguish because some memory or familiar scent reminded me of my mortal life.

Thinking of Cece made me think about Farah and my guilt grew tenfold. I remembered how easily I'd manipulated her mind, stopping her questions about why our Cece wasn't with us in the cabin. Stopping her worries about Cece, our best friend who was like a sister to us.

It was for Farah's own good, but I still felt like shit doing it.

I tried to force my thoughts away from Farah and Cece, from Cece's grieving family and friends back home, but then my traitorous mind drifted to memories of my own family.

My beautiful children—what I'd give to wake up to their bickering over the TV or to take them to all the activities I'd once dreaded in my human life. I craved to spend time with them again—listen to their chatter, laugh with them, hold them.

I could still feel little Ella's touch on my cheek as she asked me only a few days ago, *Are you sad, Mommy?*

Sad didn't even touch on what I was feeling—I was breaking apart, my heart shattered. Even if I returned to my normal life, would I ever be able to piece myself back together?

"You coming for breakfast?"

I jumped, my hand against my chest as I turned to face Ray standing in the doorway. "Yeah, sorry, let me just finish getting dressed."

A few minutes later, we sat lakeside on Adirondack chairs, bundled up in sweatshirts and blankets, sipping our coffees and eating bagels. The water looked like a pane of glass reflecting the mountains—quiet and tranquil. The last day our family was together was at this lake, the weather unseasonably warm. We spent our final moments in this place, frolicking on the lake's beach.

I sniffled, hearing their laughter echo in my memories.

Ray cleared his throat, interrupting my thoughts. "Do you know when Astrid and James are going to be back?"

"No," I said, gulping down the last of my coffee, hoping my melancholy wouldn't rub off on him. So far, he'd been more focused on figuring out a successful plan of action, and a speedy reunification with our family, than dwelling on the current separation, or the possibility of failure. But though he'd tried to remain positive, I'd see the occasional darkness cloud his features with doubt.

Even now, though he nodded, a slight frown

marred his face. The wait to reunite with my sisters and locate Sarah so we could fulfill destiny was getting to him.

"Don't you hear them in your thoughts?" he pressed.

"Not from this far away, at least not that I'm aware of. It's pretty quiet in here," I said, tapping my head and offering what I hoped to be a light-hearted smile, though it likely looked like a grimace. "I did text James and Astrid to see how picking up my sisters is going but didn't hear back."

He ran his fingers through his hair. "That sounds so weird. A bunch of ancient vampires texting."

Ah, that's right, I'd only revealed to Farah how wrong our vampire hypothesis was. Ray was still under the impression my immortal friends were the blood-sucking undead.

"They're not vampires," I said, my voice sounding overly loud in the morning's stillness, and I lowered my tone. "I made them immortal, from my essence . . . um, energy or spirit . . . I don't know how to explain it."

He stilled for a few heartbeats, the furrow in his brow deepening. I could see the wheels turning in his head as he processed my revelation.

"So, you can make people immortal as well as completely alter reality—send our family and friends into new lives," he said slowly, shaking his head. "Marci, this is so crazy. What are you?"

The *what*, not *who* statement halted my breath for a moment. Was he scared of me? Because I was scared of me—of what I was, of what I'd done, of my unpredictable powers and what I was truly capable of. All of it terrified me.

He caught my eye and must've sensed my fear. Taking my wrist, he pulled me toward him, easing me off my chair and onto his lap.

I clung to him, my face buried in the crook of his neck, breathing in his delicious scent, a hint of soap with an underlying earthy spice. There's always been an element to his scent I've never been able to describe, but it was very much his own. As odd as it was to say, the smell of Ray always soothed me; I felt protected and loved in his strong arms.

"Do you feel different? After your awakening and then the thing with our family?" he asked, his breath caressing my cheek.

I thought about that for a moment, exploring within before replying, "I don't feel different, though the memories and superpowers are weird, to say the least. Astrid made me out to be some cold, heartless bitch, but I still feel like me."

"And you're not cold or heartless," Ray reassured me, giving my waist a light squeeze.

I loved him for these words—for always supporting me, for knowing what to say to ease my fears, even when the world seemed to crumble around us.

Yet after everything that transpired in these last few months, I almost welcomed transforming into this promised unfeeling creature. Maybe then my emotions would not tear at me every second of the day.

Ray hugged me tighter, his fingers absentmindedly

rubbing my scalp. I tried to force myself to relax, take in the lake's peacefulness and enjoy this time with my husband whose soul I'd searched for in each lifetime of mine.

But my mind refused peace, not even allowing a minute of it, ruminating over all the loose threads. It pulled on each thread, fawning over the worries, until it dredged up my fight with Tarquin.

My mind replayed his anger at my plan to keep Ray with us. Over and over, it showed me the disappointment in Tarquin's eyes, his frustration and helplessness palpable.

He'd left me, his last words still echoing in my head: *It's always how you decide it to be.*

And he was right.

During this awakening, it had surprised me how little Tarquin, James, and Astrid knew about me, my immortal existence, and my millennia-long fight with the demons. But with each interaction, it had become clear I'd had a pattern of telling them what to do, information flowing on a need-to-know basis.

I had decided what they needed to know; I had dictated that knowledge. And now we were in a catch-22 of sorts, as my current knowledge was based on what little I'd transferred to them over the years.

This power dynamic was a double-edged sword. On one hand, it allowed me to keep Ray without anyone able to stop me. But on the other, it would've been good to awaken and have more information than just vague comments about sisters, Sarah, and protecting destiny.

I stood up from Ray's lap, unable to keep still and started pacing around the beach, talking to myself.

Dammit, when I need Tarquin the most he's gone!

It'd been days, and yet Tarquin hadn't returned. I couldn't help feeling abandoned and lost without him. Deep inside my aching chest, I knew he'd never done this to me before.

Many times this week, I'd subconsciously reached out to him with my mind. But the second I'd realized what I was doing, I'd stop myself. I couldn't violate him that way after all he'd done for me in this lifetime and over the centuries.

He'd come around. I just needed to be patient, stay out of his head, and give him space.

That last fight with Tarquin over Ray reminded me of the vision I'd had at the time. It was of a man— beautifully wild, with cruel eyes, and a darkness that reached for me.

The thought of this mystery man terrified me. I didn't know who he was, and never got a chance to ask, though I doubted anyone in my little party would know, either.

I suspected this man was the *him* on the lips of demons each time they caught up with me; in my dream, Tarquin commanded the other demon-possessed soldier to summon *him* as did Alastor when he held me captive in the basement. And each time, a visceral fear crawled through my belly, urging me to flee.

My brain whirled, jumping from thought to thought, from memory to memory, barely letting me finish one line of thinking before starting a new one. Recalling Alastor and my captivity in his basement reminded me of another mystery.

The demons thought I stole something from them.

What could it be? An object? Or maybe it was Sarah? Technically, I did steal her in Razma's time. But then, how could I give her back? It didn't make sense. None of it made sense.

I had so many questions and they all tangled together. The more I tried to understand, the more frustrated I became, pissed at my past life self for being so goddamn secretive with her companions.

Why the hell would I've made creatures to help me along on my journey and then tell them diddly squat? Now I had more questions than answers, and I wanted to scream.

Ray watched me pace for a while before breaking into my thoughts, "I know it sucks to just wait here and do nothing, but you need to relax. Who knows what's heading our way and you can't be teetering on the edge already."

I turned, catching his gaze and holding it as I pursed my lips. He returned it steadily, unfazed by my silent threat, instead chiding, "Stop looking at me like that. You know I'm right. You're just too stubborn to admit it."

Stubborn! God, this man had no sense of self-preservation, antagonizing me in this state. It was on brand though. He went into a den of demons to save me and our daughter and then demanded to stay with me, to protect me—a supernatural creature—in my fight with monsters that would rip him to pieces.

And he had the audacity to call me stubborn when, clearly, he was the embodiment of a stubborn ass.

I was about to unload my pent-up aggravation on him when an anxious feeling wrapped itself around me. Something wasn't right. It was like my whole reality tilted, but I didn't know why.

My anger dissipating, I sat down on the grass, examining the feeling, realizing the anxiety didn't belong to me; it was distinct from my own emotions, though familiar in origin.

It kind of felt like James.

I reached out tentatively with my mind. *James, are you nearby?*

A grunt in reply bounced around in my head, making me put my fingers to my temples. Out of the corner of my eye, I saw Ray approach, a look of confusion tightening his features.

Can you be more specific? Where are you? What's wrong? I demanded.

At the cabin. He paused, before adding, *In front of the cabin to be specific.*

I pushed past Ray, running toward the cabin at full speed.

"What's wrong? Where are you going?" Ray asked, jogging to catch up with me.

"Driveway. I don't know what's wrong, but it's James," I yelled over my shoulder.

Rounding the corner of the cabin, we found James

standing by his car, his expression unreadable, though his brow wrinkled slightly at the sight of Ray.

"What's going on? Are you okay?" I asked, relieved to see him standing unharmed in the driveway.

He gestured toward the trunk, and I made my way to the back of the car. Putting my hand on the metal, I looked at James, raising my eyebrows in a silent question.

When no clarification came my way, I prompted, "What is it?"

"Open it," he said.

Pressing the button and stepping back, I wasn't sure what I'd find. Terrified hazel eyes met mine.

"Is that Armina?" I asked, my horror growing at the sight of her gagged lips and bound wrists and ankles. "Why is she tied up in your trunk? Is this normally how you escort my sisters to me?"

James rolled his eyes. "Obviously not. When I arrived, she had no clue who she was, who I am, and didn't take kindly to my suggestion she come with me. Fought me like crazy and I had to restrain her. I did the best I could without hurting her."

"Why didn't you reply to my texts?" I demanded.

"Clearly I was busy," he grumbled, pointing at the trunk.

My hands flew to my chest to steady my erratic heartbeat as panicked thoughts ran laps around my mind. "Oh shit! Did you hear from Astrid? She didn't reply either."

He nodded. "Similar situation."

If the all-patient, saintly James brought back

Armina in his trunk, I was terrified to see how Astrid was going to transport Harlow, who from my vision appeared to be a bratty teenager.

Oh my God! What's happening? Why are they not awakened? My brain was alight with questions, but I really needed to shut it up so I could focus.

I couldn't be polite anymore and respect boundaries. Not now.

Reaching for Tarquin with my mind, I yelled into the ether, *Come back to us, now. Wherever the hell you are, you need to be here. We have a problem!*

CHAPTER THREE

Staring at the terrified woman in James's trunk, my mind raced in several directions. I didn't know what to think.

Had this happened before? From the amount of worry coloring James's energy, I'd have to guess no. But it shouldn't be surprising. Even my dream from last night suggested my sisters were getting less powerful with each awakening—and that had been many awakenings ago.

"Should we bring her inside?" Ray asked, looking from me to James.

James didn't reply, tilting his head in my direction.

Guess it was my decision.

Lifting my eyes skyward, annoyance laced my voice as I replied, "Of course we should. We can't just close the trunk on her."

James set his jaw and reached for Armina, but recoiled when she screamed, the gag muffling it. Her bound legs kicked out to fight him off.

"Will you talk to her? I'll likely hurt her if I try to haul her off to the cabin in this state."

I sighed, knowing he was probably right, but not sure what I should say. The truth sounded ridiculous: Hey lady, I'm your sister and we're both supernatural creatures that fight demons. We just have to find a person named Sarah, help her fulfill her destiny, and then we'll be on our merry way back to our old lives.

I snorted softly at my stupid joke, drawing frowns of confusion from both Ray and James.

"I was just thinking," I muttered, pushing past them to get a better look at my so-called sister.

After a long pause of eyeballing the brunette in the trunk, I finally said, "Hi, I'm Marci. Are you Armina? Is that your name?"

She nodded, tears flowing down her face, a wild, desperate look filling her huge eyes.

"Listen, we mean you no harm." I used my best soothing pediatrician voice. "Can we just go inside and talk for a bit?"

She shook her head violently, hitting it on the side of the trunk, and raised her legs as if to kick again.

"So, you just wanna hang out here in a trunk all tied up and gagged?"

She didn't respond.

This wasn't working. I was getting nowhere trying to reason with a kidnapped, hysterical woman in a trunk. At least not reasoning in the normal, human way.

I needed to try a different approach.

Reaching out with my mind, I asked, *Armina? Can you hear me? I'm Marci and these are my friends. We mean you no harm. We just want to take you inside and talk. Get you more comfortable.*

She stopped breathing, her eyes wide. I could hear her inner dialogue going a mile a minute, spurred by sheer terror.

"Please breathe," I instructed out loud.

She started moving her mouth, the gag muffling her words. I pulled the cloth out, sensing both Ray and James tense next to me, likely anticipating an onslaught of screaming.

But she only whispered, "How?"

Relief eased my tight muscles, and I smiled at her. "Can we get you inside and then we'll tell you what we know?"

She slowly nodded, but then made a sound of panic when James approached her.

Putting a restraining hand on his chest, I reached into the trunk to help Armina out myself. Her cramped legs wobbled like that of a newborn calf as soon as they hit the asphalt, and I struggled to keep her upright.

Ray jumped in to help steady us, and together we made our way toward the stairs of the cabin.

Looking over my shoulder, I realized James was not following us.

"Can you take her inside?" I asked Ray, slipping out of Armina's grasp.

Armina's eyes widened with panic, and her hands fumbled to grab hold of me again.

"I'll join you in a minute," I assured her, giving her arm a gentle pat.

With a brisk nod, Ray gripped my sister firmly, getting her back on the path to the cabin as he told her all about the beverages we had inside.

Walking back to James, I noted his usual jovial demeanor nowhere to be found. His dark amber complexion was ashen, and a shadow dulled his usually mischievous eyes.

"Are you okay?" I asked, tentatively touching his arm.

"She was scared of me," he said, rubbing his forehead.

"That's because she didn't know who you were. She probably thought you were a kidnapper planning to hold her for ransom or some other nonsense. Did you expect her to welcome you with open arms?"

"They're never scared of me. There's always some level of recognition." He shook his head, his frown deepening. "It's not right."

His words echoed my doubt and concern, and I shivered, still sensing traces of his feelings. Things were not going to plan, and it was becoming more evident we were in uncharted territory, the previous awakenings no longer a guiding light.

As if seeing his worry reflected in my eyes, James forced a smile. Throwing his arm around my shoulder, he masked his worry with exaggerated good humor and pulled me closer. I half expected to get a noogie from him on my head. We walked toward the cabin, and I couldn't help but lean into him, welcoming the change in mood even though I knew he was forcing it. I'd grown used to James's affectionate nature in this short time, and my feelings of kinship with him had strengthened after my awakening. I wanted more than anything to bask in the comfort he provided, believing everything was going to be all right.

"Where's Tarquin?" he asked, looking around as if expecting him to pop out from behind a bush. "And why is Ray still here?"

My mood soured at the mention of Tarquin.

"I don't know where Tarquin is," I snipped before biting back my annoyance. "He left when I told him Ray was staying with us. But I did try to . . . um . . . call him—you know, with my mind—when you arrived."

James's step faltered ever so slightly, but he didn't say anything, nodding as if this was an expected answer. I held my tongue. Honestly, I should've been given an award for doing so as it went against every instinct I possessed.

Stepping into the cabin, we found Ray and Armina sitting at the table having a cup of coffee, chatting as if all was right with the world. I sat down next to Ray, while James hung back to the periphery of Armina's vision, likely not wanting to upset her more with his presence.

"So, what are you two discussing?" I asked, trying to sound all nonchalant but failing.

Ray smiled, taking my hand in his. "We're just talking about work and family. We did touch upon our current predicament, though I haven't told her much, since I hardly know anything. Just said you're my wife, James is your friend, and we may be in some sort of danger."

He'd wisely omitted the supernatural bits, maybe scared she'd run out the backdoor in hysterics if she learned those details without James and me for backup.

"Great!" I exclaimed with unnecessary levels of enthusiasm.

God, I'm a bad actress.

I worried my lower lip, debating what to say next when we were still one sister short.

Armina interrupted my thoughts. "Is that really all that there's to it?" Her tone was professional and calm. "Because if so, there are so many better ways of communicating this to a person than kidnapping them from their home and stuffing them into the car's trunk. I'll have you know I'm a lawyer."

"Yes, we're aware you are a lawyer," I said dryly. "I'm a pediatrician and my husband is a dentist."

I hesitated before adding, "And I'm also your sister."

"I don't have a—"

I held up my hand. "Not by blood. You're my sister in . . . um . . . spirit."

That sounded far more lame spoken out loud than it did in my head. I tried again. "Inside us are these ancient beings that fight evil in this world; evil that wishes to destroy the destiny of humankind. And in times of crisis, the ancient beings awake."

That wasn't any better. My words now sounded

ridiculous, even to me, and I was living them. I could only imagine what Armina thought, her face frozen as she looked from me to Ray, who'd tightened his grip on my hand under the table.

She laughed, hard, really hard. "Oh my God, you're insane."

"Well, I guess you're insane right along with us, since I *know* you heard my voice in your head when you were in the trunk."

That shut her up promptly, her lips pressing firmly together.

"That's what I thought," I said with a smirk.

My smugness was short-lived.

The door opened behind me, and Armina's eyes widened, staring over my shoulder, transfixed. I didn't have to turn around to know Tarquin had finally arrived. I could feel him like a salve on my wounded soul, releasing tension from my anxious body.

He walked over to the table, standing directly behind me. Ray released my hand and turned to look up at him, but I stubbornly refused to acknowledge Tarquin's presence. Part of me wanted to punish him for his abandonment, part of me wanted to burst into tears with relief that he was back by my side.

I shifted my eyes away from Armina's frozen gaze, catching James jutting out his chin repeatedly at me, a motion that screamed "look behind you".

Subtle. I tossed that sarcastic comment at him with my mind. With a mental sigh I realized I'd need to acknowledge the dark-haired, green-eyed elephant in the room to end the awkwardness.

"You've decided to return," I said, still refusing to look directly at him, though I tilted my head over my shoulder, staring at his shoes.

"You did call for me—saying I was needed. I'm assuming this is the problem?" James and Ray nodded, and I deduced he had gestured at Armina.

"Of course," I snapped, counting to three in my head hoping to sound more blasé and less petulant as I added, "Armina doesn't know who she is or who we are."

"Well, that's a first," he replied.

A light touch on my elbow finally caused me to relent, and I turned around. Looking up into his eyes, my heart lurched at the sight of his face—the one constant in the past two thousand years of awakenings. Realization of how deep my worry had been that I'd somehow lost him, choked me, and I swallowed repeatedly.

Gulping like a fish out of water, I felt Ray watching me as I stared up at Tarquin. Leave it to me to take awkwardness to a whole new level when my intent was to diffuse it.

Breaking eye contact, I asked, "What can we do to fix this? To make them remember?"

"Don't worry, we'll put our heads together and figure out a solution. But first I'd like to catch up as to what I missed while away." Tarquin turned to face Armina, and with a slight bow, he said. "Apologies for a moment, Armina, while we step away."

Gently pulling me up, he nudged me to walk to the

other side of the cabin's living room. I tossed an apologetic look at my sister.

Ray stood up to follow, but Tarquin cleared his throat. "Maybe you should stay with Armina to keep her comfortable."

Oh, hell no. Not this again.

Shaking my head, I rose to my tiptoes and hissed in Tarquin's ear. "No, he stays with us. He's spoken to her alone and may have some insight into your questions. Besides, he's part of this team," I said, pointing to Tarquin, James, Ray, and me.

Tarquin looked like he'd protest, and I braced myself for an argument, but none came. Pulling away, he replied simply, "As you wish."

Settling into the far corner of the cabin, we compared notes on our interactions with Armina, filling Tarquin in on all he missed while off sulking. James went over the details of his initial encounter with her and then his arrival here, while I described our unidirectional telepathic chit-chat. Ray chimed in about his talk with her once inside the cabin, filling in some details about her personal life—no significant other, distant relationships with family, married to work.

My heart broke as he spoke. Armina seemed to have no one that cared about her. No wonder in my vision she'd appeared so lonely, standing in the dark watching the Manhattan skyline.

Listening to Ray speak, I smiled at how much he'd gleaned from Armina in such a short conversation. It made me realize how lucky I was to have someone so attuned to others, so willing to truly listen.

As impressed as I was with Ray, I noticed Tarquin was not, avoiding eye contact with him, even when spoken to directly.

God, we really had to get over this horrible, uneasy tension. Logically, I knew it would take time for us to gel as a team, especially given Tarquin's reaction to Ray staying with us, but emotionally, I was over it, impatient to move on.

Speaking of *over it*, Armina was likely over sitting on her butt while we stood here talking about her. Her nails clicked rhythmically on the table, and I felt her eyes boring into the back of my skull.

We needed to wrap this up. "Okay, what are we doing here, guys? It's getting late. Should we at least feed her or something?"

I hoped someone had a plan of action as my mind was blank, not able to think past having a complete unit of fully operational sisters. "Does anyone even know where the hell Astrid is?"

James glanced at his phone as if hoping the answer would materialize, though I'd seen him check it every few minutes. "I thought Astrid would be here first. Sure, she had to drive farther than me to get to Harlow. But at least her directions were clear—a sorority house in Savannah. I practically had to search around the entire Upper East Side for a goddamn lawyer. You know how many there are there, right?"

His wounded expression was almost comical, and I bit my lip not to laugh. I was about to apologize for giving him such vague instructions when the door to the cabin slammed open, startling a scream out of Armina. She covered her mouth, her chest rapidly rising and falling as she gaped.

Astrid stood in the doorway, her blonde hair billowing in the breeze, a pissed-off look etched on her face. She looked every inch the Viking she used to be.

In her arms, she clutched the lifeless form of a black-haired girl.

My stomach dropped, and my mind freaked out. *Why did we send this impatient, ruthless bitch to fetch a teenager? Is my sister dead?*

CHAPTER FOUR

"Oh God, Astrid, what the hell did you do?" I cried out, my hand clutching my throat.

Astrid held my gaze as she strode purposefully to the table, dumping the girl on top of it. The sharp movement caused Harlow's arm to roll away from her body, brushing against Armina's clasped hands. Armina whimpered at the touch, her eyes glued to the unconscious girl in front of her.

Both sisters looked as pale as corpses.

"Relax, princess, I just drugged her," Astrid replied.

I exhaled in relief, my heart settling back into its normal rhythm. "Let me guess: she wasn't awakened, didn't know who you were, and fought you tooth and nail."

"Ah, it's like you were there." Astrid rolled her eyes before her gaze latched onto Ray. Her eyes narrowed, and she put her hands on her hips. "What's he doing here?"

"He stayed with us to help," I replied, lifting my chin. "Why the drugging?" I added, hoping to distract her from asking any more questions about Ray.

"Well, she was a feisty and punchy little girl. It was either knock her out with my fists, or gently ease her into slumber with some drugs," she replied, her lips pursed in dissatisfaction as she examined her chipped manicure. "I really wanted to do the former. It would've given me great pleasure. But then I thought you'd not be pleased with the outcome."

"You'd be correct," I said, my tone dripping in snark. "But I meant why didn't you use your glamour or hypnosis or whatever you call it?"

Astrid stared at me as if I had grown a second head. "Because it doesn't work on us, and it certainly doesn't work on you and your sisters. Are you sure you've awakened? Shouldn't your memories be restored at this point?"

My face flushed at her question. "I'm very much awake and I have my memories. I just have to pick and choose what to remember," I said tersely. "Imagine a flood of thousands upon thousands of years of memories. I'd love to see how you'd react."

I stared her down for a minute, but she shrugged and walked away. God, she could be the most infuriating creature.

Turning my attention to Harlow, I went to work examining her, my physician's instincts taking over. Relief steadied my hands as I felt her slow but strong pulse, observing her shallow breaths with the rise and fall of her chest.

Armina's eyes met mine, her hands fisted and white-knuckled on the table, her gaze showing her fear.

What the hell are we doing here? My internally whispered frustration reverberated within my skull, the noise amplifying, startling me with its intensity. I pressed my fingers to my temples, soothing the growing pain within my head.

It was a valid question. How would we find Sarah and fulfill destiny if my sisters couldn't remember who they were? I needed them to succeed; I couldn't do this without them. Yet there wasn't even a glimmer of recognition in Armina's hazel eyes.

Tarquin came to my side, placing a hand gently on my shoulder as he whispered in my ear, "It will all be all right. We've faced many challenges. This is just one more."

I nodded, looking up at him sheepishly, my anger with him fading away. "Did I scream my question in your mind as well?"

He gave my shoulder a squeeze, and I sighed. "You'd think at this moment of my awakening I'd be able to know when I'm talking to you and when I'm talking to myself."

"You've always had this habit, Marcianna. Ever since I became connected to you, you've been talking in my mind. I'd like to think it's because you're comfortable with me." He gave me a small smile and lifted Harlow into his arms as if she was no more than a feather. But before he could leave, I reached out and touched his arm. "Thank you for coming back. I was worried you wouldn't."

"There's nothing you could do or say that would make me abandon you." His words were like a balm, soothing my frayed nerves, and I watched him carry Harlow down the narrow hallway into the bedroom adjoining mine.

"You okay?"

I jumped almost a foot into the air, my hand clutching at my chest as I turned to face Ray standing behind me.

"Yeah, sorry. I didn't hear you approach," I choked out, my cheeks flushed with embarrassment.

Ray frowned slightly, and for a moment, looked like he wanted to say something. He must've thought better of it though, instead directing his attention to Armina, asking her if she wanted something to eat. She nodded enthusiastically and latched onto his arm as if he were the only sane one in this cabin—which he was—and they left for the kitchen.

I plopped down onto a dining room chair. My muscles ached from today's tensions courtesy of the adrenaline spikes throughout the day. Leaning my elbows on the table, I rested my chin on my folded hands and observed my remaining companions.

James and Astrid stood in the cabin's corner, speaking in hushed voices, gesturing aggressively. I couldn't quite make out what they were saying, though they were likely comparing war stories of how they had to drag my uncooperative sisters to me. But every few minutes, James would steal a glance in my direction and frown.

Gnawing on my lower lip as I watched them, worry snaked into my belly. Was it me? Had I done, or maybe not done something, to keep Armina and Harlow dormant inside their human bodies?

Yes. Yes, it is you, my internal voice whispered, and deep within my core I knew it was right.

I had to figure this out or risk never seeing my kids again.

After dinner, I went to check on the drugged Harlow and found Armina on the twin bed asleep, curled protectively around her. For such a lonely and prickly personality, Armina seemed to be drawn to our sister. Maybe this was progress?

Trying not to disturb them, I lightly touched Harlow's wrist, reassured by the steady thump of her pulse. As I backed out the door to the sound of their rhythmic breathing, I prayed for a miracle to happen overnight, hoping they'd magically wake up as my sisters, ready to kick some demon ass.

I wandered around the cabin for a few minutes looking for Ray and found him in the kitchen, tinkering with the coffeepot.

His studious expression made me smile, and I wrapped my arms around his waist, kissing him between the shoulder blades.

"Coffee at this hour?" I asked.

He turned around and pulled me into his body, tilting my head up so I could look into his eyes. Holding my gaze for a moment, he kissed my forehead, then my nose, and finally my lips, lingering as if worried there may not be another moment to ourselves now that the house was full.

I smiled when he released my mouth, watching as a slow grin spread over his face, the single dimple in his cheek winking at me, knowing it could always make my heart flutter.

"I thought it might get pretty crazy soon, so trying to stay as alert as possible," he replied, grazing my cheek with his fingers.

I giggled. "Could it get any crazier than this?"

"Nothing would surprise me at this point." He chuckled, kissing the top of my head and drawing me deeper into his arms.

Before I could burrow any further into the warmth of his embrace, the sound of raised voices coming from outside startled us apart.

"What the hell are they fighting about out there?" I asked, peering through the kitchen window.

The darkness made it impossible to see anything. I wasn't even sure which direction the noise was coming from. The lake maybe?

"I'm gonna check it out," I said, heading to the back door which led to the lake.

Ray shook his head and blocked my path. "Do you even know where you're going? It's pitch black out there."

I pushed past him, but he didn't let me get far before he was by my side, following me to the door.

Dear Lord, this man of mine is stubborn.

Pivoting, I put my hand on his chest, forcing him to stop. "No, stay here. Keep an eye on my sisters."

He began to protest, so I added, "Please. Armina seems to trust you and, if Harlow wakes up, she'll need someone to keep her calm."

Closing his eyes for a second, he ran his hand through his dark curls before nodding begrudgingly.

"Thank you," I said, rising to my tiptoes and kissing his cheek.

Before stepping outside, I paused next to my sisters' room, pressing my ear to the door and listening for sounds of movement. It was silent, suspiciously so, and I fought the urge to open the door and check on them once more, wanting to make sure Harlow was alive and Armina wasn't planning a coup.

Catching Ray's gaze, I pointed to their door, hoping he'd understand. If they were in the middle of a mutiny planning session, I didn't want to tip them off by speaking out loud, nor did I want to enter his mind to give him instructions.

It didn't feel right going into my husband's mind without his permission; like I'd be breaking his trust.

For some reason, I was less guilt-ridden about invading the minds of my immortal progeny. But it still creeped me out, and I preferred to save the mind-hopping for dire emergencies.

Thankfully, Ray nodded. Crossing his arms, he

leaned against the wall to stand guard and winked at me as I flashed him an exaggerated grin goodbye.

Stepping out the back door, I pulled my phone from my jeans' back pocket and fumbled with the flashlight option. The phone barely illuminated the narrow path, and I stumbled several times as I followed the sound of raised voices toward the lake. With each root I tripped over, I cursed Tarquin for not installing some sort of lighting. Clearly, he wasn't concerned about lawsuits from potential renters.

The argument ceased abruptly as soon as I arrived at the lakefront, my light flashing in the faces of Astrid, James, and Tarquin.

Astrid shielded her eyes from the glare. "Stop pointing that thing in my face!"

I turned off the light, snatches of moonlight allowing me to see their guilty faces. "Why are you being so loud?"

Nobody replied. They stood there feigning innocence, as if they didn't know what I was talking about.

"Are you going to answer me? You could've woken up my sisters and we need them somewhat contained until we figure out what's going on."

"They need some awakening," Astrid muttered.

"You know that's not what I meant," I said, staring her down. "Are you going to answer me seriously?"

Astrid opened her mouth, but Tarquin quickly squeezed her wrist, and she pressed her lips tightly together as she pulled away from him.

I narrowed my eyes at the exchange. "You're keeping secrets from me? Is this how it always is?"

Astrid couldn't control herself anymore, glaring at both Tarquin and James before answering, "That's the thing—you should know this. You should know a lot of things by now. And don't give me that excuse that you have thousands of years of memories to sift through. You've done it before without an issue."

"So, this whole argument is about me not doing my part?"

"Don't be so sensitive," she said, rolling her eyes. My irritation with her grew and I had to fight to keep my fists from clenching. "But facts are facts and you're getting slower with each awakening. This time around, it's like hanging around with a damn amnesiac."

"Ah, I'm basically the broken wheel on this cart stuck in a ditch. Thanks Astrid, I can always count on you for telling me the truth."

She nodded curtly, as if accepting praise.

While Astrid had missed my social cues, my face must've broadcasted my feelings to James as he blurted out, "The argument was also about Tarquin, not just you. Astrid disapproves of him letting you keep Ray with us instead of sending him off with your family."

"Tarquin's not my parent or guardian! He's not responsible for my decisions."

Astrid looked skyward. "I'm pretty sure that is why you made him . . . to be your keeper. To literally be your guardian."

"Oh, shut the hell up." That retort was about as clever as my rising temper allowed me to be. God, she really knew how to press my buttons.

Astrid took a step toward me, but Tarquin pulled

her back by her elbow. "They were also upset that I left you," he said, avoiding my gaze.

"Well, so was I, but I don't see how that impacts the situation here."

"They think the more you cling to your human life, the longer the awakening stretches. That if I couldn't force you to give up your human lover, the least I could've done was stay with you." He sighed, raking his fingers through his hair. "Maybe my presence would've been enough to keep moving you forward."

I flushed, hearing him call Ray my lover. It was obviously the truth, but sounded wrong on his lips, almost accusatory, reminding me how I defied his request.

Find me again. The words from my dream, my last memory as Razma, crept into my mind. My temper fizzled out. I had tethered a good man to myself, a man deserving of so much better than to be forced to live as an immortal, fulfilling a destiny he didn't quite understand. Looking at Tarquin, I could see him blaming himself, not me.

Astrid was right; I was being overly sensitive. Deep down, I knew there was truth to what they said, and it wasn't fair or helpful to rant at them.

Maybe I shouldn't have been selfish, keeping Ray with me, refusing to leave that part of my mortal life behind as I'd done countless times. Maybe the reason our typical awakening plans were unraveling was because of my strong desire to stay in this life I loved.

"I'm sorry," I whispered, feeling ashamed. "Thank you for sharing your thoughts and I'm sorry I came out swinging like that. I can see why you'd be whispering on the beach, instead of talking to me. But please don't hide more from me or blame each other. I know we can fix this somehow."

They looked at each other, clearly surprised by my speech. After a long pause, they nodded, and the tension seemed to evaporate.

James even grinned, looking like he was holding back a smart-ass comment, and I couldn't have been more relieved.

"Okay, let's go through everything we know and come up with a hypothesis of how we—" I stopped mid-sentence, putting my finger to my lips. "Did you hear that?" I whispered.

Tarquin and James shook their heads and looked around us, unsure what the danger was.

"Hear what?" Astrid asked.

"I thought someone called my name." I glanced at my phone. Of course, no bars in this wilderness.

God, these pits of no reception are going to be the death of me.

"I'm going back to the cabin. Something doesn't feel right." I started running up the path to the cabin, the trio on my heels.

Tarquin got ahead of me and pushed open the cabin door, throwing out his hand in front of my chest, preventing me from going in. "Stay with Astrid, while James and I go in and make sure it's safe," he hissed at me.

"Like hell I will." I ducked under his arm, surprise

on my side as I burst into the cabin yelling, "Ray! Where are you?"

Silence greeted me. The cabin felt eerily empty.

I was about to yell again, but Tarquin covered my mouth. Holding me against his body, he jerked his head toward James and Astrid, who promptly dispersed, stalking silently throughout the cabin.

"No one's here," Astrid said when she and James returned.

I freed myself from Tarquin's grasp. "Where the hell did they go? Where's my husband?"

"I told you not to bring him with us," Tarquin snipped.

I turned around to face him, my cheeks burning as my temper flared. "He obviously did not bust them out and escape with them!"

"I'm not saying he did, but he is a liability."

We were toe-to-toe now, glaring at each other. I stood my ground, cursing our height difference as he towered over me.

"Stop it," James said, pushing himself between us and forcing us apart. "Ray staying is not the issue at the moment."

Astrid materialized by my side, pulling me back by my shoulder. "He's right. Either way the sisters would've escaped. The only difference is that Ray realized and went after them."

"How do you know that's what happened?" I asked.

"The window inside the women's bedroom was wide

open and the bedroom door looked like someone had forced it open." She paused, her brow crinkling in deep thought. "Your sisters probably locked the door and then went out through the window. But the locked door would've made Ray suspicious. My guess is he broke the door down, saw they were missing, put two and two together, and followed them out the window. The voice you heard was likely him calling you for help."

My heart beat wildly. This was my fault. I shouldn't have left him alone with my sisters. I should've been by his side.

Taking a deep breath, I tried to settle my thoughts. I wouldn't be able to help anyone if I didn't get my wits together.

"Okay," I said. "They couldn't have gotten far. We can find them if we hurry."

Astrid nodded. "Let's split up so we can cover more ground."

I nodded, my body ready to go, though my mind protested, *Split up? Haven't we learned anything from horror movies?*

CHAPTER FIVE

My lungs on fire, I raced through the woods calling Ray's name, Tarquin keeping pace by my side.

Only the faint sound of an owl answered back.

Fear overpowered my senses, my thoughts frantically tripping over each other with each passing minute. I wasn't sure how long we zigzagged through the woods, flashlights in hand. The darkness blinded me as the trees blocked out the moon and stars, and the thick underbrush snatched at my clothes, slowing my progress.

Tarquin stopped abruptly, and I crashed into his back, landing on my butt from the impact.

"Apologies Marcianna. I should've called out a warning," he said, reaching out his hand to help me up.

"Ya think?" I grumbled under my breath, trying to brush off the dirt as I stood up. Judging from the slime on my hand, I'd landed in a wet patch and was smearing mud around. "Why'd you stop?"

"We need to regroup. This is a pointless pursuit."

"It's not pointless!" I cried. "They couldn't possibly have gotten far! They're on foot in the middle of the woods."

"And yet we can't find them anywhere. We are four creatures with abilities to outrun three humans; we should've come upon them by now."

He was right, but desperation blocked any shred of reason I possessed.

"These woods are immense, and we don't know what direction they took. We may have just missed them."

Moonlight filtered in through a break in the trees and Tarquin's brow creased, obviously not satisfied with my answer. But I wouldn't give up and regroup, wasting time while my sisters and Ray got further away from us. There had to be another way.

"Maybe I can reach out to feel for them? I mean, I located my sisters thousands of miles away in separate states. You'd think I'd be able to find them in this small radius."

He nodded. "Yes, it's worth a try, even though they are not yet awakened. In truth, I don't know how you found them initially in their dormant state but running blindly is getting us nowhere. It only makes us more vulnerable to an ambush."

I closed my eyes but couldn't focus, distracted by the feeling of Tarquin staring at me.

I couldn't take it anymore and opened my eyes.

"Can you like, turn around or something? Or just not look directly at me?"

Shaking his head, he raised his eyes skyward but complied, turning his back to me. But before I could close my eyes again, Astrid burst through the thicket.

Flashing my light in her face, I saw her features pinched with worry, her hair plastered to her sweaty face making her eyes seem wild. "I can't find them anywhere!"

"Neither can we. I'm going to try and reach out with my mind."

She pressed the heels of her palms into her eyes. "Yes, do that. Do it now. Something's wrong. I can no longer feel James. Something is wrong with him!"

I'd never seen Astrid so frantic before and it scared me. Her erratic pacing also fueled my panic, destroying any possibility for the calm I needed to concentrate.

"Astrid, please stop!"

She halted mid-step, her gaze locked on me.

"I'm still new to this. I can't do much without focus and I can't focus with you panicking!"

"I don't panic," she hissed, joining Tarquin's side, her tense energy still palpable.

I closed my eyes, trying to clear my mind. *I can't . . . I can't . . . I can't.*

Oh my God, my brain needed to shut up!

I looked at Tarquin and Astrid doing their best not to watch me, trying to give me my requested space. The agitation in their stance was evident, their muscles taut as if ready for a fight, and emanating from them was a fear I could taste. It wrapped itself around me.

In this lifetime, there was not one moment, not one that I could remember when they were this fearful. Annoyed and aggravated, yes, but never full of this acute and metallic fear. Even when demons kidnapped my daughter, Tarquin seemed only on edge, in stark contrast to my terror. I remembered Tarquin did confess being afraid one time—when I was drugged and taken away. He could no longer sense me, and it scared him. Could this mean Ray, James, and my sisters were taken by demons?

The thought caused my stomach to contract, and bile burned my throat, making me want to vomit. I had to figure out how to find them. Everyone was counting on me.

Do something! my inner voice screamed.

How did I do this before? I literally just found my sisters a week ago . . . how did I do it?

The orb. I used the orb.

On instinct, I sat down on the damp forest ground, my legs crisscrossed. Closing my eyes, I placed my clammy hands on my knees and visualized the orb, trying hard to force the image. My heart drummed in my ears, and I shivered from a cold sweat as I blindly grasped in the darkness with my mind.

Finally, after what seemed like forever, it material-ized. But the orb was different than before, the space around it chaotic. I reached out with mental fingers, searching through the noise as the orb drifted away. I couldn't touch it—not like before.

I needed to calm the hell down.

Reach, I begged my mind. *Find James. Find Ray. Find your sisters.*

Another voice within me kept whispering over my pleas, *You're not good enough . . . you're not strong enough . . . you'll fail.*

Covering my ears, I screamed internally, *Shut up! Shut up! Shut up!*

My mind suddenly went silent. The incessant internal dialogue was gone, causing an odd emptiness.

It was quiet. Peaceful. My power pulsated as if freed from its restraints.

Taking a deep breath and focusing, I visualized the dark room where I'd normally seen the orb. But instead of the darkness, a door materialized in my mind in front of me.

My hand hovered over the handle, unsure of what I'd find if I opened the door. Taking a deep breath, I turned the knob and pushed hard, stepping over the threshold into a dimly lit room.

Glancing around, I realized I was in a bedroom, a child's bedroom, the orb floating in its center. What the actual hell was going on? This didn't seem right.

I stood still for a moment, uncertainty causing my heartrate to speed up once more. *Do I go and try to touch it?*

Sticking my hand out in front of me, I cautiously moved toward the orb. But seconds before my fingers could graze the shining ball, a small hand took hold of my wrist.

I was staring into the eyes of a girl, not much older

than my Ella. She wore pink polka dot pajamas, her dark blonde hair falling past her thin shoulders, curling slightly at the ends.

"Are you here to help me?" she asked, her large brown eyes widening even more. "I don't have much time, and I can't do this by myself."

"Who are you?" Though somewhere deep down inside me, I recognized her.

"I'm Sarah. Don't you remember me?"

There she was . . . this little child was the "Sarah" I needed to find to get this whole mess straightened out so I could return to my family. But why was she here now in my vision, when my intent had been to get to the orb and locate Ray, James, and my sisters? Was her time running out?

"Sarah, I need to find where my friends are and then we can come to help you. Where are you?"

"You have to find me now. I don't know where I am." Her small voice sounded scared.

"But I can't do it without my sisters," I said, my voice echoing around the room. Within my mind, vision and reality blended.

With a loud gasp, my eyes popped open, my breathing ragged. My breath echoed in the beat of wings as birds took flight from their night's nests, startled by the sharp noise.

Shit! I was sitting on the forest floor, the sunrise peeking through the trees, and no closer to locating my husband.

Astrid ran to my side, squatting down to be at eye level. "Did you see them? Where are they? Are they okay? Your jaw dropped like you saw something shocking."

Shaking my head, I averted my eyes from her intense gaze, and looked at Tarquin, hoping I'd not see his disappointment with my failure. Walking over to us, he kneeled beside me, gently pushing Astrid out of my face and giving me some breathing room.

"What did you see?" he asked.

"Sarah."

The looks on Tarquin and Astrid's faces were so comical, I almost laughed despite the dire circumstances. "Close your mouths before a fly falls in," I said, sounding very much like my mother. "Judging by your reactions, it seems this too has never happened before."

"No, you've never found her on your own. You've always needed your sisters to locate her," Tarquin replied with a frown.

"I never said I located her. Just that I saw her."

Astrid's sigh of frustration bordered on a growl. "Maybe Sarah showed up because she's getting impatient. Because this is all taking far too fucking long!"

She grabbed my arm, her desperation evident in the intense pressure of her fingers. "Stop wasting time talking and find James."

"Okay. Hold on. Let me try something else," I said, trying to wiggle out of her grasp. But she wouldn't let me go until Tarquin intervened, forcibly removing her from my arm.

Taking a deep cleansing breath, I closed my eyes, reaching into Astrid's mind, her frantic scattered thoughts about James silenced the second she felt me in there.

Can you hear me? I asked through my thoughts.

Yes, her voice replied in my mind.

Okay, now let's try one more thing. I'm going to try to see through your perspective. I did this with my mom, where I went into her head and saw memories through her eyes.

I waited for a moment, relieved when she finally replied, *Okay, do it.*

Expanding my reach into her mind, my breath hitched when I realized I was looking at myself sitting with my eyes closed on the ground.

Oh, my God, it worked! I was seeing the world through her eyes.

Pulling my power out of her mind, I cautiously entered Tarquin's thoughts. He must've known I was coming; his mind was quiet. I opened my eyes, and saw his emerald gaze glued to mine, his tension tangible.

Are you ready? I pushed my question into his thoughts and smiled when he gave me a brisk nod.

He was even easier to navigate than Astrid. We either had a stronger connection, or I was getting better at this. My excitement bubbled within my chest.

Tarquin! I squealed into his head. *It's working. I can see myself through your mind. And now I can see Astrid! You're looking at Astrid!*

This was more promising than I'd dared hope. I could control my entry in their minds, unlike previously when I'd inadvertently butted in with my thoughts. And even better, I could see everything through their eyes.

My new plan may just work . . . now time to find James.

I let my power fan out, seeking James's unique thoughts and energy, the items that made him James. I focused on his face, recollecting the sound of his laughter and the kindness of his heart.

Extending my energy far from here, I felt my power scanning forests, fields, houses, but finding nothing. Only silence. I could not feel him.

I opened my eyes in disappointment, noting Astrid watching me with rapt anticipation, her face no longer haughty and aloof, her eyes blazing with concern.

"How do you know something happened to James?" I asked her out loud, my voice sounding strange after hearing it echoing through others' thoughts.

"I can't feel him anymore. I normally do. I can feel both James and Tarquin, and I can feel you, too."

That was similar to my conclusion, but I had to ask, "Is this common for the three of you?"

Tarquin nodded. "Yes, we can't communicate with our minds as you do. But we can sense each other's moods."

"Interesting. Maybe James is incapacitated in some way. You told me when the demons drugged me, you couldn't *feel* me," I said to Tarquin, making air quotes around the word, "feel."

"Yes, but James, Astrid, and I are far harder to incapacitate than your unawakened, human body," he said.

"Maybe I could try searching for Ray or my sisters? If they're in the hands of the demons, they may see them as less of a threat than James. Maybe they left them alone."

"Stop talking about it and do it," Astrid said, wringing her hands.

I didn't take offense. Though the words seemed harsh, her tone was not.

With a quick nod, I closed my eyes again, this time focusing on searching for my sisters. At first, it felt like my power wandered aimlessly through darkness. But then, something beckoned me, tugging on my energy as tendrils of light extended toward me, guiding my path forward.

I followed without question.

The darkness soon dissipated, and I was in a dungeon-like room outfitted with stone walls and metal bars. James and Ray lay unconscious on the floor, while Harlow sat pressed against a wall, her hands gripping metal bars.

She turned her head and looked directly at me, her black hair cascading around her, obscuring the side of her face.

Everyone was accounted for except Armina, so that must mean I ended up in her mind, viewing the world from her perspective.

Seeing Ray lying helpless on the ground nearly broke me, but I fought the urge to make Armina run to his side. I wasn't sure if I even had any control over Armina's body. Besides, I didn't want to attempt it and risk freaking her out, drawing unwanted attention to us.

Voices approached the cell, with accompanying footfalls echoing down the passageway. Harlow scampered from the entryway as a man and a woman came out of the shadows, opening the cell door.

"He'd like to see you ladies," the woman said, a smile creeping onto her face.

I felt Armina's flood of terror as the man grabbed hold of her, dragging her out into the hallway. She fought him with every bit of strength she possessed, elbowing, and kicking him even after he backhanded her hard enough to blur her vision.

Goddammit! Look Marci! Think! Where could they be? Where the hell is this place?

I tried to remain calm since I wasn't sure if Armina could feel me in her head like Ray or Astrid could. The last thing I needed was her screaming that there was someone else in her body.

As she walked, her terror muddling my thoughts, I tried to take in the narrow, dimly lit passageways and the stone walls growing tufts of moss. The building reminded me of an old prison, and I wondered if there were any abandoned ones in the surrounding areas. This place had to be somewhere close by. Even if they'd driven my sisters, Ray, and James there, it still should be within an hour's ride using James's capture as a marker of time.

The winding shadowy passageways eventually led to a narrow stairwell of uneven stones framed by walls made slick with water dripping down the mortar. As soon as we arrived on the floor above, I realized this was not an old jail but a castle or some large estate.

It looked like we stepped on to the set of a gothic movie.

With Armina standing in the large foyer, I drank in the sweeping dual staircase as it cascaded to where she stood. Two gargoyles perched atop the banister above, their presence making Armina recoil. Her fear grew with each step.

Could these demons be any more stereotypical? How the hell did they find this place?

Armina sniffed delicately, and I sensed a musty smell clinging to the air.

This was so wild. I couldn't tell if it was her thoughts giving me the perception of the musty smell or if I'd somehow tapped into the physiology of her body.

Regardless of how I was doing it, the smell indicated that though the structure was solid and far from being in ruins, it wasn't a well-preserved historic building frequented by the public. Likely, it was a relic from a forgotten past, now taken over by these vile demons.

Come on Marci, think!

I grew up around these parts of New England and loved hiking and exploring historic sites. I should recognize, or at least have heard of a place this size abandoned in the middle of the woods. But try as I might, I recollected nothing about a castle-like estate where a basement contained a dungeon. Things like this didn't exist around here.

Heart hammering against her ribs, Armina stumbled into an expansive room that could've easily been a ballroom at one time. Individuals milled about, stopping to stare at the prisoners being dragged deeper into the room.

My sisters' escorts pushed past the gaping faces of the others, making their way to a large wooden table dominating this large, open space. Sitting in heavy wooden chairs, a group of creatures engaged in lively discourse that ceased abruptly at my sisters' arrival at the table.

My thoughts stilled as my gaze was ensnared by eyes as dark as the night sky, flecks of light playing upon them as if the stars themselves were captured within their depths.

It was *him*. The man from my vision.

I lurched from Armina's mind and was sucked back into the darkness.

"Her eyes are opening."

"What did you see?"

"Hush, let her breathe."

Laying in the dirt on the forest floor, I looked up into the concerned faces of Tarquin and Astrid.

"Give her a moment," Tarquin said, tucking an errant strand of hair behind my ear as he pulled me into his arms.

I leaned against him, grateful for the security he provided, not to mention the back support, as I tried to put together the pieces of my vision or whatever the hell it was. Astrid hovered over us, her mouth opening and closing now and again as if wanting to say something but changing her mind.

When my mind finally unscrambled, the first words out of my mouth surprised even me. "I saw him."

"Who, James? Ray?" Astrid asked, words tripping out of her mouth.

"No. I mean yes, but that's not who I'm talking about. I saw *him*, this man in a vision the day Tarquin and I fought about my decision to let Ray stay with us." Tarquin tensed against my back, but I continued, "I dreamt of this man a night or so ago. Both times, I was so scared. It was an all-consuming fear, a paralyzing one."

Astrid frowned, looking past my shoulder, likely into Tarquin's eyes. Turning my head slightly, I caught him shaking his head.

"What did he look like?" he asked.

I closed my eyes, picturing the man in question, my heartbeat racing as my mouth went dry.

Clearing my throat, I said, "He had dark hair, almost black, I think, and it was on the longish side. His eyes were dark and very intense. Do you know him?"

"No. In all your years, you've not mentioned anyone like him," Tarquin said.

"But you did." I said, shifting in Tarquin's lap and pulling away to face him. "A dream I had last night seemed to be a memory of when I'd made you immortal. Just prior to that moment, you told another demon to call *him*." I stressed the word "him," hoping it would prompt some epiphany on Tarquin's part. "That *him* has to be this man, the one that has Ray and James and my sisters. Do you remember anything from that time?"

I peered into Tarquin's eyes, but no spark of recognition materialized, despite my hope it would.

"I don't," he said, his tone gentle. "To be honest, I don't remember much from the time I was possessed."

We sat in silence before he asked, "Could you tell where James, Ray, and your sisters are being kept?"

"I'm not completely sure." I frowned.

Setting aside the memory of the mystery man, I focused my thoughts onto the building imprisoning everyone I needed to restore my life back to normal. "The basement where they were being held looked like an old jail or prison, but the level above seemed like a castle or large estate. It was old though, certain areas looked to be in ruins, but the main part of the building looked inhabited and pretty well maintained."

Tarquin stood up, lifting me up with him and passing me off to Astrid. "Take her back to the cabin and pack up," he instructed. "We need to leave. They'll soon realize we're here and come back for the rest of us. I'll go find this estate and get our people back."

"What? No way!" I sputtered, turning to look at Astrid for help in thwarting this ridiculous plan.

Her raised eyebrow told me I should save my breath, and she was right. Before I could protest any further, Tarquin was gone, using his insane speed to put distance between us.

What a stupid plan. He was putting himself and the others at risk by playing the hero. No good happens when you split up. We'd proved that already.

I stood in the forest fuming, left alone with Astrid, and an insurmountable amount of doubt and fear.

CHAPTER SIX

Ripping clothes off the hangers, I slammed them into my luggage, cursing Tarquin with each shove of cotton and polyester.

How could he leave Astrid and me behind, expecting us to just pack up and go? We were a team, and frankly, his only hope of success required our help. What the absolute hell was he thinking going at it alone?

I felt someone watching me from the doorway and whirled around, snapping at Astrid, "What's he going to do? Jog over there to free our friends?"

She shrugged, her tone dry as she replied, "He does run fast."

"Why didn't you stop him?" I demanded. "You know he needs us. What's he going to do by himself against a whole goddamn lair of demons!"

She stood in silence staring at me until the quiet stretched to the point of awkwardness. "You have a lot of clothes," she finally said. "It took me some time to find everything I'd thought you'd need."

My mouth dropped open. In the past week, I'd often wondered who'd so kindly assembled my things and brought them here, each item thoughtfully selected, down to my favorite fluffy robe. I was sure it had to have been James as it fit with his caring nature, but Astrid?

"Why do you look so shocked?" she asked.

"I thought you hated me and would've packed my least comfortable clothes. Or at least some mismatched socks and a painful bra."

She smirked. "Only if I thought it would've somehow quickened your awakening."

Our eyes locked for a second, and I couldn't help but burst out laughing. Astrid cracked what appeared to be a genuine smile before resuming her perfected resting bitch face.

"There's really no way to stop Tarquin once he gets something into his head. He's like his creator in that way." She lifted her beautifully manicured eyebrow, her icy blue eyes twinkling.

Her words did not leave the same sting as they would've earlier, and I nodded at the spoken truth.

Looking around to make sure I had everything I needed, I followed her out the door and into her black Mercedes. It wasn't clear from our conversation where we were heading and she didn't offer any clues, shrugging whenever I tried to weasel a hint from her.

After almost thirty minutes of driving in silence, I couldn't take it anymore; my temper ratcheting up again, breaking my will to remain reserved. "You know he's going to fail. You know he needs us! Where are you even going?"

"I'm trying to get as close to that estate you saw as I can without being noticed," she replied, her voice cool, but with a trace of rebellion in it.

Once again, my mouth agape, I stared at her. She was defying Tarquin?

"Why are you looking at me like that?"

"I'm liking you more and more," I replied, a slow grin spreading across my face.

"Well, stop it." She lifted her chin in the air, but her cheek twitched, likely from fighting back a matching grin.

Turning into a small dirt road, she parked on the shoulder and faced me, her all-business-no-fun demeanor back in place. "I knew the place from your vision the second you described it. Though in all my years of wandering through this area, I never realized it was a reunion spot for demons."

I didn't know how to respond. Shock and admiration stirred within my chest.

"Okay, here's my proposal: You reach into Tarquin's mind and see how things are going. If you cannot get a read on him, then we'll know this lone wolf savior approach failed as we suspected it would. At that point, you and I will come up with an amazing rescue strategy, possibly bordering on suicidal."

Excitement eclipsed the sheer terror I felt listening to her idea, and I licked my lips several times before agreeing. "Should I do it now?"

Astrid awarded me with an exaggerated blink. "Would you like special permission from the demons first?"

Giving her a stink eye, I closed my eyes and threw out my energy, dispersing it into the world.

Finding Tarquin turned out to be quite easy, but interpreting his thoughts was another matter.

His mind was scattered, a kaleidoscope of thoughts stemming over thousands of years. I watched transfixed as these images faded and then were slowly swallowed up by a heavy darkness.

Tarquin? I called softly into his mind, but he didn't respond.

A hollow feeling began to sap my own energy. Unsure of what was happening, I stayed anchored in his mind, hanging on to the hope his consciousness was still there, and he'd figure out how to communicate with me.

A shadow brushed my energy, and I stilled my explorations.

I was not alone. Something else lurked within the recesses of Tarquin's mind.

A strong desire to escape claimed me for a moment, but I fought against it, not wanting to leave Tarquin alone with whatever this thing was.

"Welcome, my lady," a voice whispered, twining itself around me. "I would truly appreciate seeing you once again. Face to face. We have missed you."

I didn't reply, terror choking my voice. This thing had the upper hand. It knew who I was, but I knew nothing about it.

The minutes ticked by, and the owner of the voice grew impatient with my silence, adding, "You wouldn't want me to destroy your creations, would you?"

"Don't touch them or I will destroy you," I said, sounding calm and deadly. Sometimes I surprised myself.

Laughter echoed, and I wished I could wrap my hands around whatever this thing was and squeeze, silencing its voice forever.

"Hurry now," it purred. "We wouldn't want anyone getting hurt."

My eyes popped open, my breathing ragged.

"What is it?" Astrid asked.

"It's a trap! What are we going to do? They not only know we're coming, but they're demanding we come."

Astrid frowned, shaking her head in disbelief. "How do you know?"

"There was someone else in Tarquin's head. I watched Tarquin's thoughts become muddled, then dark, and then this voice was there in his mind, talking to me. What are we going to do, Astrid?" My eyes stung, and I dug my nails into my hand, forcing myself to fight back the tears.

There was no way I was going to let Astrid see me cry. She already thought I was weak; I didn't need to give her more evidence she was right.

Astrid slammed her head against the seat, the violence of it making me jump, my muscles tensing.

Covering her face with her hands, she dug the heels of her palms into her sockets and growled, "Well, we agreed this could be a suicide mission. Let's get it over with."

Without a look in my direction, she shoved the car door open and stepped out. Her blonde hair blew in the breeze as she stalked up the dirt street, making her look like a wild Viking warrior walking into battle.

I needed to be more like her.

Razma had been a fierce Sarmatian warrior. I needed to channel her.

Because right now, I had to be a warrior, too.

Taking a deep breath, I wrestled my seatbelt off and ran to catch up.

CHAPTER SEVEN

A mansion of stone and graying wood loomed in front of Astrid and me as we hid behind an overgrown bush. The building showed decay in certain sections, but the main heart of the house was intact, smoke curling out of the chimney.

"Okay, now what?" I asked, turning to look at Astrid.

She flipped a lock of hair behind her shoulder and stared back. "I was hoping you'd have a plan," she replied.

"Me?" I pointed to my chest, my eyes wide.

"Yes, you're our leader, our maker, and by far the oldest. I'd think somewhere deep down within your memories there'd be something of use for a situation such as this."

A wave of nausea hit me. *Shit. She's relying on me. They're all depending on me. Come on, think.*

I wanted desperately for Astrid to say "just kidding,

here's the plan" but she just watched me squirm, waiting for me to come up with something brilliant.

My mind panicked as my inner dialogue overwhelmed me, telling me how terrible I was. I covered my ears, as if that could somehow drown out the noise and focus my thoughts.

Shut up! I screamed internally.

To my surprise, my mind quieted. My path forward became clearer as a parade of memories of other cat and mouse games flashed by. Nothing like this situation, but enough to give me some ideas to work with.

"I have a potential plan, but feel free to add on anything you've come up with," I said, nerves and my own insecurities stopping me from continuing.

"Are you going to tell me what it is, or should I start guessing?"

"We're going to go inside." I rushed the words, my throat constricting at the thought of being surrounded by demons yet again. If I didn't do this right, we'd all be trapped, imprisoned, and at their mercy.

"Of course, we are," she said. "I hope that's not the full extent of your plan."

"No, do you think I'd really say I have a plan and end with we're going inside?" My voice rose slightly, and I reminded myself to calm down.

"I never know with you." Astrid raised her shoulders. "Are you going to continue, then?"

"Yes. Stop being so impatient!" My commands to calm down were going unheeded by my stress-induced temper.

"I'm sorry, I can't help it," she said, her voice dripping with honey. "I've never witnessed anyone explaining a tactical operation in such a slow, drawn-out way. But do go on, I'm essentially immortal and can squat in these bushes all day listening to you."

She batted her long eyelashes, giving me a vacant smile that caused my eyes to pop out of my head. Though I wanted to question my past life's sanity for making such an irritating companion, I had to admit she was right. I needed to get to the point fast; we were losing precious time.

"Your patience shall be rewarded," I said, returning her doe-eyed smile. "Here's my plan: I'm going to go into the head of whoever is conscious enough to give me a sense of what's happening on the inside. Then once we understand their location, and how they're secured, I'll walk in there and cause a distraction. In the meantime, you free Tarquin and James, and then together you can get everyone else out."

"You think you're just going to stroll in and stroll out?" Astrid looked like she ate something sour, no traces of her previous sarcastic humor. "You know Tarquin would destroy me for letting you go through with such a plan, and I'm sure your husband wouldn't be pleased if something happened to you either."

I didn't reply, only raised my chin higher.

Twining her fingers through her hair, Astrid growled her frustration, pulling on the strands and shutting her eyes. She sat like that for a moment before leveling a steady gaze in my direction.

"I've got nothing better," she finally said, her hands dropping into her lap. "Have you done this before?"

A tingle went up my spine at her question. "No, not really," I replied. "It appears I've had a habit of abandoning my mortal body each time I've gotten too close for comfort to the demons. Especially when they wanted to bring me to their overlord."

Astrid slowly nodded, holding my gaze for an uncomfortably long time before asking, "So that's not a recent thing? Destroying your body and escaping? You've not done it often in my lifetime but enough to make me wonder why you'd do it instead of fighting. Marci, you're stronger than them. Believe in yourself and your power."

I couldn't help but smile at her compliment. "Don't worry, I will not prematurely exit this time. I have a lot to live for and am not feeling the martyr vibe at the moment."

"Maybe we need a new plan?" Astrid offered. "One that doesn't rely on you as bait?"

"No, this will work," I reassured her. "Besides, I'm strong, right?" Despite the insane amount of terror I felt at being in proximity to those creatures, I knew they wouldn't kill me. They needed me alive and cooperative to get what they wanted. To get what they thought I stole from them.

She sighed but nodded. "Fine. Let's just get this over with."

As I closed my eyes to initiate our plan, I could've sworn I saw a spark of admiration in her gaze, and it brought me a boost of confidence.

Praying our friends were once again secured in the dungeon cell, and out of the way of the swarms of demons, I reached out with my power, searching for familiar energy to latch onto.

Unfortunately, we were not so lucky.

I was once again within Armina's mind. She was not held within the dungeon as I'd hoped but sat at a table in full view of the demons, Harlow clutching at her arm.

Armina glanced over her shoulder, and I noticed Ray, Tarquin, and James chained to the wall in the corner of the room. Ray seemed alert, thank God, but Tarquin and James slumped unconscious against the wall.

Demons milled about, most within human hosts, the rest a black swirl of smoke undulating around the room. The demons within hosts taunted Ray, aiming the occasional kick into the ribs of Tarquin and James.

Forcing myself to be a passive observer, I tried not to draw attention to Armina. But it was a hard ask. Rage bubbled up. I wanted to destroy these demons for hurting my husband and friends.

With each passing minute, my heart sank further as I took in the situation. The individuals we needed to rescue were on full display, their captors on high alert, eyes darting around the shadows of the room as if in anticipation of intruders.

I noticed a few of the creatures were different from the demons within a host. They were in human form, but I couldn't detect the faceless smokey entity characteristic of a demon within these bodies. Nor was there the soft shimmering light of the human soul, or slight hint of decay of an animated corpse to indicate the soul's recent departure.

These creatures seemed to exude an energy—a power—I'd not yet felt before from any of the demons I'd encountered. And they sat next to *him*—the man haunting my memories.

My eyes fell on him at last. He was built like the other creatures without the demons inside, and by far, commanded the most reverence in the room.

His intense gaze across the table entranced me from within Armina, immobilizing me like a helpless moth tangled in his web. The familiar paralyzing fear spread throughout my consciousness, slithering around to each particle of my being.

If this was how I felt hidden within my sister, how would I be brave enough to walk into that room as myself?

Pulling out of Armina, I retreated to the safety of my body. My limbs shook uncontrollably, and I took a few calming breaths to steady my nerves before opening my eyes.

"Well?" Astrid immediately prompted.

"It's not good," I whispered. "James and Tarquin are unconscious—"

"How's that possible?" she interrupted. "We're not affected by drugs in the same way as humans. We have more control over our bodies than you do over your own, even after your awakening."

"I don't know, but I wonder if it has something to do with that creature in Tarquin's head." I immediately held up my hand, seeing Astrid open her mouth to protest. I knew what she was going to say—that the three of them cannot be possessed by demons. "Some of the creatures in there are extremely powerful; they're not like any of the demons I've seen. Instead of bodiless smoke, they appear in solid form, resembling humans, but there's no human soul inside. I can't explain it, but I know they're different. I can sense their power and strength."

Astrid licked her lips, her brows drawing in together. "What else did you see?"

"My sisters are sitting at a table with those creatures. And that man, the one I've asked you about, the one showing up in my visions and dreams, he's there with them." His image invaded my mind again, causing me to shiver.

"So, you're saying this is impossible." Astrid slammed a fist onto her thigh and gritted her teeth. "Okay, then we wait. We wait till they're not such a focus of attention. Maybe they'll put our friends back into their cells soon?"

"I don't think that'll happen. They're waiting for me. They know I'm coming." Disappointment and fear crept onto Astrid's face, and I quickly added, "We may still be able to do it. Just not what we'd originally planned." A memory of Razma setting fire to the Colosseum, snatching Sarah and her mother from under the Romans' collective noses just prior to execution percolated in my mind, giving me hope of success.

I gave Astrid the high-level rundown of Razma's rescue of Sarah, but she didn't look convinced. "You said they're expecting you and so will be on high alert."

"Yes, but a fire is simple enough to start and would cause pure chaos. Every creature for itself. We could then slip in unnoticed and get everyone out."

"Marci, an execution in an open Colosseum is one thing, but here they have a firm hold on their captives and can easily move them to safety while keeping them close. Besides, even if we catch them off guard by creating enough chaos, I doubt we'd be able to get everyone out."

She had a point. "Let's stick with the original plan where I'm bait, drawing their attention to me, and then also try the fire as cover for you to rescue the others," I said. "But you're right, we likely won't be able to get everyone out."

"What do you mean?" Astrid demanded, her eyes narrowing, a suspicious look on her face.

"I mean . . . you get my sisters to safety and as far away from here as possible. They are the priority. But you'll need to leave Tarquin and James behind." I bit my lip, hard enough to taste blood, and added, "Maybe even Ray."

She shook her head. "I can do both—I can get your sisters and Ray first and then return for Tarquin and James. You'll just need to keep them focused on you for as long as possible."

"It'll be hard when they're chained to a wall and on such prominent display. You'll have to leave them with me and trust I can get us out." Kneeling in the dirt, I held her tightly by the shoulder, my gaze locked on hers. "It's absolutely critical that my sisters and I are not captured together."

"Fine," she said after a drawn-out silence. "But please don't let them hurt you, or James, or Tarquin. I will do my best to take Ray with me, so you'll have one less person to worry about."

I gave her a grateful smile. "Don't worry. They won't hurt me. They think I stole something from them and want it back."

Tilting her head, she asked, "How do you know?"

"They told me when they held Cece, my daughter, and me prisoner," I replied. "They want *it* back, whatever the heck *it* is. And they told me I needed my sisters in order to get it."

Astrid's brow furrowed, and she asked, "Doesn't that kind of sound like they're referring to Sarah?"

"Maybe." I whispered, wiping away an errant tear as my mention of Cece caused her last moments to replay in my mind. It was a stark reminder of how dangerous the next moments would be. "Do you know anything about this? Tarquin didn't, when I asked him."

"I don't. I'm sorry." Her eyes softened, and she patted my knee. "As long as I've known you, you've been very regimented, almost militant in this process. You don't share much detail about the past, and until this lifetime, haven't been captured by demons long enough to tell tales regarding your conversations with them."

"No, I'm sorry, Astrid. I'm sorry for my past me not sharing more with you." Taking a deep breath, I decided to come clean about my disappointments with my past self in case something went awry during the rescue, and I'd not be returning to her in this lifetime. "I trust you. I trust all of you, and I should've confided all my secrets to you. We're a team."

She nodded, though she broke eye contact momentarily, her face betraying discomfort with the sentimental turn this conversation took.

I smiled. "Don't worry, we won't, like, have a sleepover and braid each other's hair or anything."

Raising her eyebrows, she replied. "I was never worried about styling hair."

Her comment caused a giggle to escape my control, and I quickly covered my mouth. "Sorry, that's a joke. Okay, enough of the chatting, let's do this."

"Finally, you're talking sense." She stood up, her face hardening, ready for war.

We crept closer to the house, and I nudged her with an elbow in the side, pushing her toward a window at the main part of the house.

Peering through a smudged pane of glass, I noted the room looked the same as I'd seen it in my mind. My sisters sat at the table, clinging to each other whenever a demon touched them. In the far corner of the room, Tarquin and James lay unconscious, the chains keeping them bound. And Ray, my poor sweet Ray, paced beside them like a caged animal, occasionally stopping to test the bindings of the chains holding him to the wall.

I had to get them out of there. This had to work.

"Go to that window," I whispered, pointing toward

the corner where Ray, Tarquin, and James were chained. "I'll walk in through the front door and cause a scene. While the creatures are distracted, you go through the window and grab my sisters. If I can, I'll open the window telepathically, but if not, just smash and grab."

She nodded and was about to leave when I grabbed her hand. "If there's a chance, please take Ray with you."

She squeezed my hand, a faint smile on her lips, and I let her go. As I moved to the front door, I thought how this whole thing needed to go off without a hitch or else we'd be in deep shit. I could do this. I had to do this.

Yet the closer I approached, the louder my internal voice screamed, reminding me how critical this moment was, how I couldn't fail, but how I was unlikely to succeed.

I was sabotaging myself with my doubts.

"Shut up in there. It's now or never," I whispered, my hand on the doorknob. Taking a deep breath, I steadied my nerves, visualizing my next steps, my naysayer internal voice fading away.

I pushed the door open, flinching as the hinges creaked, and tiptoed into the house. Moving with caution, I cursed every loose floorboard that dared make a squeak. Even my ragged breathing sounded like drums echoing in the empty hallway.

God, I can't believe a demon hasn't tackled me yet with all the noise I'm making.

Too quick for comfort, I stood at the closed

entrance of the room containing some of the most important people—mortal and immortal—in my life. Pressing my head against the door, I held my chest as my heart fluttered wildly against my palm.

Do it. Open the door.

Shoving the double doors open, I cringed as they crashed against the interior walls, the sound reverberating throughout the room.

Demon heads turned in my direction as Harlow whimpered, throwing her arms around Armina. Harlow likely didn't know who the hell I was, but Armina looked at me with relief, like I was some sort of savior, her eyes shining with unshed tears.

Looking past them, my gaze immediately locked onto the male who I feared above all other creatures in that room. He sat at the table like a statue, his dark eyes betraying surprise.

Why the surprise? Hadn't he been expecting me? Wasn't it him I'd heard taunting me in Tarquin's mind?

I watched a shadow of anger flit over his features before being replaced by a smirk tugging at his lips. He leaned back in his chair, one of his eyebrows arching seductively.

"Hello Lilith," he drawled.

CHAPTER EIGHT

Who the hell's Lilith?

Standing motionless, my confused brain unnaturally quiet and out of ideas, I found myself ensnared in the dark depths of the mystery man's eyes. They fascinated me, drawing me in against my will, despite my underlying fear. At least, I hoped it was against my will. If not, I was going insane, and we were in a hotter mess of trouble than I'd anticipated.

Whatever magic he'd cast over me, I needed to snap out of it, and at least act the part of a powerful creature. Locking my trembling knees together, I straightened my back and lifted my chin.

"I don't know who Lilith is," I said, forcing my voice to sound cold.

"It's you," he replied. The other creatures in the room had frozen, seemingly riveted by our conversation.

"Well, then you have me at a disadvantage. You claim to know who I am, but I don't know who you are." Crossing my arms, I arched my eyebrow, proud of how composed and flippant I'd sounded when my heart was in the midst of a heavy metal-style drum solo.

Unfortunately, my fledgling confidence was squashed the moment he stood up. Moving away from the table, he approached, his movements graceful, measured . . . and deadly.

With each step he took, my breath became harder to draw until I felt like I needed to hold onto something or I'd pass out.

He paused inches from my face, bringing his mouth close to my ear. "I go by many names, but the one you've known me as is Samael."

Every fiber of my being suddenly screamed for me to run, to escape by any means possible. It was visceral and I could barely control the chaos springing to life within me.

Get a hold of yourself, I commanded, digging my nails into my palms.

Glancing to the corner of the room, my eyes caught Ray's, his fear and panic fueling my own.

Don't worry, we'll get you out of here. I pushed the thought into his mind, hoping if he knew there was a semblance of a plan, he'd be less freaked out.

His response exploded into my head: *I'm not worried about me! What the fuck are you doing? Why'd you come here? Why'd you put yourself in danger?*

I didn't have time to cajole him into agreeing to our plan. *Stop worrying about me. If Astrid tells you to go, you go!*

He glared at me, refusing to reply.

God, I don't need your stubbornness right now.

Over his shoulder, I saw Astrid peeking in, waiting for me to open the window and then cause enough of a distraction so she could slip in and get my sisters out.

The creatures stalked in my direction, surrounding me as if I was a maimed animal for slaughter, leaving my sisters unattended at the table.

A demon stepped between me and Samael, her nose almost touching mine, her features scrunched in anger. "Remember me?" she spat.

Though the attractive brunette was not familiar, the swirling mass of darkness within her I knew well.

"Hello, Lamia," I said, nearly choking, my throat clenching at the memory of our last encounter.

She growled in my face. "You'll pay for what you and your fucking friends did to my family."

"Your family?" I asked. "You all kidnapped me, tortured me, tried to hurt my child, and killed my best friend. You're lucky you're not dead with the rest of them."

Lamia shrieked, lunging at me with her hands outstretched, her fingers claw-like, but Samael grabbed her around the waist and tossed her into the arms of a large beast of a man. This giant had bulging muscles and towered over almost everyone in the room.

With a flick of his wrist, the man tossed Lamia to the side as she screamed, "You stupid bitch, you killed her . . . you're the one that killed your friend!"

The giant glared at the woman, silencing her screams, then turned his attention to me. He was a creature like Samael—in human form with no demon inside him, and exuding power. His sharp features were fearsome and reminiscent of a lion, with his blond shoulder length hair and a scar on his cheek.

"My lady Lilith, we're pleased you've decided to return to us," he said, giving me a bow.

That voice. It was the voice I'd heard in Tarquin's mind. But it hadn't come from Samael as I'd assumed. It was this creature hurting Tarquin, and likely James too.

The realization caused me to clench my fists, rage simmering in my chest. I now had the perfect candidate as the target of my distraction.

Closing my eyes, I envisioned the blue-eyed giant engulfed in flames. My body tingled with excitement as a roar went out through the room, the sound blasting through my mind, forcing my eyes open. To my perverse delight, the giant was consumed by orange and yellow flames. Demons beat him with their jackets or hands, trying to suffocate the blaze.

Now! Now! I screamed in Astrid's mind as my power turned the window lock. Astrid slithered into the room, covering my sister's mouths with her hands and pulling them through the window. She quickly returned, ripping the chains from Ray, dragging him behind her. My chest tightened as I watched him resist.

Please go! I begged. *I can't do this if I'm worried about you.*

I don't want to leave you!

I know, but I'll see you soon, I promised. *Trust me. This will work!*

Within moments, they were gone. *Please go far away,* I told Astrid. *Somewhere no one can find you.*

In the corner of the room, Tarquin and James woke, stumbling to their feet, their chains clinking. So, I was right—this creature I'd set on fire had been the one controlling their consciousness.

The satisfaction of vengeance set my heart alight as well, burning with my triumph. But my glee was short-lived.

The behemoth shoved the demons trying to help him away, and drew his hands over his body, extinguishing the flames. Still smoldering from the fire, he stared icily at me. Before I could blink, he was at my side, grabbing my neck.

My vision clouded, and I cursed. I should've been focusing on the creatures in the room rather than fixating on Astrid getting her job done.

Pushing my energy outward, I thrust the creatures back, failing to dislodge the one squeezing my throat. He tightened his hold, and my heartbeat accelerated to inhuman speed as I felt him weasel into my mind.

I had to protect my thoughts. I couldn't let him within me . . . within my mind. In desperation, I punched my hand out, spewing more of my power into his chest until he finally released, slumping to the ground.

Staggering away from him, coughing and rubbing my throat, I looked around. The demons were scattered this way and that, dodging my power, which apparently had taken off like a whirlwind and was now still swirling around the room like an invisible cyclone, tossing anything that came in contact with it.

All except Samael and the handful of other non-demon creatures. They stood untouched, and aloof, watching the chaos around them.

For a moment, Samael's gaze met mine, his facial expression appeared indifferent. But his eyes held my attention. They looked almost . . . frightened. Or was it concern? Was I feeling his emotions somehow, or was this a trick?

I shook my head, confused. As I hesitated, unsure of what to do next, a movement in the corner shifted my focus.

Tarquin and James, still weak from their mental imprisonment, hadn't made much progress on freeing themselves, struggling with their chains holding them to the wall.

Shit, I forgot about them in all this chaos.

Focusing my thoughts, I forced the wisps of my exhausted power forward from my core, hoping to strike the chains and free Tarquin and James. But before I could release my energy, hands grabbed my shoulders painfully, sweeping me off my feet.

I landed on my back, a scream of shock escaping my control. Lamia leered at me, her knee jamming into my neck, pinning me to the floor.

I heard Ray's cry of rage before I saw him. He'd leapt onto Lamia, trying to wrench her away from me as she dug her fingers deeper into my shoulders.

My mind raced in fear. Why was Ray here when he should be safe, long gone with Astrid?

Before I could get over the shock, blood splattered over my face, and I cried out. Ray had stabbed Lamia! The demon's scream was deafening, vibrating through my bones.

Where the hell did he get a knife from? Lamia's going to kill him!

Lamia tossed Ray off like a rag doll and turned her attention to him. She resembled a rabid animal, teeth barred, foaming at the mouth.

My pulse pounding in my ears, I jumped to my feet. *I must save Ray! I must save Ray!*

Grabbing the handle of the knife, I ripped it out of Lamia's back.

She pivoted, rage twisting her features, and lunged at me, trying to grab the weapon from my grasp.

I slit her throat, the knife gliding smoothly over the flesh. Her eyes bulged, and she grasped her neck, blood spilling over her fingers as she fell to her knees.

This was the point Astrid had said to rip the demon out of the damaged body and destroy it before the demon repaired the body or tried to possess another person. But how? With my power cyclone long gone, the angry demons flocked around us, focusing their rage my way.

I needed to get Ray the hell out of here.

Without a second glance at the creature still sputtering on the ground next to me, her blood pooling around my feet, I grabbed for Ray. But the demons proved quicker, surrounding him and dragging him away, restraining him as he fought to get to my side.

I couldn't battle through that swarm of beasts. My

power was drained, and even if I tried to blast them with the remnants of my energy, I could hurt Ray.

"Let him go!" I screamed. "Let him go and I'll stop fighting you!"

Out of the corner of my eye, I saw Tarquin free his hands and frantically work on ripping the chains off his legs. I wanted to help him but wasn't sure if I'd draw attention to his actions. Or worse, waste the last bits of my waning power.

"Enough of this nonsense," a voice boomed, silencing the noise of the demons.

Someone caught hold of the roots of my hair, dragging me toward Ray. Struggling against the iron grip, I twisted around to see the blond, blue-eyed giant that had tried to get into my mind. He looked down at me with annoyance, before ripping Ray from the clutches of the demons and drawing him to us.

For one moment, I was close enough to feel Ray's breath on my cheek before I was tossed onto the ground at their feet. The giant held my gaze, squeezing Ray's throat in a massive fist. He raised an eyebrow, as if daring me to do something.

"Please don't hurt him," I pleaded, my arms outstretched toward them.

"Gadreel," Samael called out, his eyes darker than before, his expression still unreadable. There was no emotion in the word, and I couldn't tell if it was said in encouragement or as a warning.

Gadreel glanced in his direction, giving Samael a firm shake of his blond head before turning back to me. "Welcome home, Lilith," he said.

My breath caught in my throat, terror digging its claws into my mind. Scrambling toward Ray, I saw Tarquin had thrown off his chains and was running full speed at us.

My heart filled with hope. Together we could still save Ray and get the hell out of here. But a brilliant light exploded around us, throwing me backward. My head hit the ground, the impact blurring my vision and bringing a metallic taste gushing into my mouth.

I lay on the ground disoriented and panting, watching a strange darkness form. It enveloped the light and swirled it away, leaving an emptiness behind.

What the hell was that?

An eerie stillness permeated the room. At its center stood Samael, Gadreel, and the other creatures like them, unharmed by the blast. The demons, however, had been scattered by the light and now crept forward with their heads bowed toward Gadreel.

There was something on the ground. The demons surrounded it, poking at it before throwing back their heads shrieking like wild animals. I got to my hands and knees, my brain in a fog as I watched them.

What was the thing that held their attention? I stared at the lump on the ground, my mind not comprehending it.

There was an empty place in my heart, and within me something began to scream.

Ray. Ray was the one laying there surrounded by the demons, his body lifeless.

No, no, no. This can't be real. It can't. I have to save him. I have to get to him, be with him.

I shoved past the creatures, falling to my knees at Ray's side, holding his hand tight and placing it to my heart.

He was gone. No light was left within him. The soul that once filled him, making him my everything, was gone.

Gone. My love, my soulmate, my reason for living was gone.

A keening softly began in my chest, forcing its way through my throat, my agony ripping from my lips. That explosion of light had been Gadreel tearing Ray's soul away from his living body leaving behind an empty shell.

He took everything from me!

Hot tears streamed down my face, and I stood, fury pulsating through me as I faced my husband's murderer.

I was going to tear that shit limb-from-limb. My body shook, ready to shatter this monster, shatter him into as many pieces as he'd shattered my heart, shattered my life.

Fire pooled to the surface of my body, my blinding hatred all-consuming. I was going to kill everyone in this room, even if it destroyed me. Even if I ceased to exist.

Samael stepped in front of me, blocking my path to Gadreel. His hands grabbed the sides of my head, his strong fingers digging into my temples as he met my burning stare.

"Sleep now," he commanded, and everything went dark.

CHAPTER NINE

"Mommy! Wake up! We want some pancakes," Ella's little voice chirped in my ear as she poked my forehead. "Daddy went to get you a fancy coffee," she added, kissing my cheek.

Warmth on my face from the morning sunlight nudged me awake and my eyes fluttered open. I could hear the kids laughing downstairs over the humming of the television. Stretching out lazily, my hand drifted to Ray's side of the bed. It was cool to the touch, and I rolled onto it, burying my face in his pillow and inhaling his scent.

A light touch on my arm alerted me to someone else's presence, and I looked up, a soft smile on my lips to greet Ray or an insistent offspring of ours. Instead, my eyes met the terrified gaze of a vaguely familiar child, her dirty blonde hair obscuring much of her face.

Gasping, I sat up in bed, my hand to my chest, steadying my startled breath as my groggy brain snapped to attention. The child reached for me, tears in her eyes, and I drew her into my arms.

"Sarah?" I asked.

"Please help me," she whimpered.

My heart broke and I hugged her tight, but she pulled back, her eyes growing big. "Someone's here," she whispered.

Looking around the room, I clutched her to my chest but she slipped through my fingers, fading away like a fog under the rays of the rising sun.

I lurched up, only to be jerked back to the ground, my head slamming down hard into the cement. Chains held me tight, looping through shackles on my arms and legs, and then securing into the walls. My shoulders ached from my arms being forced over my head and I felt terrifyingly vulnerable splayed on the ground.

My throat was raw, my stomach in knots, but it all paled in comparison to the pain in my head. And it wasn't from the whack my skull just received from the ground. My brain felt like it was on fire, the level of agony beyond anything I've felt before.

I lay there staring at the moss-grown stone ceiling as reality seeped in. It had been a dream—there was no Ella, no children laughing downstairs, no one wanting me to make food or to snuggle with them.

And Ray's side of the bed would remain cold forever.

Tears spilled down my cheeks, my body breaking into heaving sobs as my mind replayed the moment Ray lay in my arms, lifeless, soulless, an empty shell.

He was no longer mine. Nothing I could do would bring him back.

It was as if someone had reached into me, tore my spirit to pieces, and stole the most precious part of me.

And I'd never be whole again.

A grunt from the corner of the cell pulled me back to my current situation. Choking back my sobs, I stared into the frigid blue eyes of the man responsible for the destruction of my heart.

"Good morning," Gadreel said, reclining against the wall, his arms crossed over his muscular chest. "I hope the chains are not overly uncomfortable. They're for your own good."

My rage flared, and the metal warmed on my wrists. Imagining the shackles disintegrating, I knew I could snap them off easily if I focused. Then I'd choke him, choke him until his cruel face ceased to exist.

"I'll kill you," I growled, pulling against the restraints, feeling them give a bit.

He wagged his finger at me as he approached and a searing pain flared in my head, squeezing until my body relented, the chains cooling and tightening once again.

Squatting beside me, he took a strand of my auburn hair, twirling it between his fingers. My hatred warred with my fear as I lay there immobilized, my heart hammering against my ribs.

"You are weak," he said. "Because you choose to

live as a human. We both know humans are not worthy of your love, that they are a menace and meant to be ruled. We could've ruled them together."

He watched my face for a reaction to his words, but I kept my features controlled.

Dragging the strand of my hair across his lips, he smiled. "You may not remember, but we're very similar, you and I."

"I'm nothing like you!" My voice bounced around the stone walls as bile rose into my throat.

Dropping my hair, he touched my cheek, stroking it. The touch was surprisingly gentle for a monster such as he, and that made it even more frightening. I jerked my face away, and he laughed, latching onto my chin and pulling it toward him, forcing me to face him.

"You were always overly spirited for your own good, Lilith."

"I'd prefer you not touch her," a steely voice cut through the dank air.

Gadreel stiffened, his face darkening. "I was only making her more comfortable."

Without another word, he released my chin and stood up, walking out of my prison without a backward glance.

Samael stood in the entryway of my cell, observing me as if I was some new insect in an already overflowing bug collection. But his eyes didn't match his reserve, burning with intensity. My breath hitched unsure of what would happen next.

Do something, goddammit, my mind cried. I couldn't take the wait anymore, the uncertainty, my body rigid as I tried to force my muscles to stop trembling, to not expose my fear.

Finally, he walked to my side, and put his hand on my shoulder, pinning it to the ground. I flinched as he ripped the chains from the shackles on my wrists and ankles.

Without a word, he took hold of my arms and pulled me up to stand, releasing me almost immediately. My legs protested the rush of blood, the burning sensation of pins and needles unbearable, and I dropped to my knees.

He knelt beside me and pushed back my tangled hair, his eyes searching my face. "You've been crying," he said, his brow furrowing.

The observation infuriated me, snapping me out of my tongue-tied uncertainty. "You helped murder the most important person in my life and you're surprised I'd be crying?"

He didn't reply, his direct gaze making me queasy, his hands on my hair overly familiar. I tried to pull away, but he grabbed onto my arm.

"Do you not remember me?" he asked.

I shook my head. "Should I?"

Samael's eyes hooded, a darkness appearing within their depths like a storm brewing, suffocating the fire that burned moments ago. He hesitated before reaching again for my head, pushing his palms hard into my temples, snaking his power into my mind.

Gasping in protest, I grabbed at him, tightening my hands around his muscled forearms. "No, please do not put me to sleep." Desperation clung to each word, and I hated myself for it.

In contrast to my vision of him, Samael's eyes were not cruel—they were hollow, almost sad, as if I'd wounded him.

Or was it pity?

Could this be a trick? A form of good cop, bad cop? Gadreel comes in and terrifies me, while Samael attempts to gain my trust?

If that was the case, then they were wasting their time. There was no way I was going to trust anyone in this hellhole of demons.

I bit my lip, the pain satisfying, remembering my instincts telling me to fear Samael. He was in the vision that unleashed a wave of terror through me, not Gadreel.

Samael released my head and pulled away from me. With his brows knitted and his mouth drawn tight, he knelt beside me in silence, as if thinking of what to do.

My breaths came in shallow pants as I waited for a metaphorical or even a literal ax to fall on my neck. But none did. Instead, he stood up and bowed his head slightly before exiting the cell. The sound of the metal doors grating against the stone was like a knife in my brain.

Once outside the cell, he faced me once more, laying his hand on the bars that divided us. "You're only pieces of yourself. When you remember who you are, then you'll remember me."

"What do you want from me?" I asked, tears of

frustration threatening to spill, and I dug my nails into my legs to keep the waterworks at bay.

He sighed. "What I want from you is far different from what the demons have been instructed to want from you. Different from what Gadreel and the other Guardians want from you."

Guardians? What the hell is he talking about?

"I don't understand," I whispered, licking my parched lips. Hatred of him and his kind conflicted with my desire to know more.

"Of course not, Lilith. You've trapped yourself within that human. How could you understand? But maybe you will once you decide to stop hiding."

I frowned, opening my mouth to speak, but nothing came out. I didn't know how to reply to him. His words were meaningless, but the implication that I was hiding, or somehow trapped, made me nervous. This was not how Tarquin presented my situation.

Being called Lilith also gnawed at my stomach. I didn't know of any Lilith of note; the name was only familiar because of a music festival. I wished I could talk to Farah; she'd know the significance of it, and who these creatures, these Guardians, thought I was.

Turning his back on me, Samael left with a warning tossed over his shoulder. "Gadreel will be coming soon to check on you."

I watched his retreating back, my confusion growing. *Why'd he say that?*

Looking down at my hands, my brain suddenly kicked into gear, the haze gone as if Samael had taken it with him.

I wasn't chained, my mobility was no longer hampered. This was my chance. I had to get out. I had to get James and Tarquin out. Assuming they were still alive.

"Please be alive," I whispered under my breath. I couldn't bear any more loss.

Though the iron shackles on my arms and legs chafed my skin, they didn't hinder my movement. It would be a waste of precious time and strength trying to get them off. Getting out of this cell was the priority.

I shuffled over to the iron bar door and realized I'd not heard the *clink* of a lock after Samael closed it. With my heart hammering in my throat, I gave the door a push. It sprang open obligingly.

My mind struggled to comprehend what was happening. *Did he mean to do this? Is he helping me, or is this some game these creatures are now playing?*

Popping my head out the open door, I peeked around the corner, relief blooming in my chest. The coast was clear.

I pressed my body against the cold stone walls and slithered around the winding hallway in search of my friends. My breath would catch at every turn, every shadow taking on the form of a faceless creature ready to force me back into my prison and into the control of Gadreel.

With each empty cell I encountered, my panic rose. *Please, please do not let James and Tarquin be upstairs on display again,* my mind begged. I didn't have the strength to fight these creatures right now.

The hallway came to an end, and my fear ratcheted. I couldn't breathe, much less think. I was about to turn around and head back, thinking I'd hit a dead end when I caught sight of a hazy outline resembling a door. It was hard to be sure in the dim light, but I sped up, exhaling deeply as I peered through the barred window, catching sight of Tarquin and James laying on the floor inside.

The door was locked, but with focus and the tatters of powers I still had, I managed to open it. Once inside, I looked around to see if there was an easy route to escape, pinning my hopes on the narrow window high above my head.

Tarquin and James looked so vulnerable laying on the cold ground and my throat squeezed closed. I'd failed them. I'd failed everyone.

I needed to protect them now.

Closing my eyes, I focused my thoughts. *Astrid, we're coming to you. Are you close? Can you hear me?*

Yes! I can meet you at the spot where I first parked my car.

Okay. We should be there soon.

Looking back at the two men lying on the floor, I debated if I should try rousing them in the cell or drag them out and do it outside. I suspected Gadreel was keeping them unconscious, and my efforts to oust him would bring the demons upon us within minutes.

I had to pull them out of here myself.

My mind was all too eager to tell me this was a fool's task, that I'd fail, that I wasn't strong enough. Ignoring the fearful naysayer within, I dragged a nearby chair under the window and stepped onto it. I was running on fumes, but I had to bend the bars. Closing my eyes, I willed them to move.

They barely budged. I took a steadying breath, looking over my shoulder at Tarquin and James, laying there exposed and defenseless. Closing my eyes, I dug deep to harvest my power.

My children appeared to me in my thoughts— their sweet faces contorted with grief, their arms reaching for me, begging for me to come home. Power coursed through my veins, building in intensity as an image of Ray filled my mind, his dimple deepening as he smiled. He pressed his mouth to mine, the vision so vivid I tasted him on my lips.

With a cry of anguish, energy shot out of my fingertips, disintegrating the bars on the window as if they'd never existed.

I pushed back the sobs that built up in my chest and jumped down next to James. Hooking him under his arms, I dragged him up the chair and into the window, grunting as I pulled and twisted his body.

I dropped him out the window and climbed out after him. Wrapping my arms across his chest, I dragged him through the weeds and between various rocks. James was going to be bruised. Pulling him was like pulling a sack of bricks, but the farther I got from the house, the more adrenaline pumped through every muscle, the fear the demons would discover Tarquin alone in his cell propelling my body beyond its limits.

In the safety of the woods, I rolled James under a thicket, covering him up with random branches as best I could, and sprinted back to the house. I ignored my pains of protest, my breath ragged with fear as I imagined nightmarish scenarios befalling Tarquin.

A whimper of relief escaped my lips the second I saw him lying unharmed. But the relief was short-lived, my internal pessimist needling me.

How have we gotten this far without anyone trying to stop us? No demon guards or Gadreel in sight? This is a trap. This must be a trap.

Trap or no trap, it was better to be free than caged by the demons and at their mercy. I'd worry later about why this was so easy.

Pulling Tarquin up to standing, I struggled with him against my body, his muscular frame dragging me down.

"Please, Tarquin," I pleaded. "Walk."

To my utter surprise, his body stiffened and did as I asked, putting one foot in front of the other, though still leaning heavily on me.

Realization dawned, *I'm an idiot.*

This whole time I could've used my power to move James and Tarquin instead of physically struggling with them. Looking at the window, I visualized Tarquin climbing through the small space and then with a steadying hand from me, his body moved, my power animating the muscle. He was far from graceful, moving like a puppet being pulled by invisible strings, but he did it.

Following quickly behind, I grabbed his hand, guiding him through the unkempt yard to the safety of the woods. Within minutes, I found James under the brush and had Tarquin lay next to him.

Now came the hard part. I needed to free their minds, which meant I needed to confront Gadreel. My mouth went dry thinking about the next steps, and I decided it was best to stop thinking and start doing.

Laying down between Tarquin and James, I fidgeted as tree roots and rocks jabbed into my back. I grasped their hands, my palms clammy with fear against their cool skin, and pressed them into my sides.

Closing my eyes, I slipped into their minds, connecting their energies through mine. I paused for a moment in the darkness, unsure where to go.

Come on, do something, I commanded. *Don't be a jackass and pick a direction.*

Yet I didn't move, the idea of confronting Gadreel in the darkness of Tarquin and James's minds freezing me in place.

My kids need me. Sarah needs me. I need to finish this and go home.

Home—what did that word even mean now? Our home would have a gaping wound left by the absence of Ray.

The thought caught me off guard, cutting me to the core, yet also bringing up a spark that lit my rage. My fury at Gadreel burned bright, and I unfurled my power, allowing it to coil through the corners of our connected minds in search of this creature hidden in the shadows.

I found him with surprising ease. Unlike last time, he was not the stalker with the upper hand—I was. I could see his power clearly—see how blissfully unaware he was of my presence, no longer a taunting voice in my ear.

Grabbing a hold of his energy, I fired my power straight at him as I screamed, *Get out, you son of a bitch!*

He flew backward as if pulled by an invisible force, disappearing into the darkness. I opened my eyes just in time to see Tarquin and James wake up, their eyes dazed, yet wild, and their breathing erratic.

"We need to go! Follow me!" I jumped to my feet, pulling them hard by their hands.

They looked weak, staring at me in a haze of confusion. I'd never seen them this way. It terrified me.

"Run!" I yelled, zapping them with my energy to try and get their limbs moving. "We can't stay here! They'll realize we're gone soon and come after us."

I moved behind them and began to push, my palms flat on their backs. With one last shove, they staggered forward and began to sprint. I led the way, navigating to where I thought Astrid waited.

Tears streamed down my face as we ran, each step away from that demon-filled house taking me further from Ray.

Cece's death had been horrific and painful, but at least James had returned her body to her family.

I couldn't do the same for Ray.

I'd abandoned him, leaving his body behind with those creatures. And I'd *never* forgive myself.

CHAPTER TEN

Astrid stood on the dirt road, tapping her foot and gnawing on her lower lip, the door of her Mercedes wide open. As soon as we breached the forest line, she spotted us, relief loosening her pinched features.

She jumped into the car, turning it on and revving the engine, ready to make a fast getaway.

Tarquin got to the car ahead of me. He opened the passenger's door and pushed me in before he and James dove into the backseat.

"Quick. Go!" I yelled at Astrid as soon as my butt touched the seat.

Astrid frowned, spinning around to investigate the backseat. "Where's Ray?"

I couldn't meet her eyes, averting my face as tears renewed their well-worn path down my face.

"Dead."

She recoiled as if I'd struck her. Pressing her lips

together, she threw the car in reverse, backing out of the dirt road and onto a major route.

I watched the forest pass by through the window, half expecting to see a creature jump out and force its way into our car. But there was no one out there. No one had followed us.

I swallowed back my fear, my heart calming its hammering beat as I immersed myself back into the sorrow, now so familiar.

Silence hung in the air, and I wrapped myself in it like a thick, suffocating blanket, ignoring my companions.

"Where are Marcianna's sisters?" Tarquin asked, after a bit, his voice jerking me from my thoughts.

Astrid gripped the steering wheel tighter, and for one second, I thought she'd say she lost them.

"Awake."

That one word stirred both hope and anger within me.

Soon this nightmare would be over, and I'd be able to go back to my normal life. But what kind of life would it be without my soulmate and best friend?

If my sisters had woken up earlier, Ray would still be alive.

I wanted to blame them, to hate them, but I knew it was my fault, not theirs. This whole mess was my fault.

Swallowing hard, I tried to think of something else, anything other than Ray right now. But my mind kept returning to his lifeless body surrounded by sneering demons. His eyes that had once looked at me with love, were shut forever.

I gulped loudly, causing Astrid to glance at me.

"I'm sorry," she said. "He turned back as soon as we got to the car. Stole my knife. But I had my hands full with your sisters and didn't realize he'd run back until he was gone." She shook her head at the memory, once again focusing her gaze on the road. "I should've glamoured him. I just thought . . . you know, he'd stopped fighting me . . . I'd thought he was on board with the plan. I—"

Raising my hand, I cut her off. I couldn't bear to hear anymore. "Please, stop. I don't blame you. It's my fault. All of it is my fault."

Tarquin's hand snaked around from the seat behind me, squeezing my shoulder. But it didn't make me feel better. No amount of reassurance could erase my pain and guilt.

Closing my eyes, I pressed my head into the seat, resisting the onslaught of emotions poised to rip through me.

I needed to fight. To plan. To do something. If I sat here, allowing them to layer on sympathy, I'd go mad.

"How did this happen?" I asked through clenched teeth. "I thought the demons believed the new reality I created. How did they remember Ray and me?"

James, who'd been sitting quietly this whole time, whispered. "They likely recognized us. Astrid and me. Watched us bringing Harlow and Armina to you." He paused, his voice pained as he continued. "We're an asset and a curse to you. You cannot truly hide when we are around."

I knew he was blaming himself, kicking himself for not being careful enough, but I only saw my own error. "I get it. It's because I only changed reality for my family and by extension for me, but not for you. The demons connected my sisters to you both, and then when my sisters escaped with Ray in pursuit, these creatures were able to put two and two together."

Massaging my temples, I sifted through the questions kicking around in my mind. "Why can't they see me? I mean my spirit . . . why can't they see it's not a human soul? I can see them within the humans they possess."

Astrid shrugged, glancing at Tarquin through the reflection of her rearview mirror. "We cannot really see you either. We see—"

Tarquin interrupted, "We feel you. I feel you. When you awaken, it's as if you're calling me home to you."

Well, that was a non-answer if I ever heard one, clearly meant to divert attention from Astrid's remark. I filed away this observation, determined to press Astrid further when she and I were alone together.

Tarquin aside, it was evident demons couldn't see me. They'd sniffed around for months before being clued in as to my identity. But Samael could see me. He'd even recognized my presence within Armina.

I couldn't hide from him. The thought made my chest tighten.

I needed to keep talking so fear wouldn't gain a

foothold within my mind. Any lapse into silence would result in toxic rumination, leading to panic.

I blurted out the first question that came to mind. "I don't understand any of this . . . how were the creatures able to get into our minds? We can't be possessed by demons . . . but they didn't feel like demons, right?"

"These were ancient creatures, far more powerful than any demon we've ever encountered," James replied, and I turned to look at him. His normal dark amber complexion was more ashen, almost sickly, and my heart clenched in worry of possible aftereffects of Gadreel's mind invasion.

Tarquin nodded. "At least four or five of the creatures in that room exuded a power I've not encountered within any demon. Hence, I agree, they didn't feel like demons, and they didn't need to possess human bodies, manifesting their own. Samael was one of them. Was he the man you spoke of earlier, the one you had the vision of?"

"Yes," I whispered, my lips numb, my blood draining from my face at the mention of his name. "Gadreel is another creature like him. Samael referred to them as Guardians, I think."

"You don't know him? None of them seemed familiar?" Tarquin pressed.

"No." The word exploded from my mouth, my head vehemently shaking as if my denial would force the word to be reality. But from the depths of my core, tendrils of awareness curled around me. *You do, you do,* they whispered to my spirit. *Remember.*

Sweat beaded on my forehead, bile rising from my

empty stomach as ancient memories tried to force their way into my mind. Razma had warned me I may not like what I see in our past, that it had the power to destroy me. And I believed her wholeheartedly, fighting against the intrusion.

Astrid interrupted my thoughts, "Do you know why he called you Lilith?"

"No. I don't know of any Lilith." I closed my eyes, not wanting to talk about this right now.

"She's a demon," James piped up from the backseat. "In some literature, she's the original wife of Adam and spurned him, embracing demonic forces. Some say she's the mother of demons, copulating with Samael—"

"Enough!" Tarquin's outburst startled us all. "That's enough, James," he continued, tempering his tone. "Can't you see Marcianna is tired? She is not the Lilith you speak of. She's clearly not a demon."

Copulating with Samael. James's words repeated on a loop in my mind. My heart quickened at the implications, my mind playing back my conversation with Samael in the cell. *Do you remember me?*

"James, who's Samael?" I asked. "From your research."

I saw Tarquin tighten his jaw in disapproval at my question, and James glanced at him briefly before replying, "There are many interpretations of him in Abrahamic religious texts—he's the Angel of Death, the Left Hand of God, the ruler of all the devils, a fallen Archangel. And that's just a partial list off the top of my head. There are more interpretations."

"Good thing you're well versed in religious fairy-tales," Astrid spat, her eyes never drifting from the road.

"Shut up, Astrid. Marci asked, and I said what I know."

"They can't all be made up; the demon part seems to be true," I said.

Tarquin cleared his throat. "I'm intimately familiar with the rise of several sects of religions, as are you, Marcianna. Though fairytales, they are rooted in kernels of truth."

Astrid's brows knitted together, her reflection in the rearview mirror getting stormier with every minute of this conversation. "Regardless of whether they're rooted in some factual event or person, they're still fairytales made up by humans, changing century after century. Humans are imperfect historians. They're fearful creatures, vilifying whatever they don't understand."

No one replied.

We drove the rest of the way in uneasy silence. I tried to occupy my mind with thoughts of my sisters, though my mind oscillated between worry over Samael to wallowing in the pain of losing Ray.

Over and over, I tried to imagine what my sisters would be like as awakened beings. I prayed they'd have enough power to help me find Sarah and fight any demonic creatures standing between me and my kids.

Amelia, Alex, and Ella were all that mattered to me now, and I'd do everything in my power to get home to them.

CHAPTER ELEVEN

A shuttered, nondescript colonial came into view beyond the front windshield of our car. Looking at the house, I couldn't help but shiver, my limbs paralyzed with the fear we'd find the house empty, my sisters gone.

I didn't want to get out . . . didn't want to see what was, or wasn't, inside.

Even if my sisters were awake and content inside that house, as Astrid had assured us, the thought of facing the women whose escape had cost me my husband's life made me want to turn heel and run. And yet I needed them desperately. Without my sisters, I couldn't get my children back, couldn't return to the shambles of my life.

I gripped the sides of my seat, my fingernails digging into the smooth leather. The next steps had the potential to make or break my hopes for normalcy.

I wasn't sure I was strong enough to take them.

Tarquin got out of the car first and opened my door, frowning with concern when I didn't move. He extended his hand and waited silently, the seconds ticking by as I stared at him, unsure what I wanted to do.

My fingers finally reached for his hand, and I clung to him, drawing comfort from his strength as he pulled me out of the car. Together we walked toward the house side by side, our steps in sync.

A light touch on the small of my back made me look over my shoulder, my gaze meeting James's. He gave me a small nod, his smile encouraging, and tears pricked my eyes.

I didn't have to do any of this alone. They were here with me.

Pulling myself out of Tarquin's arms, I squared my shoulders, deciding I'd walk into the house on my own. I'd show my sisters I was strong, that they were safe with me, and together we'd succeed. I knew we could do this. We had no choice.

Astrid passed, slapping my back, an approving tight-lipped smile on her lips. She waited for me to join her before opening the front door and stepping into the house, calling out my sisters' names.

I followed her. My hands shook as uncertainty plucked my nerves, and I clenched them against my body, hoping no one would notice.

The entryway opened to a large dark room, a musty smell of an unlived in house clinging to the air. Standing still as my eyes adjusted to the dim light, I tracked movement in the far corner of the room right before Astrid flicked the light switch.

My sisters' terrified faces stared back at me, their eyes widening with recognition. Holding tight to each other, they walked to me, their gaze never wavering from mine.

Astrid was right; they had awakened, their eyes shining with a fierce connection—a longing. They were not seeing me as Marcianna Caruso, the woman they'd met for the first time a few days ago, but as one of their own.

My body relaxed, my anxiety evaporating with each step they took. On instinct, I opened my arms and Harlow flung herself into my embrace, her body shaking with sobs as I smoothed her hair.

She was a college student, still childlike and vulnerable. As I rubbed her back in soothing circles, I couldn't help but wonder if I'd see my children at this age.

Armina approached more timidly, laying her hand gently on top of mine and pausing my rhythmic strokes on Harlow's back. Our eyes met over our sister's head, and she looked down at her shoes for a second before glancing around the room as if looking for someone.

"Where's Ray?" she asked.

The mention of Ray sucked the breath from my body. During the car ride, I'd fought so hard to bury him deep within my heart, to secure the volatile emotions triggered by each stray thought of my husband. Her words now conjured up the image of Ray fighting against the demons for my life, and then how I cradled his soulless body.

I must've pushed those last painful moments into Armina's mind. She shrank back, tears shining in her eyes.

"He's dead?" she whispered. "I'm so sorry. He was a kind man."

Kind? That's it? That's all she has to say? He'd died because she'd stupidly escaped from the safety of our cabin. He'd died because of her! I swallowed back the poisonous words forcing their way to the tip of my tongue. My pain gnawed on the tether of these words, and I reminded myself this wasn't her doing, or Harlow's.

It was mine.

And saying anything to the contrary would not bring Ray back. It would not alleviate my self-loathing or take away my pain, but it would certainly alienate my newly awakened sisters.

I nodded stiffly. "Thank you, Armina."

"Mina. You can call me Mina." She put her arms around both Harlow and me, and for a brief moment I had a sense of completeness. That is, until she straightened up stiffly, her chin jutting out, and announced, "Okay, that's enough. I need to know more about what's happening. What do we need to do? Is there a plan?"

Her abrupt down-to-business attitude caused my temper to flare yet again, and I squeezed Harlow as if she was some sort of stress ball.

Goddamn, Mina's going to annoy the hell out of me, isn't she? I understood she wanted to have a sense of control, to not feel helpless, but her delivery sucked.

Who was she to say we'd had enough? Enough of what, exactly? Mourning the loss of my loved ones or the loss of our lives as we knew them? Because I didn't think I could ever stop.

It was getting harder to choke down the nasty, bitter words forming, and I was cognizant my face looked as if I'd swallowed something foul. But Mina didn't notice my reaction and started to pace around Harlow and me.

"I have all this energy," she said, her steps intensifying with each word. "Somewhere deep inside me, there's this feeling of purpose and I don't know how to channel it. I have these snatches of memories, but I don't know what's real and what's fantasy. I need to know more. You have to tell me more."

She turned to me, and her face lost its intensity. "Please tell me." Her tone was softer, more compassionate.

Harlow peeked out from the shelter of my arms. "Marci's been through a lot and literally just got here. Leave her alone for a minute so she can get comfortable. Maybe pee or something?" Her voice was muffled against my clothes, her tone typical of a teenager. It forced a ghost of a smile onto my lips.

"I actually would like to freshen up a bit. Then we can talk." Pulling away from Harlow, I gave her arm a gentle squeeze, glancing around the room.

"The bathroom's that way," Mina said, pointing

down a dark hallway as she stepped aside, allowing me to pass, though her pursed lips broadcasted she wasn't pleased over the interruption.

I nodded and walked as fast as I could toward the promise of privacy. I didn't need to pee; I needed a good cry.

Leaning against the sink, I looked at the woman in the mirror. Pale and gaunt, pain etched in her eyes, I didn't recognize myself.

Tears fell down my face, and I let them, unleashing the control I'd imposed on myself. They poured over the wounds inflicted by my self-hatred, even as my guilt buried its claws deeper within my spirit. I welcomed the pain—it felt cleansing—yet satisfyingly punishing.

Sobs bubbled out from deep within my chest. I tried to keep them silent until I couldn't bear the burning sensation of holding them back. They ripped from my throat, and I fell to my knees, resting my face against the cool porcelain of the sink.

Lilith. Mother of Demons. It had to be true. Even in this life, I was a selfish beast, keeping the person I supposedly loved most with me, when I knew he'd be protected as far away from me as possible. I'd left my best friend unprotected, and then killed her in my clumsy attempts to save her. I'd ripped my family from the security of their reality, and forced them to live in a new one, my children suddenly without their mother and father.

And that was all from my current life. God only knew what I'd done in my previous lives, but if the creation of Tarquin, Astrid, and James was any indication, it had been equally selfish and evil.

I'm a monster. I'm a monster. I'm a monster. The mantra pounded in my mind like a drum.

A soft knock interrupted my pity party.

"Marci, let me in," James whispered from the other side of the door.

"Please leave me alone."

"You're not a monster."

Great, I must've been projecting my thoughts again. Who else heard it?

"Please just go away," I begged.

"No, I'm not going anywhere. So, you should really open the door and let me in if you don't want to draw everyone's attention to this conversation."

Reaching out blindly, I fumbled the lock on the door open, and James slipped in. He sat down next to me, propping his back against the sink, his long legs extending across the bathroom floor. Putting his arm around me, he drew me in close, and I let my head fall onto his shoulder.

We sat in silence, minutes ticking by. I sensed him waiting for me to initiate the conversation, but I didn't know what to say.

After a while, he must've given up on me making the first move, because he cleared his throat and said,

"I could hear you, crying in my head, repeating over and over that you're a monster."

He paused and took my hand in his, giving it a squeeze. "I meant what I said; you're not a monster."

"I've done some pretty shitty and selfish things," I whispered into his shoulder.

"Everyone has. There is no one perfect in this world."

"Well, I likely did shittier things in my past. Things I don't remember. Those creatures called me Lilith, and you said Lilith is a demon. Not just any demon, but the mother of all demons." My voice shook, the words tripping over each other.

Pulling away from him slightly, I turned to look into his eyes, finally saying the fear out loud that had haunted my thoughts since learning the truth about Lilith. "What if I created demons as I created you? What if I'm not the good guy but the bad guy?"

"Lilith is an ancient myth, first born from the Sumerians. Later, her legend grew as people tried to explain the disparity between the creation story in the books of Genesis."

"What do you mean by disparity?" I asked.

"One story says Eve was made after Adam, created from Adam's rib, while the other states both man and woman were made at the same time from the earth. Makes it sound like Adam had two mates, no?"

"I'm confused," I admitted, rubbing my temples with my fingers. "That would make Lilith a human . . . where does the demon part come in?"

James patted my knee, which I'd drawn tightly into

my chest. "Lilith rejected Adam and escaped the Garden of Eden. Supposedly Adam then complained to God, who sent angels to bring her back. But she refused to return, instead making demon babies with another angel, and becoming a demon herself."

"With an angel?" I asked, confused, as this seemed to contradict what he said earlier.

"Yes, with Samael." I blanched at Samael's name and James noticed, quickly adding, "But it's a myth, Marci. Lilith and Samael may be real, but it doesn't mean their story is. Astrid's right; why would we expect humans to comprehend what Lilith was and what she did?"

I looked at him skeptically, certain he was twisting his true thoughts to protect my feelings.

"Think about it," he continued. "What would humans think of Tarquin, Astrid, and me? Do you think they'd see us murdering humans and think we're good?"

"You don't murder humans. They're possessed." I drew in a shaky breath, drying my eyes with my sweatshirt sleeves, which I'd pulled protectively over my hands.

"Yes, but people wouldn't know that. They're limited in what they can see and what they can interpret."

I shook my head. "I'd like to believe you, but I made you, Astrid, and Tarquin, and that's clearly selfish and evil. I took away your life, forcing you into immortality to serve my needs. That's twisted!"

He shook his head fiercely, putting his hand over my mouth.

"Do you remember me?" he whispered. "Do you remember who I was as a mortal?"

"No," I admitted when he released my mouth, quickly adding, "But I don't want to. I'm scared to look at my past, to see what I've done."

"I was your brother. Well, half-brother to be specific," he said.

My jaw dropped as I looked at James—for the first time really looking at him in a historical context. Tarquin was from the Roman Empire, Astrid was a Viking, but who was James? I took in the handsome black man sitting next to me, trying to piece together his identity and his relationship to me.

Unlike Tarquin or Astrid, he spoke English without a hint of accent implying he likely originated in an English-speaking society. It was also evident he'd been religious in his mortal life, and he'd demonstrated a rather extensive knowledge of Christian and Judaic beliefs. And if I'd always forced my body to look similar to Razma, with her red hair and light skin tone, then it wasn't exactly rocket science to deduce how James and I could be siblings in a time and place where the color of your skin not only dictated your position in society but also whether you were considered property.

My stomach tightened. "You were a slave," I whispered, my eyes widening as snatches of memories forced their way to the surface.

He nodded slowly, watching my face as the memories came hot and heavy, playing out in my mind. Some of the memories were brutal, my throat clenching as I stepped back into that time, remembering our lives together.

I swallowed several times, trying to moisten my suddenly parched throat. "My father . . . our father . . . owned your mother. Owned you."

I was going to be sick.

He nodded, again taking my hands in his. "You had an awakening in that lifetime, and that's how I became who I am now." He paused as if unsure how to continue. "You think you're a monster, but I can tell you you're not. In every life I've known you, you are kind, loving, and fiercely loyal. Your personality doesn't change much and your heart doesn't waver."

His face pinched, the memories likely vivid and painful for him, and he looked away for a moment before continuing. "The way you treated me went against your upbringing. Your parents were not exactly good people, cruel and vain, not treating anyone with charity and respect unless it somehow benefited them. So, your attitude was clearly not shaped by your surroundings. Even the kindest human spirit brought up the way you were wouldn't have behaved the way you did toward me. To me, this means you," he pushed his index finger into my chest for emphasis, "this ancient creature that is you, is good and not a monster."

Tears welled in my eyes once again, threatening to spill over in response to his impassioned speech and his clear love for me. "Thank you," I said, wrapping my arms around him, savoring the warmth of his embrace.

Reluctantly pulling away, I asked, "How did I make you . . . you know . . . like you are now?"

"You and your husband helped me escape our Tory father. At the time, many slaves were fighting on the side of the British, being promised freedom. But I couldn't do it, couldn't fight on the side my father believed in, no matter how much I wanted papers declaring me a free man. Also, they'd probably not have taken me as I belonged to a loyalist, one of their own, and not a rebel. But by then, George Washington had overturned his previous decree banning black folk from the continental army and was using similar tactics as the British to get black men recruited. So, I joined up with the Patriots."

He had a faraway look in his eyes, as if reliving these moments with each word spoken. "It was after a particularly bloody battle that I ran into you again. You were awakened, husband gone, sisters in tow. Tarquin and Astrid tried to scare me off, but I was determined to stay with you and fight by your side. It wasn't just our shared history and blood that drew me to you . . . there was something about this group of yours on a mission that had nothing to do with the war, and everything to do with something greater than our current world. I wanted it, I craved it, it made me feel whole for the first time in my life. You must've seen me as worthy as you shrugged off Tarquin's demands to send me packing and let me stay."

He laughed, his eyes no longer dark, but back to

the usual honey warmth shining with mischief. "I died trying to protect Astrid against a pack of demons. She's still not forgiven me for it. But she begged you to save me and you did, turning me into this fine demon-killing warrior. And that's the story of how I became what I am now. See, nothing evil or sinister that would show you're a monster."

With a wink, he kissed my forehead and stood up, offering his hand to me, which I accepted with a smile.

When I got to my feet, he took my head between his hands and said with mock sternness, "Now no more besmirching my sister's good name—you *are* amazing—in each lifetime you're amazing."

My heart swelled with gratitude, and I nodded, wrapping my arms around him.

A soft knock drew us apart. "What are you two doing in there? Is everything all right?" It was Tarquin, his concern palpable even from the other side of the door.

"Yes," I called out, brushing away stray tears as I opened the door.

"Everything is right as rain, my friend," I said, smiling up into Tarquin's face, feeling as if a weight had been lifted off my shoulders. I impulsively wrapped him into a bone-crushing hug.

Peeking up at him, I giggled. I'd completely caught the poor guy off guard, his perplexed expression comical.

After a moment of standing straight and stiff, he patted my back and returned my hug before setting me at arm's length, examining me closely. "You're sure you're okay?"

"Yes. I'm good now. Ready to find Sarah." I gave him a determined nod and walked out of the bathroom in search of my sisters.

It was time to get this done and over with. It was time to reclaim my life.

CHAPTER TWELVE

We sat at the circular kitchen table holding hands. Mina's grip on my hand was light and cold, while Harlow's was tight and warm.

My plan was simple; we'd connect our energies together as I remembered doing multiple times from lives past, and then we'd use hypnosis to focus our thoughts to find Sarah. I had Farah to thank for the hypnosis idea, and to be honest, in our current state, we needed all the focus we could get.

"Close your eyes," I said. "And call out for Sarah."

Harlow giggled but did as I asked.

Mina, on the other hand, stared at me, her lips pressed together. "How will we know what Sarah looks like? Have we ever done this before? I only vaguely remember merging our powers, but I'm not sure I have any powers right now."

Good grief, so many questions. "Well, Sarah's a child," I replied. "I've seen her before in a couple of visions. We've found her by connecting our powers before in multiple past lifetimes, but it was less challenging for us, so I'm hoping a hypnotic chanting technique my friend taught me will help ease us into the right mind space. As to your power . . . well, we're about to find out what you got . . . so close your eyes."

Mina still didn't shut her eyes, her frown deepening instead. My impatience grew with each passing second, the desire to say something snarky becoming harder to suppress as we stared each other down.

Harlow peeked out from under her eyelashes, asking, "Are we doing this or what? I'm starting to feel ridiculous."

"Fine," Mina snipped, closing her eyes. "I would've liked this plan to be more concrete, so we know exactly what to expect, but I guess we're improvising."

Taking a deep breath, I shut my eyes and reached my power into Mina and Harlow's minds. *Do you hear me?*

"Yes," Harlow replied out loud as Mina said the same within her thoughts.

Harlow, try to communicate with us in your mind, I instructed.

Oh, okay, sorry!

That's better.

Changing my tone to become more singsong, like Farah had during our attempt at the Prati Prasav, I called out, *Sarah, come to us. We want to help you.* My words echoed in our thoughts as I pushed them out into the world.

Nothing happened. I felt Harlow squirm next to me as we waited.

I know you're scared, Sarah, but tell us how we can find you. We'll protect you.

Again, silence replied, made even more dramatic by the ticking of an old grandfather clock. The presence of Tarquin, James, and Astrid in the room wasn't helping either. They tried to be quiet, but their urgency to finish this quest was palpable with each breath and small movement.

I gritted my teeth, forcing myself to block out our surroundings, my mind feverishly spinning.

The orb. We need to get to the orb. The orb had taken me into Sarah's mind, or maybe it was Sarah going into my mind, or however these visions work. But regardless, she and I were together within her bedroom when I'd been trying to use the orb to locate James, Ray, and my sisters.

The dancing lights of purple and green I've come to know so well appeared in my mind and I latched on, hoping it was the orb taking us once again to Sarah.

But the lights disappeared as quickly as they'd come, and we were left standing within the dark, empty room typically housing the orb. Looking around, I did not see even a sliver of light to indicate the orb's presence.

The coolness of Mina's energy brushed against my essence, causing me to shiver as she asked, "Why are we here? There's nothing but darkness."

"It's usually here. An orb that can show us the path

forward. That can help us find Sarah," I sputtered, looking every which way within the dark room, hoping to spy the lights that had lured me here.

But no orb called to me, enticing me to touch it. What the hell was going on here?

My eyes snapped open, my head pounding with frustration. So much for my sisters' joint power. They were useless, somehow sapping my ability to connect with the orb.

"What happened?" Harlow asked, blinking rapidly as her eyes adjusted to the light.

Her innocent question annoyed me further. How could they possibly help me if they were so much more clueless than I was?

I had to get away. Now. Before I started spewing words I'd regret.

Yanking my hands free, I stood up, knocking over the chair in my haste. It crashed onto the floor with a loud crack, startling my sisters, their wide-eyed looks satisfying some primal desire to punish them for failing me.

Without another word, I stormed out the door onto the wraparound porch, grabbing onto the banister and breathing in the crisp, late afternoon air. With each exhale, my anger lessened, replaced by shame at my behavior.

Tarquin joined me on the porch. As he stood quietly behind me, I wondered if he, James, and Astrid had drawn straws to see who was going to deal with my latest meltdown. A lifetime of being my babysitters. My face burned at the thought, and I kept my back turned to him, hiding behind the veil of my hair.

"Seems like it didn't work," he said.

I stiffened. "You're very observant."

He let out an exaggerated sigh, his breath fluttering my hair. "You're wound up tightly with these emotions. It's blocking your abilities."

"Well, I'm sorry I'm not the stone-cold bitch you all are waiting with bated breath for me to become," I said, my traitorous voice cracking. "I'm apparently not there yet. I still feel grief over leaving my family, leaving my babies, without knowing if I'll ever see them again. I'm sick to my stomach at the thought of losing Ray, of taking him away from my children. And God, you can't imagine the guilt I feel about entrusting his well-being to Astrid."

Tarquin cut off my rant, turning me around by my shoulders. "Don't blame Astrid for this," he said, tilting my chin so I looked into his eyes.

"I don't. I don't. I only blame myself. You tried to warn me," I cried, my anger deteriorating as tears burned behind my eyelids.

God, I'm a mess. One minute I was flying high, convinced of my power, and the next I was bouncing between rage and despair.

Tarquin pulled me into his arms, and my hands dropped to my sides, allowing him to comfort me but refusing to actively participate in the act.

"Grief never really goes away," he said, stroking my hair. "I don't want you to stop grieving for all you've had taken from you."

"I just want to see my family, to know they're okay," I said, my voice muffled against his shirt. "I want to talk to Farah. I know she'd be able to help me figure out what's going on. Help me figure out who Lilith was and who Samael is."

"You know that isn't possible. It would be dangerous for them, and would ruin your sacrifice, Ray's sacrifice, if anyone got hurt."

A sob escaped my lips at the mention of Ray, and I burrowed deeper into Tarquin's chest.

He held me tight, his chest vibrating as he said, "I knew your husband wouldn't listen to you, to us, when it came to your safety. I knew he wouldn't listen . . . because he didn't when he was Kynan."

I pulled away from him, looking up into his face. "When? What do you mean?"

"The day you turned me into an immortal being. He came back for you."

"I don't understand. I remember sending him away." I shook my head, the memory clear as if it had just happened. "He left."

"No, he came back for you. He came back for you and found your body. I watched him go insane with grief, heard him scream with soul-shattering anguish as he cradled you. And all the while I hid out of sight, unsure of what to do, where to go."

Tarquin's face was etched with pain as if reliving this moment again. Catching me staring, his gaze hardened. "The agony of your deaths has been suffered by the many human families you've left behind over the years."

I opened my mouth to argue, to remind him I'd altered their reality, softening the blow, but he forged ahead, "You're gone, but I remain, watching their grief. This is why I'm telling you to get past your feelings, to focus, because it is the only way you'll get home to them. I know it is harsh and cruel to ask it of you, to tell you these truths, but it is necessary for you to remember the value of your life to those you love, and to the world around you."

Speechless, I stared into his eyes, my face flushed with guilt, shame, and anger—conflicting emotions battling for victory. What could I say to him? Yell at him for telling me to snap out of it so I could get the job done and get back to my children? At least then they'd have one parent to care for them.

He was right. Everything he said was right, even though it angered me and broke my heart.

I turned away with a terse nod and headed down the steps of the porch.

"Where are you going?" he called after me. "Shouldn't we go back inside and try again?"

"No." I said over my shoulder. "I need to walk a bit. Focus, as you requested. Don't worry, I won't do anything stupid. I got your message loud and clear."

I felt him watching me as I walked away.

As soon as I turned the corner, and was out of sight, I ran. Running as fast as possible, welcoming the wind in my hair, the chill in the air cooling my flushed skin. I had to get away, escape the guilt of Tarquin's words and clear my head. Maybe then, after exorcising my ghosts, I could figure out how to get us moving toward finding Sarah.

Stumbling upon a fast-flowing creek, I followed it away from the cabin, deeper into the woods. The setting sun's rays danced on the water, its last caress before another day was lost.

Slowing my pace, I took a moment to look around the forest, admiring the little buds decorating the trees with a promise of flowers hailing the change of season.

It was almost the middle of April. Weeks had passed since I'd seen my family—since I'd held my kids and laughed with friends, my mom and dad, and my brother.

If I could only see them, maybe it would tide me over until I could hold them once again. Even a small glimpse into their lives without me would suffice.

The memory of Tarquin's words halted my fantasy, dredging up fear for my family's safety, reminding me of all they'd sacrificed already.

He came back for you.

Even if I hadn't known Kynan came back for me, I should've realized Ray would never leave me behind. He'd proven it time and time again. That should've been enough for me to take away his choice, to not allow him to stay by my side. Then he'd be alive today.

Somehow, despite my grief, I noticed the woods growing still, the sounds around me fading away into silence. My heart began to hammer an all too familiar beat. The forest was trying to warn me; I was being watched.

A desire to flee pumped adrenaline through my limbs, and I turned on my heel, heading back to the house. But I didn't get more than two steps in before colliding with an immovable object. My arms pinwheeled, grasping at air as I tumbled backward. Before I could slam into the ground, strong hands grabbed my arms, lifting me upright.

My gaze locked onto Samael's dark eyes, my body stiffening under the weight of his firm fingers. He did not release me, but neither did he restrain me further.

We stood transfixed, staring at each other, unable to break the connection. An image slipped into my mind—an echo of a moment trapped in time. It was a faded memory of Samael, black hair flowing around his face, his bare body illuminated by moonlight against the backdrop of a dark forest. In the vision, he watched me with awe as if he'd never seen a creature such as I.

The memory strengthened, taking over my mind and my senses until I was reliving each emotion . . . each touch. Anticipation and fascination pulsed in my veins.

In real time, Samael let go of my arms, his hand drifting to my face, brushing gently against my cheek. I could barely breathe, reality and memory blurring together.

What am I doing? This isn't me! I jerked away from his touch.

Frowning, he took a step forward, closing the

distance I'd just created. The movement startled me, and I raised my hands in defense, shooting out a burst of energy that hit him square in the chest.

Staggering a bit, his eyes narrowed, yet he advanced again, undeterred.

Blood pumping in my ears, my breathing had gone from shallow to erratic in a matter of seconds. I pulled power from within my core and swirled it in my hands.

Throwing the ball of light at him, I repeated the motion over and over. But he easily brushed each shot away, like it was nothing more than an annoying insect.

Shit. I couldn't win like this, and he knew it. Why was he toying with me?

My helplessness enraged me, my anger growing as I watched him stalk toward me. His motions were almost feline, like a damn leopard ready to pounce on the hapless gazelle.

Well, I'm no gazelle. Blinding energy burst from my hands, throwing him off balance. I darted past him.

Pumping my legs as fast as my body would allow, I glanced over my shoulder. No one was there. *Where the hell did he go?*

My head swiveled just in time to see him materialize in front of me. I once again ran straight into him, knocking myself to the ground.

This time he didn't reach out to steady me, instead letting me fall, sprawled in the dirt. I looked up, shuddering as he towered over me. In the presence of the giant Gadreel, I hadn't fully appreciated Samael's imposing size.

Even mighty giants can fall. I swung my legs, catching Samael below his knees so that he lost his balance, landing on the ground next to me.

As I lay there panting, another memory danced into my thoughts. This one of a young Razma and Kynan lying in Tarquin's garden after she'd performed a similar maneuver. I pushed the memory away, not wanting to taint that sweet moment with this one.

Rolling to my side, I tried to make my getaway, but only managed to get to my knees before Samael grabbed my hair and pulled me onto his chest.

He wrapped his arms around me, pinning my arms with his. I thrashed about, my legs kicking wildly, hoping to hear a yelp of pain, but he didn't yield.

I needed another tactic. Calling forth my power, I tried to attack him with it, but it only sizzled around us. I couldn't concentrate enough to make any sort of impact.

My mind cried out to Tarquin, James, and Astrid, hoping the message would find them, despite my panic.

"What do you want from me?" I demanded. "Is it about me stealing something from you? Do you want Sarah for some twisted reason? What is it?"

Covering my mouth with his hand, he rolled on top of me, straddling my chest. He stared into my eyes, the familiarity making me look away. "What do I want from you?" he asked, his words strained. "I want to know why . . . why you left us . . . why you left me? I've waited for thousands of years to get close enough to you to ask this question."

The fight went out of me as I searched his face, trying to find any trace of guile. His question seemed genuine, his eyes begging me to answer.

"I'm sorry," I stammered. "I don't know what you're talking about. I don't know you."

Lies . . . lies . . . my spirit hissed.

His body tensed, and he shook his head, a look of defeat ghosting over his features. He dropped his forehead to rest on mine, and I could've sworn a soft, primal growl emanated from within him.

Laying under his body, I didn't move an inch, unsure what to do. My fists clenched as a sudden insane desire to comfort him came over me.

What the absolute hell is wrong with me?

Samael stood up, and looked down at me, dragging his hands through his hair, as if he too didn't know what to do. I should've taken this opportunity to escape, but my body refused any command of mine to move. I lay there watching him.

His features darkened, becoming more severe. "You don't need to destroy yourself to evade me," he finally said, looking away. "I don't want to see you hurt. Do what you think you need to do, but please leave now. You're not safe here. For my part, I promise I won't force my presence on you again in this lifetime, and I'll do my best to influence the others."

With those words, he vanished, leaving me alone, lying on the ground.

～

Tarquin and Astrid crashed through the underbrush to find me still lying on my back, staring at the trees. It was as if Samael had tugged the rug out from under my feet, and the fall had addled my brain.

I couldn't wrap my mind around what happened. This whole time, I'd seen him as my enemy, the ruler of the demons who wanted to use me and my sisters to get to Sarah. But he had seemed like he didn't care about Sarah, or the fight the demons were waging; he was only interested in understanding why I'd left him.

I couldn't quite remember being with him, let alone leaving. And I didn't dare push myself to remember. What would I find?

Dammit. I didn't understand the dynamic at all, didn't understand the players in this battle.

Tarquin knelt next to me, pushing my hair off my face. "Are you hurt?" he asked, running his hands carefully over my limbs.

I didn't answer. I couldn't answer.

When he was satisfied that no outward harm had befallen me, he peered into my face, his brow creasing with worry. "Why aren't you answering?"

"Because I don't know what to say," I whispered.

Astrid crouched at my side across from Tarquin. "Would you like us to help you up? Maybe you can tell us what happened? Or should we lie down and admire the trees as well?"

I turned to look at her, surprised with the laughter bubbling to my lips at her expression of mock innocence. Pushing myself upright, I sat between them, picking at stray blades of grass poking out stubbornly between the fallen pine needles.

They let me sit undisturbed for a few minutes, though I could tell it was killing them not to pepper me with questions. Taking a deep breath, I decided to end their agony. "I took a walk to clear my mind, figure out our next steps, when I ran into Samael. Literally ran into him."

Astrid made no outward reaction, but Tarquin took hold of my hand, squeezing it and then drawing me into his arms. "Did he hurt you?" he asked.

I shook my head against his chest.

"No, he didn't hurt me, he just confused me," I finally replied, pulling away and pinching the bridge of my nose between my forefinger and thumb, fighting the headache that was building. "He wanted to know why I left him."

My bottled-up thoughts suddenly spilled out. "I can't explain it, but when he looked into my eyes, I felt like he wasn't a threat to me—like he wasn't responsible for this nightmare I'm in." I looked to Tarquin and Astrid for input but was met with wariness. I continued, trying to logic my way through the confusion. "But then why in my vision was he so terrifying? The thought of him scares the hell out of me. Yet his touch, his presence, they seem so familiar. But I don't think I remember him. Why don't I remember him?"

Tarquin looked away, clearly uncomfortable. To his credit though, he continued to soothe me, rubbing my back.

"Do you think it's a trick?" he asked.

"I don't know," I replied. "He said we needed to leave, and that he'll stay away from me and try to influence the others, whatever that means. I'm guessing maybe the others he's referring to are demons, or maybe the Guardians?"

"Why would he do that?" Tarquin shook his head. "Why would he help us? It makes no sense. Where has he been this whole time?"

Astrid grunted. "Well, hopefully, he's telling the truth. We could use some help."

Tarquin and I looked at her, our eyes widening in surprise. Astrid shrugged. "What? You can't say things are going well. Can you?"

She was right. It didn't take a genius to realize our train was going off the rails. Nothing was going our way; from my difficulty in awakening, to my sisters' failure at coming into their powers. Things were not going well.

And that wasn't even including how I'd failed my husband.

Oh crap, I'm about to break down again. Not now. I needed my head in the game. Dwelling on my misery was not going to help anyone.

Tarquin stood up, pulling me with him. "Let's get out of here. We need to locate Sarah and finish this. Let's get Marcianna back to her family."

He hugged me closer to his side, guiding me back to the house. We walked together in perfect stride, Tarquin rubbing my arm every now and then as he held me tight.

Looking over my shoulder, I saw Astrid standing

quietly, watching us leave. She worried her lip, her brow creased in a deep frown. As soon as she caught my eye though, she snapped out of her musing and followed behind.

I don't know what I expected to find when we returned to the house—maybe demons running amuck all over our hideout. But stepping through the front door, I couldn't help smiling at the normalcy.

James sat in the breakfast nook with my sisters, laughing at some comment Harlow made. She seemed to have him wrapped around her finger already, like all the partygoers in my first vision of her. Mina sat beside them looking relaxed for once, listening to the conversation and nodding, while sipping from a teacup. As soon as she saw me, though, she jumped to her feet and ran to my side.

"What happened? We heard you screaming . . . in our heads," she said, her words rushed. "James wouldn't let us go with Tarquin and Astrid."

She flashed James an accusatory look.

Looking at her concerned face, I debated confiding in my sisters, telling them all the details of my experience with Samael. I decided to be as transparent as possible for once, breaking the cycle of secrecy I'd created over the years.

"Samael found me in the woods," I said. "Do you remember him? He was one of the creatures that held us captive."

"Oh my God!" Harlow cried out, hugging me tightly. "Are you okay?"

"Yes," I said, returning her hug. "It was an extremely confusing encounter, and I haven't processed through it yet."

"Umm . . . if he found you, then shouldn't we be getting the hell out of here?" Mina asked. Her hand clutched at her throat, and her eyes scanned the room as if expecting Samael to jump out from behind a couch.

"He did tell us to leave, but I think we're all right for the moment," I reassured her. "He didn't seem like a threat. In fact, he promised to try to keep the demons away from us."

Mina looked at me as if I was crazy. "And you believed him?"

I nodded. She stared up at the ceiling as if searching for her patience before facing me again, her face red. "Are you kidding me? And we're supposed to believe the word of this monster? For all we know, demons will come pouring through the door at any minute sent by this guy you barely know—this guy who held us captive, and who participated in the murder of your husband!"

I jerked, her words a slap to my face. But she was right; I sounded insane.

I'd been terrified at the very thought of Samael, visions of him eliciting a visceral fear. He'd participated in the capture of individuals precious to me, and he didn't stop the killing of Ray by Gadreel. But somehow, despite all that, his physical presence caused me to lose all sense of right and wrong. Even now, my power seemed to crave him, reaching out in search of him.

"I can't explain it," I said. "I trust his word on this. He helped free me from my cell and could've dragged me back to the rest of them if he wanted. But he didn't."

"This is crazy. He could be tricking you so you lead them to Sarah," Mina pressed, grabbing my arms as if fighting the impulse to shake me into reality. "Did you ever think of that?"

Embarrassingly, I had not, and it made complete sense. But my spirit disagreed and I pulled myself free from her grasp. "I really believe his word on this is good. I can't say why, but I feel it to be true."

"And you all agree with this?" she demanded, looking at my eternal babysitters. Tarquin and James didn't respond, but Astrid nodded.

Well, thank you Astrid. She was the last individual I'd peg as concurring with my gut regarding trusting the so-called Angel of Death. I prayed I wasn't wrong, that my trust wasn't misplaced, and this wouldn't backfire, resulting in the suffering of even more people I loved.

Mina bit her lip, looking around the room, before sighing loudly. "Fine, then what do you propose we do next?"

"I think we are on the right track, but we need to figure out what's blocking our ability to locate Sarah. So, I propose we work on relaxing, clearing our minds, and combining our powers. The sooner we identify where Sarah is, the sooner we can heed Samael's words and get the hell out of here." I inclined my head toward my immortal family. "And maybe we should go somewhere without an audience."

"Why don't we lie on a bed? That's relaxing. And we could do, like a guided meditation or something," Harlow offered.

Mina looked at her like she was crazy, but it sounded so much like something Farah would say that I decided it was worth a shot.

"Okay, let's do it." Taking their hands, I pulled them toward a bedroom.

Harlow jumped onto the bed as soon as I closed the door, bouncing several times before dropping onto her back with a giggle. Lifting herself up onto her elbows, she stared me and Mina down. "Are you joining me?" she asked.

Mina gingerly settled onto the edge of the bed, and I stepped over her, laying down between my sisters. Taking their hands in mine, I pulled them to my sides.

"This is just weird," Mina said, and earned a loud shush from Harlow.

"Please, Mina," I said. "Don't you want us to get back to our lives?"

She hesitated, then nodded, with a bit of a shrug. I didn't have the energy to interpret that.

"Okay, then close your eyes and focus," I instructed. "Leave your judgment and attitude behind."

Mina lurched up, looking down at me. "I don't have an attitude."

"Yeah, right," Harlow snorted into my ear.

I raised an eyebrow at Mina, and she jutted her chin in response.

"Stop. Please," I said, keeping my voice even despite my patience being sorely tested. "I'm sorry I said that. Just lay down and close your eyes."

She blew a strand of hair from her face, but otherwise didn't budge. A few seconds passed of us locked in a battle of wills, her staring down at me as I lay on the bed, Harlow holding her breath next to me.

"Fine," Mina finally said, flopping onto her back and slipping her hand into mine once more.

We closed our eyes. "Relax your body and focus your mind," I said, mimicking Farah's tone as best as I could. "Open up your thoughts to me."

Farah also had me chanting to help with focus, but I couldn't remember her Sanskrit words. I tried to think of an alternative.

"To focus our minds, let's repeat Sarah's name." It sounded silly, but I hoped it would work.

Our voices chanted "Sarah" until the sounds melded together, flowing through us. I felt my sisters relax, their limbs going slack as our energies entwined. We were connected, bound to each other.

An intense feeling surged through me. I couldn't quite explain it, but it was like I'd been missing a critical piece of myself that now I'd found. I finally felt right. Finally felt whole.

Before I could relish this sensation, the darkness within my mind faded as a beautiful garden appeared. Birds danced in the sky, their chirps making me smile, the sunshine warming me with its soft caresses.

Walking through the flowers, I saw a tree blooming up ahead, white flowers and fruit decorating the lush green leaves. There was a shimmer of light flowing through the branches making the tree sparkle.

Within the tree's roots sat a little girl, her head bowed, her little hand pressed against the trunk. Someone nudged me and I turned to see Mina and Harlow in their human forms.

Is that her? Harlow's voice echoed within me. I didn't reply but motioned my sisters to follow me toward the girl.

Reaching out, I lightly touched the girl's shoulder so as not to startle her. She looked up, her face puffy and covered in tears, her eyes filled with too much sorrow for such a little one.

"Sarah?" I asked.

She nodded.

"Why are you crying?" I asked, kneeling next to her.

"I can't do what you want me to do," she said, her childish voice ripping at my heart as I thought of my own children in such pain.

Harlow wrapped her arms around Sarah, and the little girl burrowed into the embrace.

"I'm so tired and scared. I can't keep doing this," she whispered into Harlow's chest.

Harlow's eyes flared, a fire within her responding to the child's words. "We'll protect you," she said, stroking Sarah's hair. "We'll fight off anything that tries to hurt you. Don't worry, you're not alone, just tell us where we can find you."

I leaned into the pair, taking both Sarah and Harlow into my arms, the urge to protect them both overwhelming me.

Sarah's little hand curled around my waist, holding on tight. Her crying had calmed, the shuddering gulps ceasing as her body relaxed. Pulling away slowly from the comfort of Harlow, she looked up into my eyes.

The garden vanished and we were in a lavender room filled with toys, a half-finished puzzle on the floor with pieces sprawled around it.

"Is this your room?" I asked.

Sarah nodded hesitantly.

Kneeling to be at her eye level, I asked, "Would you like to show us your house?"

She studied my face, touching my cheek with her finger before directing her gaze to my sisters. Her soft voice was unsure, but she replied, "Okay."

Taking Harlow and me by the hand, Sarah led us both out of her room and down the hall, Mina trailing behind us. The house was a split level, filled to the brim with frumpy, well-worn furniture and tacky floral wallpaper. I could see someone had started to peel some of the wallpaper away, a project likely on a large to-do list.

The house reflected Sarah's world—lots of distractions, unfinished projects, and hustle and bustle. And lots of love. I smiled at the little girl in the photo surrounded by a pack of brothers all mugging for the camera.

From the pictures scattered throughout the house, I could tell Sarah was the youngest of a large family. The essence of the family hung in the air, the happiness and love enveloping me, making me feel a longing for my own family.

A woman's voice called from the backyard, "Sarah . . . Sarah, I hope you're not watching TV? Come outside and play with your brothers."

I looked out the window to see the two older siblings and their parents sitting around a firepit, while two younger boys ran around the backyard, jumping on a dilapidated playground.

This was fascinating, and I wondered if this was a memory or if we were in Sarah's head in real time.

I turned and saw Mina scanning the papers on the kitchen table, trying to identify our location as I'd done when I'd located her in the Upper East side of New York City. But I knew where Sarah was, knew I'd be able to find her and her family with no issue. They were etched into my spirit now.

It was time for us to go and physically travel to her, help her fulfill whatever destiny was necessary to keep humanity on track.

Giving Sarah a hug, I whispered into the top of her head, "We'll be back. We'll help you. It'll all be okay."

The room tilted and darkness eclipsed the light. The three of us lurched up in the bed still holding hands.

Mina panted hard next to me. "What the heck! I didn't get a chance to figure out where she was."

"I know where she is," I replied. "We didn't need to stay longer. I had everything I needed to find her again."

"Oh, you did, did you?" Mina challenged.

We eyed each other, neither of us saying a word. I started feeling awkward in the stare down, wondering if I should apologize for pulling us out of the vision without consulting with anyone else.

Before I could say anything though, Harlow placed a hand on my arm, drawing my attention to her.

"I'm sad for Sarah," she said, her ink-colored hair framing her face, not one strand out of place despite us laying on the bed. "She seems so scared. We have to protect her. Promise me we will."

Looking into her dark eyes, I saw such desire to help, to fight for this child, and my heart warmed at her passion and fire. "Don't worry, we'll take care of her and her family. We'll make sure nothing bad happens to them."

I patted her arm, and she smiled, giving me a kiss on the cheek before bouncing off the bed.

Mina followed her off the bed and headed to the door. Pausing with her hand on the handle, she turned to look at me. "Well, if we're going to make good on this promise of yours, we should get going, or is this your sole decision, too?"

"I'm sorry," I said. "I should've said something before pulling us out of there. I promise I'll do better. We're a team."

A small smile appeared on Mina's face, smoothing out the signs of tension, her shoulders visibly relaxing. "Thank you." She fidgeted as if unsure what to say next. "I . . . um . . . appreciate it."

She pulled open the door and bellowed, "Tarquin, James, Astrid! We know where Sarah is! We have to go now!"

My heart quickened its rhythm in anticipation. It was starting. The wheels were in motion, and soon this nightmare would be over. I could practically feel my children's arms around me.

CHAPTER FOURTEEN

We rushed to pack our scant belongings, anxious to get the hell out of there. The house was a symphony of creaks and groans, each floorboard screaming good riddance and readying for another long slumber.

Stepping outside, I was surprised to find two cars parked, Astrid's Mercedes and Tarquin's SUV. I frowned, unsure how I'd missed Tarquin's car when we'd arrived or how'd it even got here from the cabin.

Harlow wrapped her arm around my waist and, as if reading my mind, said, "We awakened pretty quickly once Astrid got us here. And then we helped her get Tarquin's car while waiting for you to contact us. Is that what you're thinking? I figured since you were staring at the SUV and getting all frowny."

Looking at her, I asked, "Do you know what made you finally awaken?"

Harlow averted her eyes, jabbing at the dirt with the tip of her shoe.

"You were screaming in our minds," Mina replied, joining us outside. "We could feel your pain ripping us apart until we thought we couldn't bear it anymore. And then suddenly you were gone."

"We didn't know what happened," Harlow whispered, her words rushed as tears pooled in her eyes. "We didn't know why you were in so much pain. And the awakening was so scary."

"It was horrible," Mina added, rubbing Harlow's arm lightly in a soothing motion. "We were finally cognizant of who we were, and that we needed to be with you, yet we could no longer feel you, couldn't find you."

"I'm sorry; I must've become lost to you when Samael went into my mind, and I lost consciousness." The pain they felt was Ray being taken from me, but I couldn't say this out loud. I was barely holding the pieces of my heart together as it was.

"Astrid was scared," Harlow added.

I looked at the blonde in question. She currently looked annoyed, bickering with Tarquin. Fragments of their conversation caught my ear enough that I knew they were arguing whether we should all go in the SUV or split up into two cars.

Astrid must've convinced Tarquin it was safer to split up in case of an attack. She now strode toward us, her chest puffed out in victory and her voice cracking like a whip, "Tarquin, you take Mina and Harlow. James and I will take Marci."

She grabbed me by the elbow, pulling me away

from my sisters before any of us could protest. As she ushered me to her Mercedes, I glanced over my shoulder and saw Tarquin's frown. I suspected he wanted me to go with him, but Astrid's speed didn't allow any opportunity for further discussion. She had me in the passenger's seat in no time, even leaning over to buckle my seatbelt.

My eyes met Tarquin's through the rearview mirror, and he shot me a comforting smile before loading my sisters into his SUV.

James slid into the backseat of our car, tapping me on the side of the head affectionately. "Ready," he said as Astrid revved the engine.

Adjusting the rearview mirror before pulling out of the driveway, Astrid said, "So, North Carolina. Too bad you didn't have that epiphany before I hauled ass with a teenager all the way from Georgia."

I don't know why I felt guilty, but I did. "Sorry, but you know it would've been impossible. I needed my sisters to locate Sarah in the first place, right? A chicken and egg thing."

Turning to me she grinned and winked. "I know," she said. "I'm being difficult. It's what I'm good at."

James snorted. "I'll say."

Looking at the two of them, my heart squeezed with happiness, and I laughed despite my kaleidoscope of emotions. We soon settled into an easy banter, James and Astrid regaling me with their many adventures in between my awakenings. They behaved almost like siblings, or an old married couple, one minute arguing and the next laughing hysterically over something the other said.

I relaxed for the first time in what seemed like forever.

Time flew by quickly, and I was surprised when we passed New York City, James startling me out of my daydreams with a loud declaration. "I'll add my complaints to Astrid's. Wish we could've grabbed Armina as we drove past Manhattan. Maybe she wouldn't have tried to emasculate me if you'd been there."

"I'm so sorry," I said, turning in my seat to face him. "She was rough on you, huh?"

"She usually is," he laughed. "But it's easier when she's awake and knows who I am. She's always been fiercely independent."

"Always the same personality?" I asked.

He nodded, glancing at Astrid. "Harlow is different. She embodies sweetness, passion, and is extremely persuasive."

A smile flickered over his face with that last statement.

"He means she has all men eating out of the palm of her hand," Astrid snorted and then tilted her head as if in thought, after a moment adding, "And women, for that matter."

"Am I always the same, too?" I asked James, not sure if I wanted to hear the response.

"You're very much the caretaker, always thinking about everyone else, thoughtful and motherly."

"Wow, I seem incredibly boring compared to fierce

independence and sweet passion," I said. Not sure why this bothered me. I mean, I was the things James said —I was a mother—but that couldn't really be the extent of my whole personality.

"I can add on if you'd like," Astrid said.

"Oh, I know what you're going to say . . . cold, heartless bitch . . . no pesky human emotion. Isn't that what you told me before?" I plastered a forced smile on my face in hopes it would mask the hurt and worry I felt over her previous observation.

"I don't remember saying *those* words exactly," Astrid huffed, lifting her brows high, impressively so, given her tightly pulled back ponytail. "But you *are* very much the leader of your sisters . . . you're the one who knows what is right, how everything should be, and when you awaken, you become that much more unyielding in your vision."

"You really could've stopped at *boring vanilla* and didn't need to go to *bossy jerk*," I said, my tone as dry as a desert.

"But I didn't want to disappoint you since you didn't like James's depiction," Astrid said, showing off all her pearly whites.

"Ha—well, then I made you in my image."

Her eyes widened, and she burst out laughing. "Sometimes I wish you did, but I seemed to have gotten the 'bossy jerk' part, as you call it, without any of the kinder parts."

I knew she said that as a joke, but something about her statement pulled at my heart.

"You've got kinder parts to your personality too," I

said softly. "You don't want us to see, but we've had glimpses between the prickles and thorns."

James sat uncharacteristically quiet in the backseat during our exchange. Peeking out of the corner of my eye, I noticed a slight smile tug on his lips. He was pleased by what I'd said, and I realized as much as James and Astrid fought, he had a soft spot for her.

Astrid pulled the car over at the next gas station. "We need gas and I'm sure you require tending to your biological needs."

As if on cue, my stomach growled, and Astrid made a "told you so" face. Getting out of the car, I stretched my limbs, realizing I could also use a bathroom right about now. Making a beeline for the convenience store, I quickly used the restroom, trying my best to ignore the pale, disheveled woman staring back at me in the bathroom mirror. The past few days had made me almost unrecognizable.

Leaving the bathroom, I browsed for some snacks and drinks, settling on some chocolate-covered peanuts and water. I was surprised Astrid and James hadn't followed me into the convenience store, and I looked out the window at our car. They were standing outside of it talking. Astrid looked determined, but James kept looking away, his brow creased, his head occasionally shaking in disagreement.

I continued to watch their dialogue over the shoulder of the cashier as I paid for my purchases. For a moment I considered invading their thoughts, but the ick factor of doing so without good cause was a bit much. For all I knew, they were discussing the best route to follow, or maybe the best restaurant choices. I hoped it was the latter as I couldn't live on chocolate-covered peanuts.

As I approached the car, they halted their conversation. James looked nervous, his shoulders tense, and his eyes unable to hold my gaze as they tracked my progress.

"I'll be right back," he said when I arrived by their side.

He headed toward the convenience store, leaving me standing with Astrid, though he looked back at us a couple of times.

"What's going on?" I asked.

"With what?" Astrid replied, her eyes widening in innocence.

"What were you two disagreeing about?"

"You know us," she smiled, and flicked an imaginary speck of lint off her designer jacket. "We're always fighting about something."

"Okay, fine. Don't tell me." I gritted my teeth and resisted the urge to stamp my feet like a toddler. "Are we waiting for Tarquin here or we gonna meet him somewhere else?"

"Somewhere else. Here, sit down," she said, patting the hood of the car as she leaned against it. "We can relax while James does whatever James is doing in that store."

We sat there not talking for a bit as I drank my water. Digging the chocolate peanuts from the kangaroo pouch of my sweatshirt, I offered some to Astrid. She took one, eyeing it suspiciously.

"Do you have a peanut allergy?" I asked.

"No, just never had one of these before." She popped it in her mouth, closing her eyes, savoring the candy. "It's nice. I like it."

Reclining against the hood, she propped herself on her elbows and peeked out at me from under her eyelashes. "I always wanted to ask you a question."

"Ask away," I said, my chest tightening as if anticipating the worst.

"What do you see when you look at them?" She pointed to a group of teenagers loitering outside the convenience store.

"Who? The kids over there?" I squinted, seeing nothing out of the ordinary.

Bobbing her head, she replied. "Sure. What do you see? I'm just curious."

My palms got a little sweaty. The way my body was reacting, you'd think I was being asked to take the medical board exam again. "Umm . . . I see kids, teenagers. I'm confused, what am I supposed to be looking for?"

"Don't look at them with your human eyes," she instructed. "Do it with your Lilith eyes."

Turning to face her, my cheeks flushed as I sputtered, "Don't call me by that name."

"Fine. Settle down, I meant no offense," she said, rolling her eyes at my reaction. "How about you do it with your Razma eyes then, or your creature eyes, or with your whatever-kind-of-supernatural-being-you-are eyes."

Raising an eyebrow, I bit back my sass, my curiosity overriding my anxiety. My mind racing a mile a minute, I worked on silencing my inner voice before relaxing my body and focusing on the teenagers.

Soon every cell, every synapse within me hummed as the bodies of the teenagers blurred into the background, shimmering lights of a multitude of colors taking shape in their place. It was their souls. I'd never really looked this closely at them before, only noting their presence—or absence. They reminded me of the orb.

Through my trance, I heard Astrid's voice as if in the distance. "Can you tell their souls apart?"

"They're each a slightly different composition of colors . . . some subtle differences in hues, and maybe the way they shimmer." My voice seemed like it wasn't part of me, floating off somewhere in space.

"But would it be memorable in any way? Would you recognize them by these colors?"

I looked closer at the glowing shapes of energy, rippling as if pulled by a current, and I realized that like the orb, the sheen of the colors varied with each passing moment. "Their colors are changing. I'm not sure I'd recognize them."

With those words, I came out of my trance to find Astrid's face mere inches from mine.

"Shit, Astrid!" I yelped, clutching at my chest. "You scared me! I wasn't expecting you all in my personal space."

She didn't acknowledge my comment or startle. "So, you'd not be able to recognize them again, be able to differentiate them by their souls?"

I shrugged, feeling oddly uncomfortable by her question.

"What about you?" I asked.

"Even if I interacted with a human soul for a long period of time in one of their lifetimes, I'd still find it difficult to recognize them in the next one." She emphasized each word as she spoke, her icy blue stare piercing me. "Actually, not difficult; it would be impossible. Those hues of color change with their experiences in life, with their feelings. They're not distinct to me. It's because they're part of the One Spirit."

I didn't understand why she was saying this, what the significance was. Or perhaps I didn't want to understand. "I've never stared at the souls of humans before. Maybe if I'd spent more time at it, I'd be able to recognize them like I do the demons," I replied, turning away from her gaze.

She grabbed my arm, pulling me back as if not yet done with this conversation, but James arrived at that moment, his eyes flickering between Astrid and me.

"Everything okay?" he asked, his voice strained.

"Yeah," I replied, yanking my arm out of Astrid's grasp and opening the car door, sliding in quickly. I saw them exchange a look, a conversation passing between two creatures bonded together for hundreds of years. But I couldn't decipher it.

They got into the car, and we drove off. This time

we sat quietly, the atmosphere no longer jovial, but tense.

Something of importance had transpired—I knew it, and part of me wanted to examine the data further, but an even stronger part of me refused. And this part forced me into silence, signaling to everyone there'd be no more discourse about humans and their souls.

CHAPTER FIFTEEN

Speeding down the highway, I watched the trees fly by as I pressed my head against the window. The car ride had turned somber. No one spoke, and Astrid had put on death metal to fill the silence.

The music was far from soothing, but the warmth from the sun shining through the window coupled with the sway of the car made my eyes droop. Realizing I hadn't slept in a few days, well, at least not in a manner where I wasn't knocked unconscious first, I allowed myself to be pulled into the darkness, succumbing to my exhaustion.

The dreams started almost immediately, vivid and all-consuming.

I sat in a room, snuggling a baby as a fire burned in a hearth. The child made sweet gurgling sounds, its dimpled arms reaching out toward my face.

Humming softly, I realized my voice didn't sound like mine, the pitch and timbre different. And when I began to sing, the words were unrecognizable. Until suddenly, like magic, everything—the music, the place, the child—became familiar. I closed my eyes, clutching my sweet babe to my breast, relishing this tender moment.

My flaming red hair surrounded the child like a protective curtain, the shade far more vibrant than my muted auburn. It was a blood red, even richer than Razma's shade, thick and shining brightly in the firelight.

The baby grabbed the strands in its tiny fist, laughing with each tug.

"No, give Mama her hair back," I giggled, untangling my curls from between chubby fingers. Standing up with the child, I walked to a little basin filled with water and began undressing him.

"My son," I said, my voice echoing around the sparsely furnished room. "It is time for your bath."

Planting raspberries on his plump tummy, I was rewarded with squeals of delight, our laughter melding together.

Holding him on my hip, I caught my reflection in the water. It was not my face staring back, and not Razma's either. The woman in the reflection was truly lovely with her dark green eyes and delicate features, a cloud of curly hair cascading down her back.

Another face appeared in the basin next to mine, and my heart squeezed in recognition. Samael smiled back at me, pressing a kiss to my neck, his lips trailing down my shoulder.

My hand stilled, the wet cloth I'd readied to bathe the child dropping into the water.

In this dream, he did not terrify me, his touch bringing pleasure and sparking a longing within my stomach. Turning to face him while still holding my squirming child, I couldn't help but admire his beauty, so raw and wild, his eyes blazing with passion as he leaned in to claim my lips.

His kiss deepened, his tongue exploring my mouth, drawing a sigh from me. A squeal of laughter interrupted us as my son kicked his feet into the basin, splashing water over us.

Samael chuckled against my mouth. He released my lips, trailing his fingertips down my cheek before fishing the washcloth from the basin. "Let me bathe him. His eyes belie mischievous plans to soak his mother from head to toe."

Giggling, I moved to pass him our son, but my hands were empty. Lifting my eyes to Samael, I realized he was also no longer by my side. The room was fading away.

Frantically I looked in all directions for my child and Samael until I realized I was in a luscious garden, a little boy running circles around me, screaming, "Look at me Mama!" as he changed his appearance, flitting between shapes—one minute a child, the next an animal, and then back to a human form.

"Stop," I laughed breathlessly, catching him in my arms and twirling him around. "Be careful who you do that around; we're too close to the mortals, and these humans wouldn't understand what you are if you kept shifting your form like this. They'll think you're a demon, or some other creature of the night sent to hurt them. Scared humans can be dangerous, my love."

"Mama, but I like it, and they like me. I showed the human children, and they weren't scared." He showered my face with kisses, and my arms tightened around him, worry eating away at my happiness. Gazing into his sweet face, I opened my mouth to tell him yet again to be cautious.

"Marci." A voice broke into my dream, strong hands jostling me awake.

Gasping, I jerked upright, my hands flying to my face. My cheeks were wet with tears and my throat still clenched with the need to protect my child.

My child . . . my child with Samael! Was this dream real? It most certainly felt like a memory, not a fantasy. My stomach lurched as James's words echoed in my mind, *some say she's the mother of demons, copulating with Samael.*

Though the child was not a demon, at least not in that memory, his existence supported the reality of my copulation with Samael.

Astrid snapped her fingers in front of my face, and I reflexively slapped her hand away.

"What's wrong with you?" I hissed.

"You were moaning and groaning, thrashing around in your seat. You were so loud, even James was getting uncomfortable. You know, in his eyes, you're still his little sister."

I flushed, wondering if those moans were sexual in nature as my dream-self relived Samael's touch. Probably, if they mortified poor James.

Turning apologetically to him, I found an empty back seat. "Where's James?"

Astrid gathered her belongings, answering distractedly as she searched the nooks and crannies for her phone. "Getting our room key, we're in North Carolina."

"Shouldn't we get to Sarah, then?" I asked, putting my hand on her arm, forcing her to look at me.

"No," she replied. She looked like she was going to leave it at that, but then caught my eyes narrowing with disapproval. "It's best to regroup and plan, rather than showing up at the poor kid's house in the middle of the night with no idea what we're doing. Don't you agree?"

Her answer made sense. As much as I wanted to get this over with, we needed some rest and planning instead of rushing in, potentially botching the job.

I nodded and got out of the car, staring at the motel. It was definitely the type of place I would've happily stayed at as a teenager during spring break but would scoff at as an adult.

James called out from the second story porch, disappearing into an open door as Astrid and I trudged up the stairs to join him. The room, though utilitarian, turned out to be a pleasant surprise—clean and well maintained, not at all what I expected from the outside.

"Are Tarquin and my sisters here already?" I asked James.

"They should be in twenty minutes or so." He

threw himself on one of the beds with an exaggerated bounce.

Astrid emerged from the bathroom, scowling at James. "What gave you the idea you'd be sleeping there?" she asked, throwing a hand towel at him. "Marci gets one and I've claimed the other."

"Dream on. My body on this bed clearly shows I've claimed it." He grinned. "Besides, I'm bigger than you and deserve to relax on something that doesn't squash me like an accordion." Covering his face with the towel, he added, "Now be a dear and use the couch."

The interaction surprised me. I was either unobservant or self-absorbed, or likely a little of both. I'd been with them for weeks and somehow hadn't noticed they slept. They'd always seemed to be lurking about everywhere.

"You sleep?" My question stopped Astrid from dropping a bag onto James's head.

"Yes. Despite our immortality, strength, and speed, we still have some mortal vulnerabilities," she said, kicking James in the hip with her heel, only to be rewarded with him faking a loud snore.

"You can take this one," I offered, gesturing to the remaining bed.

"No," Astrid and James said in unison, James leaping off his bed as if it was suddenly on fire.

"Don't be ridiculous." I shoved James back onto the bed he'd claimed. "I'm fine. I slept half the ride here, remember?"

They exchanged looks, their features like reflections in a mirror, eyes tracking my every move. "You both relax; I'm going to sit on the porch a bit and wait for the other car."

They still looked like they were going to protest, their gaze bouncing between me, the door, and each other.

"Seriously—relax—because when I return, I'm going to pull someone's ass out of the bed," I said, deciding to be firmer in my proposal. "Or maybe Tarquin can stay in this room, and I'll stay with my sisters. I'm sure one of them won't mind sharing the bed with me."

Not letting them reply, I grabbed a blanket from the bed, wrapping it around me in lieu of the sweatshirt I'd left in Astrid's car, and stepped out into the crisp night air.

As I sat down on the flimsy plastic chair, Astrid popped out of the room. "You'll be sitting right there, and you won't move?"

I nodded. "Please go inside and catch some z's. I need you spry."

"I'm always spry," she snorted, but ducked back into the room.

The door didn't remain shut long, James stepping out within seconds of it closing. Putting his hand on my shoulder, he forced me to look up at him. "Is something wrong? Do you need to talk?"

"I'm okay, really," I assured him, but he didn't budge. "I'm just not tired and want to enjoy the night air. Is that weird?"

He grunted. "No. It's understandable." Patting my shoulder, he gently tousled my hair before giving me a mock stern look. "But come straight to us if anything seems wrong. And scream."

Flashing him a thumbs up, and a hopefully reassuring smile, I watched him leave, hamming up my smile when he hesitated at the door. "You know I have powers. I've destroyed demons. Don't underestimate me."

"I'll never underestimate you," he said, finally twisting the handle and pushing the door open. "But still scream."

"Will do," I replied, exhaling a sigh of relief as soon as I was alone, finally able to think without being scrutinized.

Wrapping myself tighter in the blanket, I stared out onto the front parking lot, wondering what the heck was taking Tarquin so long. The motel was situated off the beaten path and the night, though chilly for an April in this part of North Carolina, was still and peaceful.

"Hello, Moon," I whispered to my constant companion, the stars adding an extra twinkle as if not to be outdone by the serenity of the moon. How many lifetimes must I've looked up at the same stars, never remembering them, or that I've walked these paths before?

Somewhere out there, my family lived their new life, waiting for me and Ray to come home. My breath hitched, thinking of our kids' devastation when their daddy didn't return. Reminding myself it would break them even more if they lost their mother to boot.

Squeezing my eyes closed to force back tears, I

vowed to myself, to the blasted moon, that I'd make it through this, that I'd survive for my kids. I didn't really know what I was doing, what everything meant, and who the players were, but I'd figure it out, putting together the pieces of this jigsaw of memories that spanned millennia.

I had to.

If only Farah was here by my side, she'd know how to make the pieces fit. Her brain was made to understand these types of mysteries.

"I need you, Farah," I cried out. I desperately needed her—my clever best friend who'd not only helped me through this mess but through life in general. Covering my face with my hands, I wept for all I'd lost and all I still had to lose.

A sound in the parking lot caught my attention, and my head jerked up, hopeful Tarquin was pulling in. Scanning the parking lot, I noticed nothing amiss, only stillness. Gooseflesh decorated my skin as I shivered. Again, it was this feeling I knew too well.

Someone was watching me.

I leapt from my chair, squinting into the dimly lit parking lot. There was no one . . . I couldn't see anyone out there.

Shit. Something's wrong. Scream! Get back inside the room, my brain yelled. But my limbs failed to comply, my body stiffening as I continued to look into the darkness past the parked cars.

There, under a thin beam of light provided by a lone lamp, stood a figure.

My heart raced into my throat as the individual

made eye contact with me. I'd know that frame, the hair, the face shape, anywhere—even under the scarce light surrounded by utter darkness.

It was Farah, standing there as if I summoned her with my tears.

Was that even possible? *No, you idiot*, the words echoed in my mind. Yet, I paid no heed. It was a sound theory—one minute I'm crying, begging to see her and the next she appears. But then why the creepy posturing next to the lamp, standing on the outskirts of the parking lot almost on the road? Why didn't she call out to me? Wave to me?

I needed to get a closer look; maybe I was hallucinating, seeing what I wanted to see. My mouth was dry with anticipation and fear as I went down the stairs, cautiously crossing the parking lot until I was halfway to her.

Stopping in my path, I turned to look over my shoulder at the motel. My internal voice battled furiously, begging me to go no further, to go back to my room and to the safety of Astrid and James.

"Marci?" the figure called out. "Is that you?" That was definitely Farah's voice.

Breaking out into a full-on sprint, I ran to her, flinging my arms around her shoulders and sobbing into her neck. "Oh my God, Farah. How'd you get here?"

"I don't know," she sputtered. Her face scrunched up in confusion. "One minute I was getting the kids ready for bed and the next, I'm standing in a parking lot in my pajamas."

High beams from a car approaching in the distance illuminated our surroundings, distracting me. Farah grabbed my hand, her voice taking on a tone of urgency. "We have to go. Will you come with me?"

"Where?" I shook my head, pulling her toward the parking lot. "No, you come into the motel with me. It's not safe here."

Digging in her heels, she pleaded, "Please, I need you to come. Don't you trust me? I thought you were my best friend."

Guilt pricked at my conscious, and I looked around, unsure what to do. This is Farah, I reminded myself, my confidant and spiritual lighthouse, my sister from another mister. "I trust you," I finally said, my voice as emphatic as I could make it, and her face brightened. "But where do you want to go? I'll go with you wherever you need me to go."

The lights of the oncoming car grew brighter, reflecting strangely off Farah's dark eyes as an eerie smile spread over lips, her features contorting in a sinister way.

Her mouth curled and she replied, "We're going to hell. Where you belong."

The light exploded above us, raining glass on our heads. Somewhere in the distance, someone screamed my name, but a loud buzzing sound drowned them out as an electric current zapped through me.

Darkness enveloped me, and I had a sensation of spinning, wind lashing at my clothing. My stomach heaved, and I shut my eyes. The wind strengthened, and it felt like my skin was sloughing off.

Two seconds away from puking my guts out, from screaming *I can't take this anymore*, everything went still. My ears popped and I cautiously cracked my eyes open.

I was no longer in the motel parking lot. Flickering floating lights illuminated the contours of a cave, and my breathing turned ragged.

Shit! This place was crawling with demons, and they only had eyes for me.

CHAPTER SIXTEEN

Shadowy figures pressed in on me, and my heart rammed painfully against my rib cage. How did I get here? One second, I was in the parking lot holding hands with creepy Farah and the next I was in a vortex to wherever the hell this was.

Oh, God, hopefully not hell. My mind panicked. *Please let me not actually be in hell.*

Farah was still standing next to me. Outwardly she looked like my Farah, but now that I looked at her with my Lilith eyes, as Astrid would say, I could tell she was not human. It wasn't even a case of human possession, as I'd initially feared while tumbling through the tunnel of doom.

"What are you?" I demanded.

"It's a mimic, you silly creature. Can't you even recognize that?" A woman came out of the darkness, lingering wisps of the former occupant's shimmering soul still clinging to the flesh.

Lamia! That smug, faceless demon within this

unfortunate body would pay for destroying another human life. Another family.

"I told you I'd make you suffer for what you did to my family," she spat in my face.

"And what are you going to do? You know I can destroy you." I looked at the rest of the demons and puffed out my chest, hoping they bought my confidence. Most of the demons in the cave were bodiless, free-floating through the dim light. This cave seemed to be their shelter, keeping them safely away from the daylight and allowing them to move about without the need for a human host. Were they less powerful like this? What was the strength of their power in this form? Could I attack them and win?

"You're going to destroy us all? I highly doubt it. Besides, we have something to discuss as I'm getting—"

"Lamia!" A familiar voice boomed from the entrance of the cave, causing me to jump, my hand clutching at my chest.

Oh please, no.

Cold sweat beaded on my forehead as my husband's murderer strode into the cave, his long legs shortening the distance between us at an obscenely rapid pace. His hands were fisted as if ready to fight and, judging by his giant arms, he was powerful enough to tear a person to shreds in any battle.

"Gadreel," Lamia crooned.

"What the fuck are you doing?" he asked, his tone eerily calm.

Lamia shifted uncomfortably, the bodiless demons

around her swaying as if a breeze had entered the cave, drifting them away.

"I'm taking my revenge. As you—"

His hand sliced through the air, demanding silence. "Whatever you think I said was clearly wrong, you idiot. Why would I ever want you to harm her when we've searched so long for her to rejoin us?"

She watched him silently. The uncertainty in the air was thick as if manifesting a corporeal form itself.

Gadreel's fingers wrapped around my elbow, and my skin crawled with an immediate desire to wrench my arm free. I suppressed the instinct, my internal voice telling me to wait and watch.

"You do not dictate what we do and don't do," Lamia hissed, grabbing me by the wrist and pulling me close.

Great, this was fast becoming a tug-of-war. The demons and Gadreel were having some sort of stand-off, and I was the prize.

Gadreel wrenched me away from her and slammed me against his hard body, bruising my back. "Should I call Samael here? What do you think your lord and master would say if he heard you were planning to hurt her?"

Lamia blanched while her smoky form wrapped tighter within her human host. The other demons recoiled as if calling out Samael's name would bring him here to make good on Gadreel's barely veiled threat.

"That's what I thought," he snarled, his toothy grin terrifying against the coldness of his blue eyes.

Like the lion he resembled, he'd staked his claim, showing his rival beasts this prey was all his. When no one contested further, he yanked me toward the opening of the demon's cave. My feet, unable to match his gait, barely touched the ground.

I peeked over my shoulder now and again, convinced the demons would attack our flank. But they did nothing, only watched our departing forms, Lamia's face barely containing her hatred as our eyes met.

As soon as we made it out of the cave, I fought for Gadreel to release my arm, punching him in the shoulder when he didn't comply.

"Is this the way you thank me for saving your ass?" he asked, his voice like gravel.

Saving my ass! I desired to rip out his heart and feast on it for what he did to my husband. And he expected gratitude from me?

"I could've handled the demons," I snapped back.

He tightened his grip and continued to pull me along. "Not with your human body intact. And I get the sense you really want to go home . . . . continue playing house with your mortal children," he growled over his shoulder.

I sucked in my breath, my cheeks burning as if he'd just slapped me with his words. Something wasn't sitting right. This whole situation was wrong. Why would my husband's murderer protect me from demons? Why would he allow me to go back to my family when he'd just stated his desire to have me rejoin their group? I dug in my heels, fighting against his brute strength until he paused and turned to acknowledge me again.

"How did you find me?" I asked. Try as I might to keep my tone curious, it came out demanding and accusatory.

His jaw clenched, making me think he wasn't going to answer, but he surprised me saying, "Lamia was bitching to anyone who'd listen that she'd get even with you . . . that she didn't care about who you were, or why we needed you. Of course, I needed to follow her. That stupid demon couldn't be trusted, and I was right."

Yanking me back into motion, he continued dragging me again to wherever the hell he was going. It was infuriating. He was treating me like I had no say in what was to happen to me, like I should happily comply in whatever he dictated.

It was time to stop struggling against his physical strength and fight him with my magic. Channeling energy through my arm, I zapped him. He stopped in his tracks and glared, but didn't release my elbow.

"Where do you want to go, Lilith?"

Was he kidding? "I want to go back to my friends. Back to where that mimic thing found me."

He looked like he was considering my request, his brows knitting together. "No," he finally said, after a drawn-out pause. "I have a better place. Somewhere where we can talk in private without being disturbed."

Before I could protest, his arms wrapped around me like iron bands and, to my absolute shock, dark gray wings materialized from his shoulders as if out of thin air. For a crazy second, I prepared for him to launch us into the air, but the wings merely wrapped around my body as the world tilted. With his giant wings shielding me from the outside world, I was relieved to discover that the travel wasn't as painful as it had been with the mimic.

After a few minutes, the tilting feeling stopped, and his wings unfurled from around us. I stepped away from Gadreel and spun around the room, taking in my surroundings, unsure of where he'd taken us.

I noticed the light outside the window. A glorious sunrise kissed the early morning dew, making the droplets sparkle across a lawn I knew very well.

How could this be? This was my house—the decorations were different, another family plastered on the walls, but I'd recognize it anywhere.

Standing in the living room, I half expected to see my kids fighting over the TV, maybe begging for me to make pancakes. Waves of sadness assaulted me as my whole life flashed before my eyes—laughter, tears, cuddles, Ray's beautiful, dimpled smile making my body thrum with happiness each time he directed it at me.

"Why'd you bring me here?" I demanded, holding back my tears, not wanting to show weakness to my enemy.

Gadreel shrugged. "The family living here is away, so it's a quiet spot for discourse. Also, you have a connection here. Perhaps it'll help you remember other critical events."

How did he know I had a connection to this place?

I'd manipulated reality, and from my memories of my past lives, my distorted realities were believed by humans and demons alike. "I don't understand how you'd know this house has any significance to me," I asked after my mind ran through several possible theories.

"I've been in your mind, in your friends' minds, remember? I saw this place and your family living here." He shrugged dismissively, pulling me to a couch and pushing down hard on my shoulders, until he forced me to sit.

"Do you remember me?" he asked, peering into my face, his giant body towering above me.

Shaking my head, I attempted to stand up, but he pushed me down again.

"Just tell me who the hell you are and stop manhandling me!" I said, my temper flaring.

"I'm Gadreel, one of the Guardians. I'm tasked with protecting humankind since the beginning of days."

My mouth dropped open, literally. Protect humans? Was that a joke? He was a cold-blooded murderer.

"You are Lilith," he said, jabbing me in the chest with his index finger. "A Guardian responsible for the well-being of the humans, making sure they thrive and grow." He spat out those last words, as if they disgusted him, scanning my face for a reaction. I kept my expression neutral, and he continued. "You were once considered a goddess by the humans—their Mother Goddess—revered until you set their world on fire, stabbing me in the face when I intervened."

Okay, what the hell did that mean? I sat in stunned silence, blinking up at him, not knowing how to respond. His words, "you set their world on fire" kept playing over and over in my mind. My fears crept up from the depths of my banished memories, the same ones Razma instructed me not to seek out.

"My words have shocked you." The fearsome beast before me hid behind a calm demeanor, his tone sounding sympathetic. "The humans almost destroyed you, seeking your power and knowledge. I had told you time and time again that we needed to reign them in, that they couldn't be trusted with access to such power."

I didn't reply. His features darkened, smoothing out so quickly I may not have noticed the change if I'd blinked.

"I can help you remember. It would make our conversation more productive if you were to remember our shared past." He extended his hand toward me, but I evaded his touch.

Not liking the vulnerability of my position on the couch, I stood up, shoving him away. He barely budged an inch.

"Why would I trust you?" I asked, taking a sidestep and making my frustration clear, distancing myself from him.

"In order to understand the present situation, you must understand the past," he said.

Pinning me with his eyes, he closed the distance

between us once again and reached out to touch my head, but I jerked it away. My mind screamed not to let him touch me, to rip him limb-from-limb for what he did to Ray, and what he did to my family. But there was a part within me desperately wanting to know what he was talking about, to finally be on the same footing as everyone else in the know.

Looking around the room that until recently had held my whole life, I wondered if this could be my opportunity to truly understand what was happening, maybe my only hope of getting back to my children.

Gadreel grabbed me by my wrists and pulled me into his body. "Just let me show you," he cajoled.

Closing my eyes for a second, I forced myself to relax and give in, to stop fighting him.

I opened my eyes. "Okay," I said.

A slow grin spread across his scarred face, and I almost instantly regretted my decision. But it was too late. Releasing my wrists, he squeezed my head between his hands and looked down into my eyes.

"Good. Now remember, Lilith."

CHAPTER SEVENTEEN

Gadreel's touch brought burning pain, my body seizing up with the violation to my thoughts. I fought against him, demanding he get out of my mind. But reason soon cut through my resistance. I had to stop fighting or this wouldn't work; he wouldn't be able to help me remember.

Yielding my mind only worsened the pain, setting it on fire. Memories flashed by like stars swooshing past at warp speed. Soon though, they slowed to a trickle, the scenes taking on recognizable shapes.

My breath hitched as Samael's face came into focus. His hair was tousled around his handsome face, and an easygoing smile tugged at his lips. His dark eyes watched my every move, crinkling at the corners every now and again as he laughed at something I said.

There was so much warmth and love radiating from him. I wanted to bask in his light, to take him into my arms and never let go.

Little hands wrapped around my legs, and I looked

down into the impish green eyes of our son. "Mama, I want to play at the tree. My friends will be there!"

Touching his cherub face, I pushed back the dark brown curls. "No, my sweetling, you cannot go. It's too dangerous for you to play near our tree in the presence of the humans. We must hide your magic . . . hide your power from them. Remember what Gadreel has told us."

The little boy stuck out his lower lip and stomped his foot. "I don't care what he said. He just wants to keep us from being happy and having fun."

"Sariel, you're too little to understand now," I said, kissing the top of his head. "But when you're grown, you'll know Mama was right to keep you safe."

Someone cleared their throat behind us, and I turned to see Gadreel. With his blond mane and muscular frame, he had a look of a ferocious lion, but his full lips softened the sharp angles of his face. He was perfect in appearance even if his behavior at times left much to be desired.

"My lady Lilith." He bowed his head in greeting before continuing, "The humans are demanding to see their beloved goddess. They're insistent she give them the knowledge she promised so they may prepare accordingly for the near future."

"Thank you, Gadreel." I said, with a dismissive nod. Though I appreciated his desire to keep us informed and safe, it annoyed me how he always lurked about in the shadows.

"Do you think it's wise?" Samael asked, pulling me gently by the hand to face him. "We're here to guide, protect, and challenge humans to be better. But this is not our path. We shouldn't allow them to mandate how we use our power, nor should we give them access to all this sacred knowledge."

"They need me," I said, my voice sounding defensive, and I sweetened the tone before continuing. "I came here to be with you and left them behind. I've never been away this long, and without me, the humans grow frightened, and they despair. As soon as they see me, they'll be appeased; I'll only give them a peek into the future, nothing more. Just a little help with the harvest."

I smiled up at him, my fingertips lightly smoothing the concern off his brow. He worried far too much about me.

"Why do you coddle them?" Gadreel's tone was sharp, and I turned to look at him.

He was about to launch into one of his speeches—one of his never-ending lectures about my behavior and duty. Digging my nails into my palms, I bit my lower lip as he continued, "We rule this world. These humans were created for us to have dominion over them, to do what we demand of them, not the other way around. I don't understand you—to have such power yet grovel at their feet."

His words angered me. He always seemed to ridicule me whenever Samael was by my side, embarrassing me in front of my mate. Yet when we were alone together, he spoke respectfully, kindly, as if we were friends.

"I thank you for your counsel. But I do not grovel

at anyone's feet," I replied tersely. "I think you'd both do well to remember your roles, as well as mine, when it comes to the humans. Gadreel, you teach the humans how to defend themselves and are tasked to protect them from outside forces wishing to harm them. But that does not subjugate them to your domination."

Facing Samael, I placed my palm on his chest. "And you're responsible for leading the Guardians, as well as your demons, striking a necessary harmony between them and the humans. But you do not dictate the destiny of the humans."

I turned to face them both before continuing. My mate nodded, accepting my words. But Gadreel narrowed his eyes, his expression darkening with each passing second of my speech.

"I'm the one responsible for the well-being and future of the One Spirit's creations, for these fragile humans," I said, raising my chin high as I pressed my hand against my chest. "They're in my charge, and I must ensure they grow in wisdom, in love, and in strength. Each generation must be greater than the next. It is my decision on how I handle the power bestowed upon me. Not yours."

I made a production of turning on my heel to leave, dismissing them with a wave of my hand.

I knew Gadreel wanted nothing more than to force me into using my power to enslave the hapless humans, make them bow down to the Guardians. It wasn't a secret. He talked about it all the time. But he could save his breath, for I'd not bend on this. It was not what the One Spirit would want from us, and ultimately, we owed this powerful being our lives. We'd aligned our paths together, and accepted the responsibilities given to us.

A heavy hand gripped my shoulder, spinning me around. "Who do you think you are? The great Queen who dictates our lives here ever since she's mounted our leader? Your power doesn't belong solely to you anymore!" He shook me by the shoulders, his eyes bulging, a vein throbbing in his temple. "Once you become a member of the Guardians, your power is to be shared with us."

He'd never behaved so viciously toward me, and I was momentarily stunned before my temper sparked to life. My breath hissed out between my teeth and my hands fisted, ready to strike him for the disrespect.

Samael beat me to it. Grabbing Gadreel by the back of his neck, he growled, "Get your hands off my wife."

Gadreel froze, his fingers digging into my shoulders to the point of pain, but I refused to cry out and give him the satisfaction of a reaction.

Samael must've strengthened his hold on Gadreel's neck as well. With a frustrated roar, Gadreel released me, and Samael slammed him hard against the wall, bits of rock crumbling around his frame. Though Gadreel was more muscular, he and Samael were similar in height, and Samael had the advantage of fury, his protective instincts on full display.

"How dare you speak to her this way! She owes you nothing! She lives amongst us in this tower, set away from all she's ever known because she's decided to do so as my mate and the mother of our child. She's not here to do your bidding, nor the bidding of any other Guardian."

My stomach churned as I watched them face off, regret at my heated words surging through me. I was grateful to Samael for defending me, but he never would've had to if I'd just kept quiet. With each day I lived amongst the Guardians as one of them, the rift between them and Samael grew.

Though Samael was the natural ruler of the demon world, the Guardians had chosen him as their leader. And he treated them as his equals . . . as his friends. That is, until I came to this mountain-embedded keep a few years ago and became a source of contention between them.

These Guardians found my interactions with the humans curious, and my unique gifts stirred their imaginations, stoking in some a desire for more power. This was especially true for Gadreel.

I should've stayed with the humans, living amongst my animals and plants. Every day I longed to bask in the sun's rays once again as it warmed the earth, and then soak up the moon's soothing glow. My occasional visits to the mortal realm did not sit right with me. These visits were rushed and tainted with a fear pressed into me by Gadreel's lectures and Samael's worry. With each visit, I felt a darkness growing within the humans, taking hold like the seedlings I'd nourished and then left behind to rot.

"Please, stop," I called out to my husband and his

best friend. "I'm sorry, I don't belong here. I shouldn't have come, pretending to be one of you. I'll leave and then the Guardians can have peace once more."

My hands trembled at the thought of leaving. But the fights over my power were escalating. I had to face the reality that my departure would be best for everyone. "I should've left long ago," I whispered, tears spilling onto my cheeks.

Samael released Gadreel, shoving him one more time into the wall before his long strides brought him to my side. Holding me at arm's length, he searched my face before crushing me to his chest, cocooning me in his arms.

"If this place makes you unhappy, we can go elsewhere, just our small family . . . no other Guardians," he said, the vibrations of his words pleasing to my ear as I pressed against him.

Oh, how I wanted this fairytale he spun to be a reality. But it could not be. The demons would wreck this world if left to their own devices, and the Guardians relied on Samael's leadership. I'd already made it difficult enough for him with my presence and taking him away would make things worse.

With sadness in my heart, I shook my head and pulled away. "You know it's not possible and I would not ask it of you."

"Nothing is impossible." Squaring his jaw, he took on a look of pure stubbornness, a look I'd seen reproduced on his son's face countless times.

For a moment, I thought it could be so. Gently

caressing his cheek, I let myself hang onto this thread of hope he'd extended.

A female voice broke into my daydream. "The demons are getting restless, Samael—you must come. They wish to speak with you and only you."

Jophiel stood in the entranceway, her pale blue eyes meeting mine before returning her attention to Samael. Her pursed lips and pinched features showed her disapproval of me.

The Guardian of Beauty had never warmed up to me. It wasn't just physical beauty she commanded, which she possessed in excess, but beautiful thoughts too. For the humans she created feelings of love and warmth even when the days were bleak. She was pure positivity, except when it came to me. And it made me sad to think we could've been friends, if she'd only given me a chance.

Samael caught my hand in his and kissed my palm, then my wrist. "I'll be back in a moment. Please wait for me, and do not do anything rash."

Watching them leave spoiled my mood once more, and the nagging feeling I was ruining Samael's life amongst the Guardians returned in full force. It seemed so simple when we'd first met, deceptively so. But now I feared he'd grow to resent me, and I him if we continued like this.

"I'm sorry for my words," Gadreel's gruff voice said behind me. "We do not know what lurks out there that may want to destroy us, destroy the humans. Your gift is very precious, very powerful. We need it to protect ourselves . . . to protect this world we've built."

His voice trailed off, and I felt his fingertips graze my back, causing me to shiver. But I didn't turn to face him, hoping he'd get the hint and leave me alone.

"Didn't you tell Sariel to not play at the sacred tree?" Gadreel asked, his tone suddenly sharp.

He moved to the window, looking down the mountain onto the garden I'd created with Samael, the tree containing the sacred fates and destiny blossoming in the center. Joining Gadreel at the window, I clutched the stone wall, my fear rising as I took in the scene below. There, clear as day, was my son, who'd only moments ago heard me tell him not to play with the humans at the tree. And yet, he ran around with a group of children, entertaining them by transforming into different animals—a pig one minute, a dog next, then a goat.

"You should reign him in better," Gadreel grunted, and I glared at him.

His eyes suddenly widened, and he grabbed my arm. Pulling me closer, he directed my gaze toward the sacred tree.

A crowd of adults had gathered. From where they'd come, I did not know as there were only children there moments ago. They surrounded something, their hands raised in anger as their children cried, trying to push through the adults. The crowd parted, and a man emerged from the center, hefting a bleating goat high over his head.

A knife caught the light of the sun, and the screams of the children echoed with my own. At that moment, I knew beyond a doubt the little goat was my son.

Wings emerged from my back, propelling me quickly down the mountain, Gadreel by my side. The powerful beating of our wings pushed the people away as we landed amongst the crowd.

The humans fell on their knees, touching their foreheads to the ground in fealty. I'd never seen them behave this way before, but I didn't have time to ponder this; I needed to make sure my child was not hurt.

"Where's my son?" I cried out. The people cowered in fear, their faces blank and drained of blood.

The man who'd held the goat stood up. "What son?" he asked. "We discovered a demon, a beast of some sort, desecrating your tree of knowledge and power. We took its life in your name as a sacrifice, so you'd once again bestow upon us your blessings, our kind sweet Goddess." Bowing low in deference, I saw over his shoulder the little goat laying in a pool of blood, its legs bound. Gadreel was already by its side, his palm spread over the creature.

Lifting his head to meet my eyes, he said, "He's gone."

A scream ripped from my lips, and I rushed to the little goat, but Gadreel grabbed my waist, stopping me from touching my child. I screamed in his ear, punching him. Over and over, I yelled that it was not possible—my child was immortal like myself, like his father.

"Do not look," he whispered in my ear. "It does no good to look and you do not want to show your weakness in front of these lesser creatures."

He raised an odd-looking knife into the sky. The blade was made of an iridescent black and white stone, and my eyes fixated on the blood dripping down it.

Still holding me tightly to his chest, Gadreel's voice boomed as he addressed the crowd, "Where did you get this knife?"

No one moved a muscle, their eyes reflecting fear and uncertainty. I hated each one of them.

"Let me go," I cried once more at Gadreel, trying, and failing to pull myself from his grip. "I need to hold my baby. Please, please let me go." When he didn't relent, I grabbed the knife from him and jerked it wildly, accidentally slashing the blade over his cheek.

He released me, grabbing his face and screaming. The blade was capable of injuring an immortal. My eyes widened with realization.

Pushing aside my shock, I ran to my son, throwing myself on top of him. Why was he still in the form of this animal, why had he not turned back to his natural form? I wanted to see his beautiful face one more time, to kiss him and hold him. Each sob of mine felt wretched out from the depths of my heart as a fire ignited within my chest.

The stupid man spoke again, his voice whiney and high-pitched with nerves. "We thought you'd be pleased, our great powerful Mother, and you'd reward us with the knowledge we need to survive the next cycles of the moon."

A choking rage took over my body and my mind. I couldn't think or speak, I could only scream and scream. The sound was unnatural, ripping from my very spirit and shaking the ground around us. Light emanated from every particle of my being and the world around me began to burn, screams joining my own in a symphony of agony.

The pain around me felt so good. I wanted to feel the whole world burn with me in it. I should be punished for losing my son as much as these wretched humans I'd trusted.

Someone grabbed ahold of my shoulders, shaking me. Through the chaos of my mind, I heard a voice repeating, "Stop, stop. For the sake of the One Spirit, stop."

I wouldn't, I couldn't stop. Not until I bathed this world with my pain. I needed everyone to suffer as I was suffering.

The harsh grip of steel fingers was replaced by firm yet gentle hands. They pulled me into a familiar body, and I heard Samael's voice whispering in my ear, "Lilith, my love. It's all right. Everything is all right. I'm here, no one can hurt you."

The energy flowing out from me in violent bursts slowed to a trickle and then halted. Opening my eyes, I looked around. I stood in a wasteland of carnage. The people who'd only moments ago cowered before me were fragments of bone, their burnt flesh now ash dusting a garden of ruin. And my beautiful tree holding the sacred fates and destiny crumbled as the power seeped out of it.

Beyond the hill that housed my garden lay the village of the humans, its occupants stumbling from their homes, looking around confused. They turned their attention to the hill, their mouths agape as they saw the destruction. Running in our direction, they called out the names of their loved ones.

What had I done? I'd destroyed what I was meant to protect, my willfulness causing the death of my child. Turning to face Samael, I saw the other Guardians standing behind him, Gadreel's face bearing an angry laceration—a testament to my darkness.

I couldn't look at any of them; shame and disgust at what I'd done rolled within me.

Samael took my face between his hands, trying to force me to look into his eyes, but I couldn't. How could I tell him I was responsible for the death of our son? How could he ever forgive me? How could I forgive myself?

I pulled away, avoiding his touch.

A look of surprise washed over his features, his eyes reflecting his pain at my rejection. The hurt I'd caused him slashed at my heart, pulling my spirit apart. I couldn't be here anymore . . . . I needed to escape.

With one last glance at the devastation I'd created, I called forth the shimmering power leaking from the once luscious tree and pulled it into my own body.

Samael reached for me, crying out, "Don't." But it was too late. I was already gone.

CHAPTER EIGHTEEN

My eyes opened. The world around me was spinning, the effect dizzying.

Someone held my head tightly, and I clawed at their hands, trying desperately to free myself.

"Stop Lilith. It's me. You're safe."

Disoriented, Gadreel's face slowly came into focus. My gaze drifted to his scar, and I stared at this physical representation of the memories I should've never unearthed. The mere sight of it was too much for me.

All of these memories were too much. Too much at once.

With my stomach twisting in pain, I wrenched from Gadreel's grasp and fell on my knees to the floor. "I can't breathe," I sobbed, clutching my neck as I gulped air into my lungs.

He squatted beside me, patting my shoulder awkwardly. "I'm a monster," I cried. "Those people—I killed all those people . . . my son died because of me."

I went from breath holding to hyperventilating with each word I uttered, vomit crawling up my throat.

"No. The fault lies with the humans. They craved your power. They were addicted to knowing their destiny, their fate . . . they longed to manipulate it."

I couldn't look at Gadreel in my shame, keeping my face covered with my hands as I shook my head. "I left with Samael to live with the Guardians. I abandoned the humans, leaving them alone to suffer, no longer nurturing or caring for them. They'd wait for my visits to give them scraps of knowledge to help them survive. Of course, they'd do anything to win me back, to get my attention, and I punished them brutally for it."

"Of course, you punished them. They murdered Sariel to win your favor and get at your power," he said, his tone incredulous. "This is why they can't be trusted. This is why we must rule them. This is why we need you to come back."

Uncovering my face, I dropped my hands into my lap and looked into Gadreel's eyes. "I should've never listened to you about keeping Sariel away from them. I should've introduced him to them when he was born, and they would've known he was part of me, and accepted him as they accepted me . . . accepted the Guardians. Then they would've never misconstrued him as an evil creature desecrating the sacred tree. He'd still be alive."

"Or they could've killed him sooner," Gadreel growled. "Have you forgotten how possessive they were over you? Over your power? You think they'd not use everything they could to force your attention solely on them? They could've used Sariel as leverage to steal your gifts over the fates and destiny. Did you think of that?"

I shook my head, my brain muddled with confusion. I didn't know what was up or down, and definitely couldn't grasp what was wrong or right.

"No . . . I didn't think . . . I don't know," I whispered, tears spilling over my cheeks.

His voice softened as he gently brushed my tears away with his large fingers. "It is understandable what you did. Sariel was your only child, and the only child born of a Guardian and another powerful creature. With your extraordinary gifts, you should've been part of us from the beginning. I have no idea how you stayed hidden amongst the humans for so long before Samael found you. I think in our own way, we all wanted to protect you and your child. But we failed you, and we failed him. Yet I promise, if you trust me now, I will not fail you again. I can help you with your burden, and then you can go back to your new family."

Something blocked out the morning sun's rays streaming from the window, and an unfamiliar voice said, "Murdered Sariel? How interesting."

Gadreel stood up quickly, dragging me with him. The bright sunlight shone behind the man, obscuring his features and turning them into shadows.

"What are you doing here, boy?" Gadreel spat.

The figure laughed, stepping closer. "I heard rumors you'd brought the thief of the sacred fates and destiny to our residence in Vermont. Curious that you'd send me away on a wild goose chase when you had such an intriguing guest. So, I thought I'd follow you around to see what else you were hiding from me." He paused, directing his attention to me. "And I wanted to make sure you didn't hurt my mother. Despite her abandonment of me, I still owe my existence to her."

No longer backlit, I gasped when I saw the stranger's face. Though a grown man, his green eyes and dark brown curls were unmistakable to me. My son. The child that minutes ago I mourned was standing clear as day before me.

My eyes were wide, my head shaking in disbelief. "How's this possible?" I whispered.

"A fantastic question, Mother. I think both my father and I would love to hear how it is you thought I was dead." Sariel's eyes narrowed on Gadreel.

Gadreel tightened his hold on me, and my ribs protested, my vision blurring. My human body was losing oxygen and I should've fought back but I was too stunned, my brain frantically trying to make sense of the situation.

"Even as a child I'd always known you couldn't be trusted, Gadreel . . . especially not around my mother," Sariel said and lunged at us.

Gadreel jerked me behind him, unsheathing a knife he'd hidden.

My jaw dropped, and for a moment I was paralyzed. It was the knife from my memory, the one dripping in my child's blood, the one I'd scarred Gadreel's face with so many millennia ago.

I couldn't let him hurt Sariel! I wouldn't let him take my son away again! Channeling all my pain and rage, I twisted my body, throwing myself at Gadreel's hand holding the knife, my power pulsing out in a flash of light.

Gadreel lost his grip on me, and I grabbed the knife from him, rolling to the side and onto the floor as Sariel collided with him. A sharp pain bit into my side, but I ignored it, watching helplessly as the two men fought. I wasn't sure what to do, how to help without accidentally hurting Sariel with my unwieldy power.

Someone materialized next to me, and I gasped in relief at the sight of Samael. Scanning my body, his eyes lingered on my side, his jaw tensing. I looked down, surprised to find my navy shirt ripped, a dark wetness saturating the material.

With a startling roar, Samael rushed into the fray, his strong body crashing against Gadreel. Shoving Sariel away, he yelled, "Get her out of here!"

Before I could protest, Sariel pulled me into his arms, his wings wrapping around me. We flashed away, and I clung to him, a tangle of emotions choking me as I tried to make sense of all I'd learned in the last few hours.

Raised voices permeated my cocoon, and I realized we were no longer propelling through space; my feet were on solid ground. As Sariel's wings receded, I looked upon the faces of my immortal family and sisters staring slack jawed at us as we stood in the middle of their motel room.

My sisters cried out, running toward me, but James and Astrid blocked their path, holding them back, their eyes narrowed in distrust.

"Pack up. We're leaving this shithole," Sariel said. His voice had a bite to it, and I noticed the harsh looks he gave my immortal family.

Tarquin approached us cautiously, then his arm shot out with the speed of a viper strike and he pulled me away from Sariel. "Who the hell are you, and why would we listen to you?"

Tarquin and Sariel silently glared at each other, the others on alert, ready to fight at the first sign of danger. The tension was suffocating. I needed to fix this quickly, so we could get out of here and to safety.

Opening my mouth to explain, I found I couldn't utter a word. Only a whimper escaped my lips as pain spread like a trail of fire from my side. The room spun around me, and my legs gave out. I sagged against Tarquin.

Looking down with surprise, Tarquin gently lowered me to the ground. He examined his blood covered hands, confusion and shock written on his face.

He pulled up my shirt, exposing my wound, and sucked in his breath. "She's injured. Badly. What happened?"

Sariel joined him by my side, taking away the knife I still clutched in my hand. "She must've been injured by Gadreel trying to get this away from him." He examined the knife with a frown before putting it down and touching my wound.

Tarquin pushed him away. "You haven't explained who you are."

"He's my son," I croaked through dry lips, feeling as if I was floating away from this conversation. I could see shocked faces blurring in my vision as the darkness battled to take me away. My eyes closed, until one of them screamed.

Samael stood in the room, looking disheveled but thankfully intact.

He fell to his knees beside me. I noticed James and Astrid lurch to attack, and I called out to them with the last ounce of energy I possessed, "No, please leave him alone. He's not a threat."

Samael ignored them, his attention focused entirely on me. Smoothing the hair from my face, he lifted me gently onto his lap and examined my wound closer.

His brow furrowed, and he tightened his arms around me. "We need to get somewhere safe."

Turning to Astrid, he asked, "Do you know somewhere Lilith—Marcianna—wouldn't know about? Somewhere Tarquin and James wouldn't know about? If so, tell my son and he will begin to transport you all there."

I could barely focus on the conversation, my eyelids heavy as I faded in and out of consciousness.

James and Astrid must've released my sisters, their terror-stricken presence pushed against my side. I forced my eyes open to see Harlow holding my hand while Mina sat next to her, a look of concern etched on her face, her eyes fixated on Samael.

I tried giving them a reassuring smile, but was pretty sure I failed. Their anxiety was palpable as they huddled together by my side.

Sariel walked over to us, whispering something to his father before pulling my sisters up by their elbows. He silenced their protests by embracing them within his massive wings, and together they flashed away. He returned within seconds, appearing behind Tarquin and James. Grabbing them roughly, he disappeared with them before they could protest.

I was left alone with Samael, my brain struggling to stay awake.

His lips grazed my forehead, and he stood up effortlessly with me in his arms. "Hold on, we'll have you safe soon enough."

"The knife," I whispered. "Did Sariel take it with him? He put it on the floor next to me right before you arrived."

That little speech almost caused me to pass out, but I clung to consciousness, feeling it was critical to keep the knife with us and not let it fall back into Gadreel's hands.

He glanced around the floor, adjusting me as he picked something up from under a chair. "Got it," he said.

As his wings materialized around us, a crackle of energy caught my attention. My heart lurched as Gadreel and two other Guardians appeared in the room.

One I recognized as Jophiel, her beauty unmistakable, as was the hatred in her gaze the moment her eyes latched on me. The other Guardian also seemed familiar, but my brain was too scrambled to remember his name.

They lunged in unison toward us but were too late. Samael and I were already propelling through the ether, Gadreel's scream of rage echoing around us as we flashed to safety.

CHAPTER NINETEEN

Floating in darkness, I didn't know who or where I was.

My body burned. Pain like I've never experienced clawed at me, ripping me into fragments until I thought I'd go mad with this slow torture.

I was growing tired of fighting. And death's embrace called me, louder than I'd ever heard it. Would I find Ray waiting on the other side? I wasn't quite sure how it all worked, how I found him each time, but I found comfort in the fact I'd been successful for two thousand years.

Sarah weighed on my mind. She was waiting for us, for me, to help her. The world needed us to help her. But at this point, I felt expendable. There was a little army ready to fight for her—they didn't need me, not really.

Voices faded in and out. Every now and again, I felt hands on my body and energy pulsating through me. Someone was trying to heal me, but it didn't seem to be working.

Darkness held me close, pulling me further from this world, my pain drifting away. I sighed, ready to let go.

Losing pieces of myself slowly, bit by bit, I gave myself permission to disintegrate. But an essence within me railed at my body, instructing it to hold on, to not succumb. It desperately grabbed onto the parts of me floating away, tethering me to my body.

Your children need you! Fight. The words pounded against my mind, thumping my heart to keep going. If I let go, I'd not only lose my human children, but I'd also lose Sariel.

I needed to fight through this, whatever it was, this thief of both my mortal body and my immortal being. Focusing my energy on the wound at my side, I tried imagining the healing process of my flesh—the cauterization to stop the bleeding, the battle against infection, the stitching of skin.

The fire-like pain rushed back into my body. I let out a scream.

I wasn't strong enough; my power weakening with each passing moment. The shadows taunted me, urging me to follow them on a path far easier than the one some part of me was determined to forge.

Tears seeped from the corner of my eyes, and I heard murmurs around me as someone wiped my face with a damp cloth. A warmth permeated my bones as strong arms encircled my body, soothing away some of the pain.

I fell into a void filled with silence and blackness, my body relaxing despite the pain.

Something brushed against my lips. The feeling was so unexpected that I managed to force my eyes open. Ray smiled down at me. Somehow it wasn't odd that my dead husband was here with me.

Was this a dream? A delirium? I didn't care, wrapping my arms around him, I lost myself in his touch.

He tasted so good, a taste of laughter and love—a lifetime of memories playing out in one kiss. I frantically pressed him to my body, addicted to his touch and taste, missing this moment so much that it calmed my spirit.

And destroyed it.

His fingers trailed a path up my side, and I shivered in anticipation, closing my eyes to savor every touch. He cupped my breast into his palm, his other arm pillowing my head, and I wrapped my legs around his waist.

He laughed in my mouth, "Slow down, love. I want to enjoy you thoroughly."

The voice was different, yet the same, and I fluttered my eyes open to find myself locked in the gaze of Kynan. My tears spilled freely at seeing his playful grin, this moment wiping away my last memory of him, of when I forced him away, telling him he was not my equal.

"Why are you crying?" he whispered, kissing my wet cheeks.

"Because I'm happy," I replied. "Do you forgive me?"

He replied by hungrily devouring my mouth, his teeth grazing my lips as he started a path of hot kisses down my neck, licking and nipping as he explored my body.

He drove me wild with ecstasy and I begged him to stop teasing me, to give me what I wanted—all of him, completely. He traveled back up my body to claim my mouth once more and when I looked into his eyes, it was the dark eyes of Samael looking back.

It didn't shock me, though. Being with him felt as natural as breathing, the rhythmic movements of my hips matching his thrusts. I remembered every moment with him, every caress, my fingernails digging into his muscular back, trying to pull him deeper into me, to join our spirits as well as our bodies.

I screamed my release, my body on fire, and he captured my cries with his mouth, giving all of himself to me.

Rolling onto his back, he pulled me on top of his chest, holding me and lazily stroking my back. "Sleep now, my Lilith," he whispered.

As if on command, my eyes became too heavy to keep open and I quietly drifted off to a dreamless and pain-free sleep.

The hum of whispers drew me from the darkness, and I cautiously opened my eyes. A full bedside audience stared back at me. Given the things I'd dreamt about, I prayed I hadn't given them an orgasmic vocal performance, or I might as well die now from embarrassment.

"Oh, thank God!" Harlow cried, beginning to throw herself across my bed. Thankfully, Samael was faster than she was, catching her before she landed with all her weight on me. He pulled her up, passing her into the waiting arms of James.

"I'm so sorry, Marci, I was just so scared you were going to die," Harlow said, her cheeks red and her eyes glistening with tears.

Forcing my cracked lips to curl into my best imitation of a smile, I gave her a small wave, hoping it adequately conveyed a "don't worry about it" sentiment.

I cleared my throat, testing out my voice and choked out a question. "Where are we?"

"Can we tell her?" Tarquin asked, looking uncomfortable directing his question to Samael.

"Her mind is her own now," Samael replied.

I averted my eyes, careful not to make eye contact with him. Yes, he'd been my husband several millennia ago, and clearly, we'd been intimate in the past, but I wasn't sure if what I'd experienced while unconscious was some sort of dream, or memory, or if he'd been an active participant with me in my head.

"We're at a house in Georgetown, on the outskirts of D.C., that Astrid owns," Tarquin said, sitting down on the edge of my bed. His eyes brimmed with a haunted mixture of concern and guilt. "Apparently, she's full of surprises as none of us knew about this purchase." He smiled faintly as if attempting to lighten the mood, but his gaze belied his discomfort, straying between Samael and Sariel, both stationed at either side of my bed's headboard.

This must be so difficult for him, forced into a situation with creatures he didn't know or trust. Thousands of years doing something more or less predictable, and now he'd lost his sense of direction. He wasn't the only one; James and Astrid fidgeted behind him, unsure what to say or do.

The awkwardness was killing me, and I'd only been conscious for a few minutes.

"So, have you all chatted?" I asked. "Do you know each other now? Are we good?"

I felt like an idiot asking these questions. But I needed to know where we stood. The last time I saw everyone together in a room, distrust and a desire to fight mired the atmosphere. I hoped while I was knocked out, we all got on the same page.

They all stared at me. No one said a word. So, I guess we hadn't been sharing our life stories.

Moving away from the wall, Samael folded his arms across his chest. "I know them all," he said tersely. "I know them better than you do, and I may even know them better than they know themselves."

Well, that was quite the statement, and I couldn't help but laugh when Astrid replied with, "Well, I know you sound like a jackass."

To my utter amazement, Samael's stone-faced demeanor cracked, his features visibly softening and a smile tugging at the corners of his lips. Watching him from the corner of my eye, I couldn't help but admire his beauty—the way strands of his shoulder-length black hair grazed his high cheekbones, his strong jawline . . . and those dark eyes, they mesmerized me each time they caught me in their gaze.

What the holy hell am I thinking? I shook my head, trying to get these shameful thoughts out of my mind. The situation I was currently in was absolutely insane—a newly minted widow sitting in a room with not one, but two, former husbands and having lustful thoughts about one of them. The soap operas I'd watched as a kid after school didn't match this level of crazy.

My brain felt like it was pounding against my skull, and I pressed my fingertips to my forehead, hoping the counter-pressure would alleviate some of the pain. I'd only uttered a few words, and it had already tired me out.

Tarquin put his arm on my shoulder. "Are you okay? You scared us. We thought we were losing you, all of you, not just your mortal body."

I nodded. "I'm okay now. Truly. Don't worry, you can't shake me that easily." My wan smile was hardly convincing as he started babying me—feeling my forehead, tucking in the sheets, and adjusting pillows. I soon found myself propped up by several fluffy pillows like a queen in visitation with her subjects.

"Tarquin, I'm fine. Stop stressing."

"I never should've left your side," he said. Standing abruptly, he glared at Astrid before pacing around the small bedroom.

So, I hadn't imagined the guilt in his eyes earlier,

and he was making me dizzy trying to exorcise it.

James stopped Tarquin's pacing with a hand to his chest. "It was our fault, we let her out of our sight. We should've known better."

Great, now I was feeling guilty because they were feeling guilty. It was my fault, all my fault . . . I'd stupidly gone to go investigate that mimic creature because I'd wanted it to be Farah so badly. And let's not forget, I brought Ray with us despite Tarquin's protest because I desperately didn't want to leave him. So really all the blame for all the fuckups lay squarely with me.

"Stop it. Please," I cut in. "No one's at fault. I'm a grown-ass woman and, as I said when I left you, I've taken out demons. There was no reason to think I couldn't sit alone on a porch a few minutes before Tarquin arrived."

Astrid nodded as if seeing the logic in my words, but James was not so easily swayed. "If anything happened to you, we'd never forgive ourselves."

"Oh, come on, James, don't be so melodramatic. I've died in the line of duty multiple times—I can't even remember how many, as most of my deaths have blurred together by now."

"This was different," Tarquin said. "It truly looked like not only your mortal body was dying, but you, the essence inside, this Lilith, was dying." He turned to Samael and Sariel. "How could that be possible when she's immortal?"

"It was the knife that impaled her," Sariel replied. "I had thought it a myth, a mere ranting of an obsessed Gadreel. Our legends say there's a stone that when forged into a weapon can destroy immortals."

"And that this stone was given to the humans as protection against us," Samael added.

"If it's for the protection of humans, why would Gadreel have it?" Astrid asked, her brow creasing. The wheels were already spinning in her head. I could only imagine the giant connect-the-dot yarn board in her thoughts right now.

Samael's face hardened. "I don't know the answer to your question, but I promise you, I will find out. He'd told us Lilith had it and used it against him. That she'd escaped with it."

Astrid looked satisfied with his response, but I couldn't help but shiver. Though I was comforted to have our new allies, the possible answers as to why Gadreel not only had the knife in his possession, but had also brought it with him to meet with me, made me nervous as hell.

But what scared me even more was how close I'd been to giving up as I'd lain dying, my life draining from me. I had vowed to do everything in my power to get back to my kids, especially now that Ray was gone. And yet I'd almost failed.

"He had the knife because he likely stole it after the humans used it to kill Sariel, or whatever I thought was Sariel. The last time I saw the knife before now it was dripping with what I'd perceived to be my son's blood." I frowned as I forced myself to relive that memory. "Gadreel had looked stunned when he'd found the creature dead at the hands of the humans.

If it had been his plan to trick me, maybe the death of that creature was not part of it."

An uncomfortable, heavy silence permeated the room. All eyes focused on me.

"You know what," I said. "Enough talk about this doom and gloom. I, for one, am grateful I was taken by that mimic thing. Because at least now we know Gadreel is as big of a monster as I thought him to be when he'd killed Ray." I paused and extended my hand to Sariel. He took it without hesitation as I added, "And it also brought me back to my son."

I still couldn't wrap my mind over the fact I had a son—a son thousands upon thousands of years old. A son I'd unwittingly abandoned. None of it made sense, but I was still grateful.

"Let's worry about next steps and stop beating ourselves up over what happened," I said, hoping that would be that, but they still stood there, tense, and uncertain.

All except Astrid, who immediately took charge. "Okay, let's let the grown-ass woman relax a bit and then we'll figure out our next course of action." I silently gave thanks to her as she pushed James and Tarquin out of the room.

Mina and Harlow followed quietly behind, casting concerned glances in my direction. I felt so bad for them. These poor women certainly have had a wild ride.

Sariel glanced at his father, then smiled at me before closing the door behind him. Left alone with Samael, my heart pounded like the entire percussion section of an orchestra as he sat down on my bed, taking my hand in his.

"Sariel told me what Gadreel said to you. About his supposed death," he said, rubbing his thumb over my hand.

"It seemed so real. I saw our son die, killed by the humans with that knife." I pointed to the vile weapon on the nightstand.

He touched my cheek. "It was a trick."

I closed my eyes for a moment, fighting to keep my emotions in check. "How? How could I have been tricked in such a way?"

"Did you see a body?"

I nodded, taking a steadying breath. "Yes, a little baby goat."

"And it didn't turn back to a boy once dead?" he asked.

"No, it didn't." I shook my head, the image infiltrating my mind as if it happened yesterday, the pain still raw. "Even in my grief, I'd thought it odd. I remember crying, begging to see our son's face once more."

His hand drifted from my cheek to the back of my neck, his fingers rubbing rhythmically as I leaned into him.

"It was a mimic. Like the one that tricked you into believing it was your friend. They don't have a form of their own, so it stands to reason if one were to die it would remain in the last form it took on."

"Have you not seen one die?" I asked.

"No, I've only seen demons killed, destroyed by

you or by your creations," he replied.

I shivered in response, unsure of his thoughts on my culling of his demon herd. His face didn't betray his feelings, and I closed my eyes, surprised at how I welcomed his touch on my neck, rubbing away my tension and fear.

"Why did you not come to me?" he asked after a few seconds of silence. "Why didn't you let me help you? I would've done anything for you then, just as I'd do anything for you now—now and forever. Lilith, I'd burn this world down for you."

Opening my eyes, I looked into his tortured face. There was so much shared hurt between us.

"I already did that. Remember?" I could barely speak, my chest ached with the memory. "I burned those villagers' world down over a lie. I killed so many innocents."

I relived those moments of pain—the moments when I'd lost myself completely—when I'd thought I'd lost my child.

And done the unthinkable.

He drew me into his arms, letting me sob into his chest, my tears flowing freely as he stroked my back. He was so familiar, his presence calming and comforting, in a way I'd only felt with Ray. The thought of Ray brought my guilt, and I pulled away, wiping the tears with the back of my hand.

He smiled softly and brushed a strand of hair off my face. "You should follow your own advice and not beat yourself up over what happened in the past. We can't change what has already happened, but we can choose to change our future. Nothing is written in stone."

"My mom used to quote something similar to me," I replied, my lips faintly returning his smile. "She'd say, 'You can't go back and change the beginning, but you can start where you are and change the ending'. She's told me that ever since I can remember."

My mom. My family. I missed them all so much.

Digging my nails into the palms of my hand, I tried to steady my emotions, but it was all undone when I met Samael's eyes. The sympathy and love I saw within their depths took my breath away. My body tensed as I watched him lean in slowly, cautiously, his lips meeting mine.

I should've pushed him away, but I didn't. Allowing him to kiss me, my heart raced as I tentatively parted my lips.

What's wrong with me? My brain screamed to stop, but my body refused, following Samael's lead. He felt so right in this moment, as if he was a part of me, a part of my spirit, calming my anxiety and making everything appear so much clearer.

Pushing against his chest, I pulled away but my lips hovered close to his. I took in a deep breath, letting his scent fill my lungs.

I froze as a realization crept in. His scent was familiar, and not familiar in the, we-hooked-up-thousands-of-years-ago way, but a scent that had surrounded and comforted me my whole adult life as Marcianna.

Ray's.

CHAPTER TWENTY

The scent was not Ray's earthy spice—it was the fragrance I'd never been able to identify, yet was uniquely his.

I'd recognize it anywhere.

Gasping, I pushed Samael away. "Why do you smell like him?"

I twisted the wedding band on my finger, cutting into the skin. Was this why everything seemed so familiar about Samael? Just days ago, the idea of him, the very image of him, terrified me on a visceral level. But the second I came face to face with him, the feeling had dissipated.

"I can explain," he said, reaching out to me. My expression must've clearly said, he'd-better-not-lay-a-finger-on-me. He wavered, uncertainty decorating his features, before fisting his hand and resting it on his leg.

I stared at him through narrowed eyes, my teeth pulling on my lower lip as my thoughts went full throttle into panic. He knew who, and what, I was talking about without me having to specify. What did this mean?

If I had the strength, I would've leapt out of bed and run as far away from him as I could go. But I was trapped, propped up against fluffy pillows, exposed in my fear of the truth.

"Will you give me a chance to explain? Or have you passed your judgment on me, ready to flee again?" he asked.

Silencing my panicked mind, I forced myself to meet Samael's gaze. His eyes were locked on mine, not flinching away from my accusatory stare.

As much as I wanted to lash out in my reply, I knew it wouldn't help the situation. Instead, I nodded, croaking out one word, "Explain."

The tension holding his facial muscles rigid released, and for a moment I saw echoes of him across the millennia. From a time when we were happy, living together amongst my forest, not thinking of the consequences of our love. But this was before he took me to live with the Guardians.

Inhaling deeply, he said, "When I arrived at the sacred tree, I found you beyond reason. You'd decimated a large group of humans, of children, and attacked Gadreel, stabbing him in the face with a weapon believed to be able to kill immortals. A weapon Gadreel said you stole from the humans."

I opened my mouth to defend myself, feeling sick at the images his words evoked, but he shook his head, lifting his hand to let me know he wanted me to let him finish. "Then, without a word of explanation, you destroyed the tree we'd planted together. We'd secured the fates and destiny of humanity into that tree when you decided to leave the human world and live amongst the Guardians. And you took the sacred fates and destiny and disappeared."

My eyes widened with each word he spoke, my cheeks burning in shame at how it must've looked from his point of view.

"To say the other Guardians were displeased was and is an understatement," he added dryly.

"Why didn't you defend me, or at least try to find me? I thought you'd burn the world for me. Didn't you just say that?" I knew I was being unfair, but I didn't care.

Instead of answering my question, he posed one of his own. "Do you remember when we planted the sacred tree together?"

Frowning, I started to shake my head when a hazy memory floated into my mind. I remembered his smile. And the way he'd held my gaze, his eyes shining like the star filled night sky. His spirit had called to my heart, and mine returned the call—a song of happiness at being by his side. I remembered seeing his power mixing with mine as we drew forth a sapling from a seed. And I could feel the trust and love I had in him, as I poured my power of the fates and destiny into the bark and roots, until each iota of the tree blossomed with my gift.

He'd made me feel safe, loved, as if with him I'd found my home.

Swallowing hard, I whispered, "I do. I remember."

His fingers touched my cheek, wiping off a tear. I didn't even realize I was crying. The memory had been so real and raw, it consumed me.

"I had instructed Gadreel to keep watch over the tree," Samael continued. "The task suited him as the protector of the people of the One Spirit, teaching them to fight and to survive. I thought if he could keep the tree safe, then you could be free of the responsibility contained within it. The Guardians had always trusted him, and when he described what transpired at the tree, the tree he'd sworn to protect, everyone believed him and questioned my leadership when I defended you."

"What did he say?" I asked, barely able to choke out the words, fearing the worst.

"You fought with the people because they'd wanted the power of the tree for themselves. Tired of being fed scraps of knowledge, of suffering without the help of your passing charity, they'd revolted against you." Samael paused, his eyes searching my face. "Is this too painful to hear? Do you want me to continue?"

I nodded, leaning closer to him as he spoke again. "Gadreel said he begged you to give the sacred gifts within the tree to him for safekeeping, to allow him to restore order. But you attacked him with the blade and then incinerated the humans. He said you were a danger not only to the people of the One Spirit, but also the Guardians, as you possessed a weapon that could destroy us all. And he demanded we bring you back to our mountain keep and force you to relinquish your power to us."

Listening to these words, my heart thumped wildly against the prison of my ribs, my mind struggling to make sense of these accusations. I was likely as pale as a corpse, my hands cold and numb as they gripped each other within my lap.

"Since the moment I met you, I've only known you to be good and honorable. Your love for these humans was evident in your every word and action; that is until you met me, and I took you away from them." For the first time, he averted his gaze, his eyes taking on hues of gray, reminiscent of an approaching storm.

I reached out, my movement hesitant, and took hold of his hand—the same hand I'd pulled away from just moments ago. Giving him a small, tight-lipped smile, I hoped it would be enough to encourage him to tell me more. As much as I feared and hid from the knowledge, I needed to know more from this time, this time I couldn't really remember, though it held so much trauma for us both.

It worked. Taking in a ragged breath, he once again lifted his eyes to mine. His hair obscured part of his face, making him look vulnerable, and I resisted the urge to wind my fingers into the inky black strands.

"I'd secluded you. I've justified it many times over the years, but I recognize it now for what it is—placations to my conscience. I convinced myself I was protecting you—your power was tantalizing to the immortals, and I'd worried they'd grow to lust for it, causing division."

It was fascinating being in his mind, listening to his perspective, but my anxiety grew with the knowledge this story would soon crescendo to something I'd not want to hear. Gripping his hand tighter in anticipation, I reminded myself to breathe with each word he uttered.

"But in reality, I was jealous. Jealous of the humans who'd claimed you as their own. Jealous of your all-consuming devotion to your power."

That confession made no sense. "Jealous of my power? But you're so powerful."

"I wasn't jealous in a coveting sort of way," he replied. "The sacred fates and destiny were your gift; yours to protect and yours to do with what you will. But when contained within your body, it had a strong hold on your conscious self and you'd fall into long trances. Each day I'd lose you to the realm of what was, what is, and what could be. You were the most amazing creature I'd ever seen, so wild and free, so pure, and I wanted to have you all to myself. I convinced you to place your gift within the tree, the tree we'd forged together and protected by our entwined power. Then I took you from the moonlight and the sunbeams you thrived in, away from the worship bestowed on you by the people of the One Spirit, and I locked you up in a fortress, where under my nose Gadreel sowed seeds of doubt and fear."

He paused as if the words were getting more difficult to say out loud, and I reminded him of my original question. "I appreciate you telling me all this, but I don't understand how this relates to what I'd asked.

Why when I breathe in your scent is it like I'm breathing in Ray? Why do you elicit the same familiar feelings in me?"

"If I were to answer you without telling you my story, you may want me to leave and never return. This is the closest I've ever gotten to you . . . the most I've spoken to you, in thousands of years."

Closing my eyes, I grabbed onto the threads of my unraveling patience and steeled myself for the inevitable truth. With his response, he'd already signaled I'd not like the answer to my question.

"When you looked into my eyes mere seconds before you disappeared, you looked so scared, so pained, that I felt you hated me. So, I could believe you'd left me. But I couldn't believe you'd abandon our child. You doted on Sariel, loved him with all your being. And because of this, I followed you, and I kept following you, trying to catch you, to speak with you. But each time you'd refuse, looking at me with terror, doing everything in your power to escape me."

Memories buried within the far recesses of my consciousness surfaced, drawn by Samael's words. They were jumbled, yet vivid, bringing with them emotions that cut into me now as they'd done then. I could feel the acidic fear of Samael's judgment at my failure coursing through me, incinerating any hope of rational thought. It wove with my guilt, each stitch tightening around my heart as a mantra played within my mind.

I didn't protect our precious child. I failed my sweet Sariel. I failed Samael. I failed all the innocent humans that put their trust in me.

Suddenly I was tumbling through lifetimes, my thoughts twining together, my memories fading until I no longer knew why I feared Samael, only that I needed to get away, that I'd shatter if he spoke to me. The fear evoked by the thought of him gripped me by the throat, raking its claws across my mind.

A cold sweat soaked my body, and I had to remind myself this wasn't real. Though these feelings were tangible and urgent, they were memories of times long passed.

Forcing myself back to the present, I tuned back into his words, noting the anguished look on his face as he said, "I watched you rip yourself into pieces and hide in the human world. And then you slowly began to fade away, weak and lost, lifetime upon lifetime. It broke me that I couldn't help you. That I'd somehow done this to you."

He drew a breath and strengthened his hold on my hands as if to prevent me from fleeing before he spoke another word. "I was there when you met Kynan. I watched you grow together and fall in love. In this chaotic new existence of yours, I'd never once seen you as happy as you were with him. And I wanted you to have that happiness forever . . ." Samael's voice faltered, and I could feel him tensing within my grasp.

"What did you do?" I asked.

"I marked his soul with my essence."

And there it was: my whole life, my whole existence, was one big lie. Nothing in my life was real.

Pulling away from Samael, I drew my knees into my chest, flinching as the pain in my side intensified. I covered my face with my hands and sobbed. It was as if I was mourning Ray's death all over again.

"He didn't love me. You had to force him to be with me." I kept my face covered, my words coming out stilted. "Has everything been a lie?"

"Whatever feelings you had toward each other were your own," he said, gently prying my hands away from my face, forcing me to look at him. "I only helped you find him. My mark on his soul did not force him into anything."

This was too much—all too much, and all at once. My mind swirled furiously as I tried to digest his words, the conversation with Astrid in the gas station parking lot dancing its way into my mind, playing on loop like a bad movie.

Was this what she was getting at? Forcing me to stare at people and asking me if I could differentiate between their souls . . . if I could identify them? Did she do this because she couldn't understand how I'd found Kynan in every lifetime when the souls of the One Spirit creations are indiscernible to immortals?

How in all these years had I not seen this mark? Or had I and just didn't want to acknowledge it?

I wanted to believe Samael's reassurance that all the iterations of Kynan loved me, that what I had with them was real. But I wasn't sure I could. Humiliation and betrayal crept up on me, replacing my initial shock and etching rivets of insecurity within my spirit.

Stop it! I couldn't let my pride overshadow the bigger picture. I had to set my hurt aside, get my shit together, and move on. I couldn't cry in the corner over the past; I had more important issues to tackle, like how to get everyone out of our current predicament alive.

Get the job done and then mourn properly. You'll get to go back to your kids and hopefully live the rest of this life in relative peace. The words banged a staccato cadence in my mind, reminding me where my priorities lay.

I kept my legs pulled into my chest. They were like a shield protecting me from the magic Samael spun around me. For despite all his revelations, there was something deep inside me that craved nothing more than to be with him, and it grew stronger the closer I got to him.

I had to get control of this situation.

Blowing a strand of hair off my face, I narrowed my eyes. "The demons hunting me over the years . . . was that your doing?"

He shook his head, his face hardening. "No, that was Gadreel. I'd renounced you publicly for your actions and didn't intervene with his hunt, only instructing the demons not to harm you. I didn't want the other Guardians to suspect my love for you was still strong, even though my words were to the contrary. I feared they'd find you if they looked closely in my direction."

When I didn't reply, he continued, his eyes darkening with each word. "You're my mate, my wife—you are a part of me. All the years you hid, your spirit still called to me, pulling me to you. I've always been within your orbit."

Dammit! Tears pooled in my eyes, but I stubbornly refused to let them fall despite their sting. I didn't want to let him know how his words affected me, and yet my heart fluttered, a little bird taking flight on battered wings.

I viciously shoved these feelings aside. "You instructed your demons not to harm me? Well, they did harm me. Aren't they your creations? You are the Prince of Demons, after all."

He let out a tired laugh, shaking his head slightly. "I watch over these creatures, but I didn't participate in their creation. I'm the so-called enforcer of the One Spirit, punishing humans when it's required by allowing the demons to bring darkness into the world. Using that darkness to push humans to evolve into better versions of themselves."

My face was likely broadcasting my confusion, for he continued to explain, "There's no light without darkness, no growth without discomfort. If the humans were in a perpetual state of bliss, would they ever strive to learn, to advance? Happiness is intensified when felt after the sharpest pain, just as a warm day is savored after the bitterness of winter."

I nodded slowly, turning his words over in my mind. It made sense, kind of, but still seemed cruel.

He watched me, probably hoping I'd say something profound. Instead, I cracked a stupid joke, "Oh good, so we didn't make a bunch of demon babies together as the legends say."

"None that I'm aware of, but Sariel can behave as rashly as one." A teasing smile played on his lips, but I didn't return it, his words reminding me how much I've missed—all of the stolen moments of my little boy growing into the strong immortal who'd had come to my rescue.

This conversation was an emotional rollercoaster, and I really wanted off the ride. But since I was primed for tears, I asked the question that would likely send me over the edge.

"Does Sariel hate me for abandoning him?" My voice broke, and I cringed, terrified of what the answer would be.

The second my voice faltered, Samael broke the unspoken barrier between us and pulled me into his arms, careful not to disturb my wounded side.

Cradling me against his chest, he replied, "He worshiped you . . . in his eyes you could do no wrong. He believed to his very core Gadreel did something terrible to you, forcing your hand to create such destruction and flee. He tried to convince me, begging me to tell him where you were, and threatening to find you on his own if I wouldn't help. But instead, I told him you didn't want to be found. That you never wanted to see us again."

"Why? Why didn't you let him find me?" I whispered against his chest, my hand fisting against his shirt.

Resting his chin on the top of my head, his arms tightened around me. "I needed to protect you. If I helped him find you, it would've led Gadreel straight to you. That traitor convinced the other Guardians they were entitled to the sacred fates and destiny, and that you posed a threat to them. Some devoutly followed him, but most only humored him, searching for you for a few centuries until they eventually grew weary and abandoned the cause. I didn't want to do anything to renew their interest. Nor did I want my authority to be questioned as I still had enough sway to steer the majority away from you, keeping you safe."

Samael squeezed me closer, and I felt an overwhelming feeling of tenderness for him. He'd sacrificed so much for me.

"Gadreel was my best friend, my brother, a Guardian warrior, and apparently a liar and a traitor. At the beginning, I didn't doubt his words, rather I believed my actions were responsible for what happened. I should've immediately seen right through him. The second he laid eyes on you, he wanted you— he wanted your gift."

I didn't know what to say to that, so I opted to sit quietly as he stroked my hair, listening to his heart beating under my cheek. I smiled at the sound. In some ways, he felt so human, and at the same time not. An immortal creature with a beautifully beating heart and power at his fingertips primed for destruction.

Peeking out of the corner of my eye at his profile, I noticed his jaw was clenched, a lethal look in his eyes. He looked like he was plotting a murder.

"How did they find me so easily at the motel?" I asked, breaking into his thoughts. My voice sounded muffled against his chest, and I pulled away slightly, tilting my head to look into his face. "I'm so confused, Samael. The mimic knew what Farah looked like. How's that possible when I'd altered reality? To them Farah isn't Farah and I'm not Marci. I've not been anywhere near her to connect the new me to the new Farah. At least that's how it worked with demons. Are mimics different somehow?"

"No, they're not different. Both demons and mimics are simple creatures," he said. He frowned and thought for a moment. "Gadreel had been in control of Tarquin and James's minds. He'd entered your mind back in Vermont. That type of power lingers, and in your human state, you're more vulnerable to his manipulations. I had to purge him from your mind when we arrived here, his essence still clinging within your thoughts. It was why I asked Astrid for a hideout, as she was the only one not tainted."

"My sisters also. They didn't have him in their heads," I reminded him. Samael stilled, a thoughtful expression furrowing his brows before quickly smoothing away as if I'd imagined it.

He didn't comment on my observation, instead continuing to muse about Gadreel. "Gadreel has proven himself a master manipulator. It appears he's formed a stronger alliance with the demon world than I gave him credit for. Again, all this happening right under my nose. I've failed you with my short-sightedness."

"Oh, stop it," I said, bent on interrupting his pity party. He'd done nothing wrong. "Clearly, the other

Guardians were taken in by Gadreel's lies. You weren't the only one to misplace your trust. Though, I'm amazed with all these Guardians and demons looking for me at one point or another, I'd somehow managed to elude them."

"It's easier to see you when you've awakened. Your power is more visible then. But normally, the soul in the body you possess obscures you."

I went stiff, staring into his eyes, horrified.

What in all of hell did he just say to me?

CHAPTER TWENTY-ONE

"What did you say?" I asked, my jaw tense as a ringing in my ears intensified until it was deafening.

Samael frowned, hesitating before replying, "Which part?"

"The part about a soul obscuring me." The words came out choppy and high pitched, my breathing irregular as my mind sped away into a very dark place.

Please, please, I begged, *don't mean what I think this means.*

"The soul you share this body with hides you from demons and Guardians. They have a difficult time seeing past souls originating from the One Spirit— you've hidden in plain sight, blending in amongst the humans."

Shit. It meant exactly what I suspected. To say I was stunned was an understatement; you could've knocked me over with a feather.

Tarquin lied to me. He'd lied when he laughed off

my comment about the meat suit when I first met him in this lifetime.

Without a thought to my wound, I scrambled off Samael's lap, disentangling myself from the bedcovers and leaping out of the bed.

"What are you doing?" he demanded. With a worried glance at my injured side, he grabbed my arm, pulling me close, trying to restrain my movement. "Get back into bed. Your mortal body needs to rest."

"No!" I struggled against him. "I need to talk to Tarquin, and you better let me go or I'll hurt myself even more fighting you."

With a frustrated growl, Samael released me, and I ran to the bedroom door, throwing it open with such force it slammed into the wall, causing everyone in the room to jump in surprise.

Tarquin rose from his seat to greet me, and I jabbed him hard in the chest, causing him to stumble back down into the sofa chair. "Did you lie to me? Or did you not know how fucking wrong you were when you said I wasn't masquerading in a meat suit."

He looked away from my accusatory stare, and I had my answer. He lied.

Glancing around the room wildly, my eyes rested on my sisters sitting frozen in their seats. I could almost hear Astrid telling me to look at them with my Lilith eyes.

Harlow and Mina fidgeted under my stare. Looking past their nondescript light that shown from all creatures, I saw hues of souls materialize, sharpening in vibrancy the closer I looked. They filled their human forms in the same way the souls of the teenagers hanging outside the gas station did. But on the periphery of that light, something familiar shimmered, peeking out further as my power called to it.

Unwelcome tears slid down my cheeks, and I quickly wiped them away. I noticed through their sheen that not only did Tarquin look guilty, but so did James and Astrid.

They knew. They all knew I was in here with the rightful owner of this body. That I was behaving no better than the demons I was supposedly fighting.

Anxiety tightened my chest as a strange sense of cognitive dissonance swept over me. My thoughts went wild, racing in different directions, but all driving back to the same question: Where did I end, and my body roommate begin?

I gulped in air, forcing breath into my body as the stranglehold of a panic attack crept upon me. In my mounting hysteria, a random thought popped into my head of how I should've picked a less anxiety-prone brain than that of Marcianna, and I almost cackled like a maniac.

Piece by piece, I was falling apart, while everyone stared at me, unsure of what to do.

Samael's scent wrapped around me, and he laid his hands gently on my shoulders. I'd become hypersensitive to his scent now that I'd identified it, and I leaned back into him until I was cradled against his chest. I welcomed the calming spell he seemed to cast over me, hoping it would pull me from this spiral of chaotic emotions.

Whatever he was doing was working—my body relaxed as my breathing and heartbeat synchronized with his. The voice inside my head ceased running its incessant dialogue, demanding answers I didn't have.

Harlow got up from her seat, her movements measured as she approached me and took my hand in hers. "What's wrong? You're scaring me."

What should I do? Tell my sisters what I'd learned, and risk terrifying them more, or keep quiet, finish what we started, and consider revealing the truth once we're in a safer situation?

Leaning toward the latter, I turned away from Harlow, feeling as if I were betraying her and Mina, my earlier anger at Tarquin, James, and Astrid fading away. I could almost see why they'd withheld this from me. *Almost.*

Though in Astrid's defense, she'd tried her hardest to clue me in. Earlier I'd thought her questions at the gas station were about Ray, but maybe her intention was to force me to look critically at my sisters—to look within, and see the human souls pressed up against a supernatural presence. If I'd done that, would I have connected it back to myself and revealed this secret earlier?

Probably, if I was being honest with myself. I always could see the truth, but instead, had chosen to remain blind, living my human life blissfully ignorant, not looking back at my trauma.

My eyes drifted to Sariel sitting perched on the arm of the couch, his brows pulled together with a mix of curiosity and concern. He looked like he wanted to help but didn't know what was needed. And he didn't know how to interact with me, nor I with him. We'd lost so much time together because of secrets and lies.

Pulling my gaze away from Sariel, I looked onto the faces of my creations.

Poor Tarquin's face was crestfallen as he sat on the plush sofa chair staring at his hands, the epitome of guilt and regret. Standing on either side of him, Astrid and James looked at me expectantly, having gotten over their initial guilt, their eyes never wavering from mine.

They were my family, woven with my essence, as much a part of me as I was of them.

My attention drifted to my sisters as Harlow squeezed my hand, her worry for me plain to see. She and Mina had been through hell and back these last couple of weeks. Their lives had been turned upside down as much as mine.

In all my relationships, it was our love and desire to protect each other that had led us astray, creating a tangle of secrets and misunderstandings. We'd done so much wrong in the name of what's best—what's best for me, what's best for the immortal family, what's best for humanity—without including each other in the decision.

Maybe these secrets should be things of the past. I could decide right here and now to rewrite this story into one where we trust each other implicitly. To stop doing things that impacted others in our group without their knowledge, forcing each other's hand in fear we'll fail if we didn't. We were only as strong as our weakest link, and it was time to make our links as well forged as possible.

It needed to start with me. Now.

Taking in a deep breath, I said, "No more secrets. To get through this, we need complete trust in each other. Do we all agree?"

Samael released my shoulders and moved to stand by my side. He nodded, his eyes narrowing as he glared around the room as if to threaten agreement from the others.

I guess I can't expect an immortal being to change overnight, I thought, suppressing an eyeroll dying to make an appearance.

The room filled with head bobs and grunts of agreement. My gaze caught Astrid's, and she arched her eyebrow, inclining her head in a slight bow. I smiled, acknowledging her acceptance—and dare I say it—satisfaction in me.

"Harlow." I tightened my hold on her hand. "Mina." They both looked at me, their concern palpable. "We are apparently living within bodies inhabited by souls."

Their mouths dropped open, their faces reflecting the horror I'd felt earlier at this realization.

"What do you mean? Are we demons?" Mina choked out, her face pale as she scurried over to Harlow and me.

James strode to our side, and Harlow tucked herself into his shoulder, looking like she was about to cry. He rubbed her back, all the while repeating, "No, no . . . not demons."

"He's right," I said, interrupting James's words of comfort. "We're something different, I think." I looked around the room, hoping another immortal would chime in and help explain.

I doubted Tarquin or Astrid would know much more, but I noticed Samael and Sariel exchanging looks.

Looking at them pointedly, I asked, "Do you know? Are my sisters and I the same? In my memories from when Sariel was small, I saw myself as similar to you both—solid flesh that could grow wings and fly or flash away. A form that was virtually indestructible. Not human, but maybe made in their image."

"More like they were made in our image," Samael said. "But yes, you and your sisters are the same."

Though his answer was direct, and his tone without a hint of subterfuge, he looked uncomfortable. His eyes shifted away from mine when I tried to make eye contact.

There was something he was holding back. I felt it. Whispers within my spirit told me to open my eyes.

"So, if I were to leave this human's body, I would manifest into a corporeal form . . . a supernatural creature?" I pressed.

Samael cleared his throat, running his hand through his hair. "Yes, *you* would."

My brain on alert, I furrowed my brow, wondering why he'd placed an emphasis on the word "you". I searched his face for clues when Astrid's voice startled me. "Why'd you say 'you' like that?"

She heard it too. I wasn't imagining it.

"Are you saying I'd manifest as Lilith, and if so, what creatures would my sisters become? Are they Guardians?" I added my questions to hers.

"Stop." Tarquin begged, standing up abruptly. He looked equally lost and surprised by his own outburst, as if he didn't know where to go or what to say next. After a few awkward beats of silence, which Astrid graciously didn't break, he added, "I know we just said no secrets, but we still should temper this bluntness, particularly when talking about such matters. Are we sure this wouldn't be too much for you? For them?" He pointed to Mina and Harlow, still clinging to James. "What if this fracture of reality is too great?"

In the past few months, he'd told me things that would make a person's stick-straight hair curl into ringlets, yet, this conversation concerned him. We were clearly heading into uncharted waters.

Walking over to him, I lightly touched his arm. "It's okay. You don't need to protect me anymore. I'm stronger than you think. Trust me."

His expression looked so forlorn that I wrapped my arms around him. "And please know that I trust you," I whispered into his chest as he returned my hug. "I should've confided everything to you, while I still had the memories . . . maybe then we'd not be in this position of uncertainty."

He nodded, his chin tapping me on the top of my head before he released me. Turning to face Astrid, he gave her a curt nod. "You get your way."

"I think that was permission to answer our questions," Astrid said, pinning Samael with a pointed stare.

We all looked at him, the tension in the room growing with anticipation of this great reveal.

Out of the corner of my eye, I saw Astrid holding her breath, her hands clenched at her side, her eyes a vivid blue. She definitely had a hypothesis.

"Are you sure you really want to know this very minute?" Samael asked. "Is this the time to pull you from your familiar world? Perhaps do what you normally do in these awakenings. We can discuss everything after you've completed your task and are safe from Gadreel and the other Guardians."

"Absolutely not," I said at the same time as a "tell us" exploded from Astrid.

Before we could have the satisfaction of an answer, a violent pain seized my head, blinding me, and I dropped to the floor on all fours. It felt like someone was trying to rip into my mind. My body seized up, and my arms collapsed out from under me.

Was this Gadreel? Did he have such power as to drill back into my mind after being ejected by Samael?

Bright lights flashed in my head, swirling in familiar hues of greens and purples, as a voice cried out, "Help me! I can't do it! Please come!"

It wasn't Gadreel. It was Sarah. She needed us. Now!

CHAPTER TWENTY-TWO

Jerking up in a blinding panic, my head slammed into something painfully solid, and I ricocheted backwards. Hands broke my fall, cradling my body and gently guiding me back to the ground.

I opened one eye cautiously, peeking through a haze of what felt like a severe migraine remnant. I'd rammed my face into Samael's head. He hovered over me, a look of concern in his eyes. He didn't appear the worse for wear because of our head collision, but the metallic taste on my lips was a testament to my damaged nose.

In addition to the nose and head pain, my side burned with renewed fervor, and I could barely suck in a breath without feeling like someone was stabbing me. Laying on the ground, breathing shallowly, my body threatened to give out at any minute.

Forgotten was my anticipation, and frankly, trepidation over Samael's big reveal, replaced now by guilt and worry over my mortal body. How long would I last continuously patching it up? It had already been through so much. If I was a good creature, I'd vacate this flesh and bone before I destroyed it.

Marci deserved to go back to her family, not to be pieced back together by a clingy creature craving to be human. But was I brave enough to do it—to leave behind the life I knew, and go live as Lilith? Lilith, the creature capable of destroying humans in a fit of rage, while in the same breath being lonely, pitiful, and easily manipulated?

The answer was no, not now. In all honesty, this Lilith from my distant past scared me. I didn't recognize myself in her, and I didn't want to.

Pushing these thoughts away, I focused on everyone huddled around me, their expressions projecting various degrees of fear.

"What happened?" Samael asked. "Was it Gadreel?" The concern in his eyes was overshadowed momentarily by a murderous zeal as he spat out that name.

I shook my head, wincing in pain. "Sarah. She needs us," I rasped. "She's becoming more persistent. Whatever we need to help her with must be happening now. The situation is urgent."

Astrid elbowed her way through the cluster of men. Kneeling down, she looked me over. "Do you think you can move?" she asked.

"Yeah, give me a sec," I said. "I didn't realize Sarah was so powerful. She really knocked me on my ass."

Sariel frowned. "Is her name Sarah in every incarnation?"

I never really thought about that, but it sounded ridiculous.

"Probably not," I replied. "It's just a name we use. It was destiny's name in Razma's time, and that time seems to hold a lot of significance for me." I smiled wryly. "Maybe it's a code word to get through to Lilith, to me, telling me I need to deal with destiny."

Sariel nodded, though his brows were still knitted together in deep thought. "I can hear her too," he confessed. I looked at him, surprised. "It makes sense some of your gifts would have transferred to me. You're my mother, keeper of the fates and destiny of humankind. Though I do not have your power to influence them, I can both see and hear them. I'm like an observer of the forged path of humanity and the decisions you've made to alter it."

"Do the other Guardians know this?" I asked.

He shook his head and looked toward Samael. "My father made it clear I shouldn't divulge such information."

"Probably a wise decision," I said, elevating myself onto my elbows, a precursor to standing.

The room spun. My side spasmed with a sharp pain, causing me to collapse back onto the floor.

"You're bleeding, again." Astrid clucked, pressing her hand into my side. I flinched under the pressure.

Samael pushed Astrid's blood-soaked hands aside, and scooped me into his arms, carrying me back into the bedroom.

Now that the adrenaline from all the self-discovery had faded away, the burning pain was almost unbearable. The wound was gapping open and seeping reddish-clear fluid, a sign my body was trying to heal itself but failing.

Reclining against propped up pillows, I watched Samael work on my side, pouring his magic into my body to yet again close the wound. The light touches of his fingers brushing the skin after each burst of power caused me to shiver, though I tried to control my reaction as each twitch seemed to worry him.

I noticed after each healing session he'd frown, shaking his head at my wound, clearly not pleased by my lack of progress. He'd then push his hair behind his ears and continue mending my body, his jaw set in determination.

How long would he be at this? It seemed like he'd never be satisfied with the progress we'd made, looking at me as if I'd shatter at the first moment of adversity.

Despite him tending to me without uttering a word, the more I was near him, the more right it felt. I didn't mind using the time spent in silence to admire his odd mix of beauty and ferocity—the man looked like he could rip an enemy limb from limb, yet his long eyelashes softened his appearance.

Raising his eyes, he caught me watching him work, a slow smile spreading over his face, his eyes crinkling. "You know it would be easier if you'd just leave this body behind."

"So I've been told." I said wearily.

He looked surprised by my statement. "By whom?"

"Astrid," I replied.

We held each other's gaze for a few beats of silence before he threw back his head, laughing heartily. My heartbeat accelerated. Settling into a lopsided grin, he said, "I could imagine her demanding 'you get your ass out of that body and fight'."

I returned his smile. "Technically, she expressed her desire for me to stop snoozing all the time and stay awake. I don't think she realized I could exist without being in a human body. She probably imagined me being more like her. To be honest, though, I'm not sure how to get out of this body without it dying and become corporeal in my Lilith form."

He opened his mouth but I didn't let him speak as fear surged within me at the possibility of an eviction from this body. Despite it being a lease, it had given me a happy life, and I wasn't quite ready to let go.

"We can talk about that later," I said, rushing the words. "Am I healed enough for now?"

He inclined his head. "You are."

"So . . . um . . . do we flash outta here to Sarah's house or back to the motel to get our cars?"

He didn't address the reason for my sudden change in topic, but his smile faded. His eyes, which had softened to a rich brown as we'd joked, were now his typical dark, stormy color.

"How important are these cars?" he asked. "Sariel could take one of your creatures to the motel and pick up the cars. Though it's likely Gadreel has a demon, or perhaps even a Guardian, watching our last known location."

That was a good point, and I felt dumb asking about the stupid cars. I'm sure somewhere within me, the great warrior and battle strategist, Razma, cringed. "Okay. Fair enough. How many individuals do you think you can transport at once?"

He frowned as he considered the answer. "Three at most, and it would be best if they were smaller in size. They could get hurt if I can't shield them appropriately. Human bodies aren't well adapted to such travels, even ones held together by immortal glue."

I balked at the glue comment, but the mischievous look in his eyes silenced the snark about to fire from my mouth. I rolled my eyes, biting my lip to mask the smile forcing its way through.

Looking down at his fingers still on my side, I watched as they absentmindedly traced patterns on my skin, and my cheeks flushed at the familiarity with which he touched me. His fingertips trailed over my ribs, and I swallowed hard, my mind struggling to think of my next words.

"We could . . . um . . . arrive at Sarah's house in groups," I stuttered, horrified that my face was likely visibly on fire. "And um . . . and take her away."

"Where do you think you'll be going with her?" he asked. God, his fingers were driving me to distraction. I wanted to slap them away as much as I wanted to close my eyes and lean into his touch.

"I don't know . . . to wherever we need to go in order to help her keep destiny on track."

His fingers stilled, and he frowned. "Let's just go there and figure out the next steps. For all we know, we won't have to do much," he said. "I've noticed many times you and your sisters just need to evaluate the possibilities with Sarah—to understand what needs to be done and support her through the difficult parts of pushing that reality through. Help her do that which she cannot do by herself."

Covering his hand with mine, I asked, "Have you always been with me? Watching me?"

He flipped his hand to grasp mine and rubbed his thumb against the softness of my inner wrist. Raising his eyes to meet my gaze, he replied, "Always."

That word was like a match thrown into a pile of kindling—a fire ignited within me, and I looked away, terrified at the passion I saw in his eyes and my reaction to it.

Clearing my throat, I extracted my hand and continued our conversation, doing my best to ignore the desires of my spirit. "That seems overly simple. Where are the demons? Where's Gadreel? I vividly remember everything from Tarquin's time with the original Sarah, though my memories prior to that are fuzzy, at best. But then the demons were very much in the picture . . . they had Sarah and her mother . . . they were going to execute them . . . and they also possessed Tarquin to hurt me."

"I can understand how you'd see it that way," Samael said. "But the demons were in Rome for an unrelated reason. Sarah was to be executed because of who her father was, not because she was identified as destiny. Remember, the demons don't see what Sarah is . . . she looks like any other human to them. And

Tarquin, well, he was a fortuitous accident for them. Someone they didn't realize was a perfect pawn until you awakened, and your essence eclipsed the human soul, so they could finally see you for who you were."

His words conjured scraps of images within my mind, and I closed my eyes as they weaved together like a quilt. At first, I was an observer watching Razma and her two sisters with the orb, their arms entwined, the orb's energy flooding their bodies. But then the perspective changed, and now I was Razma, the visions within my mind vibrant, almost tangible. Sarah was communicating with us, showing a new destiny, a new path forward. She and her mother were to die in the Roman's Colosseum, but a new branch of fate had sprung forward—an alternate destiny bringing with it a hope of a more fulfilling future for humanity. A decision needed to be made, stay the course, or follow the new path. But the new destiny required Sarah to live, and she could not save herself from death without our help.

Opening my eyes, I wondered why the connection with Sarah was so much stronger back then. In this lifetime, it was muddled, uncertain. Sarah hadn't reached out with a defined proposal, only a fear that she had to do something but couldn't.

Astrid had said that with each lifetime I was becoming more human. Was Sarah like me and the same could be true for her? Or was I the one weakening the connection?

Before I could ask Samael, the door opened, and Tarquin walked in. He paused at the sight of Samael sitting on the bed with me, his mouth tightening into a thin line.

My cheeks flushed at Tarquin's disapproval. "Samael's just trying to patch me up a little more. My stupid wound doesn't want to heal properly," I said, my voice sounding guilty, a little too airy.

I should feel guilty—playing doctor with a devil, while my children wait for me . . . their father dead. Disgust at my actions grew as my brain raged.

"Is it time to go?" I asked. I could feel tears of shame pool in my eyes, and I covered my face for a second, trying to hold them back, not wanting to showcase how raw and unstable my emotions were in this moment. I didn't need everyone worrying about my mental health when we had more important things to do.

Get a hold of yourself, I commanded, raising my chin in hopes I looked more the part of an awakened warrior, ready to fight for the destiny of humankind.

Tarquin nodded. Walking to my side, he offered his hand to me, and I accepted, allowing him to gently pull me up to standing. Adjusting my clothes, I followed him out of the bedroom and into the living room, where everyone else looked anxiously toward me, ready to head out.

"Thank God you're all right," Mina said, looking me over. "Let's get this whole thing over with so we can get back to our lives. I think I'd rather battle figurative demons in a courtroom than actual ones, especially with the fate of the world hanging in the balance."

Harlow rolled her eyes but didn't chastise Mina. She looked exhausted, and likely wanted to get back to being a college freshman partying it up at her sorority house, rather than being waist deep in this craziness.

Samael came up behind me, and though he didn't touch me, I could feel his reassuring presence. "I'll take Lilith and her sisters with me to meet with Sarah. Sariel, can you take the others? Remain outside of Sarah's house and ensure Gadreel and his followers do not disturb us."

Sariel frowned. "You're stronger than I am. Maybe I should take the sisters and you take the others? I don't want to accidentally hurt anyone during our travels."

Samael hesitated, but then patted his son on the shoulder, motioning for Astrid, James, and Tarquin to join him. Astrid and James gripped onto him, but Tarquin stepped back, looking unsure if he wanted to be part of the Samael sandwich.

"What are you doing?" Astrid snapped. "Stop being a child. Just hang onto James and me." She pulled Tarquin forcefully against herself, and James drew his arm tightly around his shoulders as Samael's large wings encircled them and they disappeared.

"Mother," Sariel said, opening his arms to us.

As Mina, Harlow, and I wrapped our arms around him, I couldn't shake the feeling that the comment wasn't solely directed at me.

CHAPTER TWENTY-THREE

Sariel's wings unfurled, and I stumbled into Sarah's room, my eyes adjusting to the moonlit darkness. A hodgepodge of toys was strewn across the floor, reminding me this was a child's room—a child no different than my precious babies waiting for me back home.

My resolve steeled. I had to protect Sarah at all costs from Gadreel, by any means, as I would my own children.

A noise from the corner of the room drew our attention. Sarah sat in a pool of blankets at the center of a princess poster bed. She rubbed her eyes, her tangled hair shining like silver in the soft glow of the moon.

"Hello?" her sweet voice called out.

Harlow immediately ran to her side, wrapping the child in her arms. "We're here . . . just like we promised. Tell us what you need."

"I've had bad dreams," Sarah whispered as if

confessing a dire transgression and hid her face in Harlow's shirt, her little body trembling with sobs.

I sat down next to Harlow on the bed, placing my hand on Sarah's back and making small circles in hopes it would help her relax.

To my surprise, Sariel joined us, his voice soothing as he asked, "Sarah, what's your real name?"

"Katie," she mumbled into Harlow's shirt.

"Do you know who Sarah is?" he asked.

At first, she shook her head, but then nodded. "It's someone inside me . . . talking to me . . . showing me things . . . bringing the bad dreams."

"Katie, would you like me to help Sarah show everyone the scary dream? I've seen what Sarah's shown you, too."

Katie peeked out from Harlow's chest, staring up at the imposing man standing next to her bed, his hand outstretched. She took it tentatively, still holding onto Harlow's shirt, dragging Harlow with her, as she crept to Sariel.

"Do you recognize me?" he asked.

Katie shook her head. "No, but you feel like I know you."

He smiled, tucking a lock of hair behind her ear. "That's how I feel about you, too."

Though it pained me to hear this child talk with fear in her voice, pride bloomed within my chest watching my son soothe her. He'd grown into a kind, strong man. Looking at him, I couldn't help but see the child I'd grieved, blaming myself for his death, fleeing with such fierce conviction of my wrongdoing that I'd inadvertently abandoned him.

Sariel caught me looking at him, a small smile on his lips as if he could hear my thoughts. "Like I said before, I've inherited some of your gifts, Mother. I've been able to hear Sarah calling out. Over the years, it seemed to correlate with strange lights in the night sky that I'd thought only I could see. Though I never knew where she was or who she was, I could see the shifts in destiny she was trying to communicate."

"How did you happen to notice the lights?" Curiosity got the best of me, distracting me momentarily from the task at hand.

"You taught me to love the night sky, weaving legends of our origins from the fire of stars and the sands of moons. When I was a boy, you'd point to our moon and tell me stories of how she watches over us." He paused. "And if ever we were to be separated, I should look to the moon as you'd be gazing at her as well. So, I did, and I still do."

He shattered me with those words and the vulnerability I saw in his eyes. I imagined him as a small boy staring out into the night sky, wondering why I'd left him. I fought the urge to throw my arms around him and never let go.

"I'm here now," I whispered, taking his hand in mine. "And I'm so sorry I left. I never would have if I knew you were alive."

A gentle smile pushed away the sadness from his face. "I know. Don't worry, Mother, I always knew."

Sniffling caught my ear, and I realized Harlow was

crying, which wasn't surprising, but what shocked me was the sheen in Mina's eyes as she stood near the doorway watching us.

No-nonsense Mina was crying. If I hadn't seen it, I may not have believed it. I motioned her to come join us on the bed, and she crept nearer but still stood at a distance from us.

Reaching out, Sariel pulled Mina in closer by her elbow. "Sit," he said, motioning to a spot on the bed next to Harlow and me.

She complied, her back stiff in protest as she arranged her limbs to fit on the twin bed.

Looking at my sisters and me, Katie's little face scrunched in confusion. I gave her a reassuring smile. Poor kid was likely confused why the adults who came to help her were now crying.

Sariel sat down across from us, and Katie settled in his lap, her little head bumping against him as she fidgeted nervously.

"Are you scared?" I asked. She nodded, a tear spilling down her cheek.

"We're here. We'll face this dream together." I reached out, taking her hand in mine. She squeezed it tight, her fingers so tiny in my palm.

"Don't worry, I'll help you and Sarah show them the dream," Sariel said. Katie whimpered in response, and he added, "You're not alone. We'll be with you the whole time."

She nodded and reached her hand out to Mina as I took hold of Harlow's hand. Sariel covered Katie's hands with his, wrapping his fingers around mine and

Mina's hands.

Glancing around the circle of people surrounding her, Katie closed her eyes, and we all followed her lead.

Our energies connected, thoughts intertwining into one consciousness as we waited in the darkness for a vision. I could feel Sariel's energy pulling a thread of light forward, and I latched onto it. Suddenly a bright glow blinded us, and we saw a fuzzy image of Katie's parents looking at us with love, our newly born limbs squirming and reaching.

Katie's life played out for us like a movie reel—sometimes we were in the point of view of an observer, while other times we saw things through her eyes, feeling what she felt.

We watched her grow up with her family—laughing with her brothers, being spoiled by her parents as their only baby girl. We went into the future with her, our collective heartbeats drumming in excitement as she met her husband. Happiness spun around us, as we danced in a raucous wedding surrounded by the faces of loving friends and family. We cried as she welcomed her children and then grandchildren. And our spirits were heavy, watching as she buried her parents, her brothers, and then her husband.

Soon, darkness obscured our vision again.

It was a simple life filled with laughter, thrills, successes, and touches of sadness—a life anyone would've loved to have lived.

Suddenly, visions of her last moments on earth replaced the darkness. Then it was like someone hit a rewind button, speeding in reverse through her life, until we were back at the beginning, starting again.

We replayed the early years in double speed, everything the same as the first time. But then the movie reel slowed down. We were in the present.

Katie squeezed my hand, her fingernails digging into my skin. My heart quickened as her fear pulsated through me.

We watched Katie's mom telling Katie and her brother, Mark, she'd make them macaroni and cheese after her shower. The siblings pouted as their mom left the kitchen and headed upstairs, stopping to yell down into the basement. Katie's older brothers were downstairs with their dad, hooting and hollering. They paused their game long enough to hear the shower turn on, the pipe noise signaling the all clear.

Katie turned to Mark, nibling on her lip nervously when she saw he'd turned on the flame. But thoughts of being grown up dispelled the bad feelings of disobeying their mom, and Katie dived enthusiastically into helping make the snack.

They laughed as they cooked, and when the macaroni was tender, Mark lifted the pot to pour off the water. He burnt his fingers on the metal and howled at Katie to get potholders.

She ran to the drawer, pulled them out, and passed them quickly to him over the stovetop. But before he could take them from her, one glove fell onto the burner, catching fire.

The kids screamed, jumping back from the flames as the fire spread quickly to a pile of mail near the stove. "Put it out, put it out!" Katie cried. But the twisting red flames grabbed onto the kitchen curtains next, the heat causing the electricity to spark. The fire alarm blared in their ears.

"I can't stop it!" Mark screamed. They ran to the front door as the fire bloomed around them. Over the shriek of the alarms, they could hear their brothers and dad running up the basement stairs.

Hands suddenly grabbed Katie's arms and she was hefted up over the shoulder of a neighbor, who carried her and Mark to safety. As soon as their feet touched the ground, they screamed for him to help their family.

We watched in horror as the neighbor ran back up the porch, yelling the names of people that were like his own family. But before he could get to them, the house exploded, sending him hurling through the air. Heat scorched the faces of Katie and her brother as the explosion threw them into the dirt. Flames shot out of their home.

More neighbors arrived, followed by fire trucks and police, but no one could save Katie's family. Katie wailed, the type of high-pitched screams that cut up a soul. But Mark stood silent, even after the police pulled him away into an ambulance.

Bile climbed up my throat and I gripped tight to Harlow's hand, hearing her labored breathing as she choked back sobs. The sound grounded me to reality, taking the edge off the pain I felt within Sarah's vision of Katie's possible life. I wanted to open my eyes and stop watching this alternate future, but I couldn't.

The movie continued to play, forcing me to watch

as Katie and Mark were shuttled to various foster homes. Forcing me to experience Katie stand by helplessly as her brother spiraled into self-loathing and torment.

Clawing herself out of her own misery, over the years, she tried to save Mark. She failed, losing him to addiction, and drowned out the pain by studying hard and eventually becoming a psychiatrist, specializing in childhood traumas.

The vision sped up, fragments flashing by of Katie finding love, getting married, having children— her life regaining a semblance of peace and normality.

And then the pace slowed down again, the vision halting to focus on one moment.

Katie sat on a couch in her home, watching the news with her husband. He lifted the remote to change the channel, but she gripped his wrist, her eyes caught on a child, his sad face filling up the screen. The child was located nearby after a nationwide search, the news anchor describing the young boy as the sole survivor of an unspeakable act of cruelty. Tears ran down Katie's face as she listened to his story. Going to her boss the next day, she was assigned to the boy's case within the week.

My eyes flew open, and I struggled to breathe. I could hear Mina gagging as she fought down nausea.

Katie's gaze met mine, tears streaming down her face. "I don't want it to happen," she cried.

I'd been physically ill watching these visions. How could this child bear seeing this about herself . . .

about her whole family? What had she been forced into? This was beyond cruel to do to a child.

Mina's voice jolted me from my thoughts. "What just happened? I don't understand what we saw?"

"It seemed to be two different futures," I replied. "One path is the one Katie is currently on and the other appears to be a new future. But I don't know what the difference would be between these two futures."

"I do," Harlow whispered.

Mina and I looked at her wide eyed. "What do you mean?" I asked.

"I can't explain it, but when we were watching the vision, I was seeing the different futures of the two versions." Harlow pressed on her temple with her index fingers. "I thought everyone saw what I did."

"I could see it," Sariel said. We all swiveled our heads toward him.

"How's that possible?" I frowned.

Harlow opened her mouth, beginning to say, "I don't know," so I shushed her with my finger on her lips. "Not you. Him."

Sariel looked me in the eyes and said, "Because I can see all the fates—the fate of what was, the fate of what is, and the fate of what will be."

Worrying my lower lip with my teeth, I wondered why I couldn't see this "fate of what will be". The closest experience I'd had to seeing the future was at the start of my awakening when I'd heard a voice in my dreams telling me about the plane crash, and then the malfunctioning toaster oven.

I held my questions back though, when I saw Katie anxiously listening to the conversation. Instead, I said, "Okay, that's interesting. Umm . . . what did you both see then?"

Harlow looked to Sariel, but he waved his hand at her as if to say, "after you".

"The boy Katie rescues in the alternate future, becomes someone very beneficial to the world. He's an influential person. Not like a president or anything, but he makes this tech that saves people."

"So, we're going to destroy Katie's life right now for tech?" Mina hissed.

Harlow shifted uncomfortably, her eyes darting to Sariel before answering, "That same boy in the current future—the future where he does not meet Katie—is also very influential and charismatic, but he does horrible, evil things to people when he grows up. And not like on a small scale . . . I mean on a whole world scale."

We stared at each other not moving, barely breathing, until Katie's whimper broke the silence.

"What . . . what kind of evil are we talking about?" I stammered.

"I don't wanna say in front of Katie," Harlow whispered, her eyes speaking volumes. My heart fell into my stomach. It was an impossible decision—allow Katie's family to die now and potentially save countless people or let them live as originally planned and set humanity back.

"I can't do this," I said, jumping off the bed and

falling to my knees on the floor, my mind racing. "I don't understand any of this."

Sariel joined me on the floor. "What don't you understand?"

"So many things," I said, choking on my anxiety. "But what bothers me most right now is not remembering this duality with Katie and Sarah. Before, there was just a choice to be made, no emotions in play. Is Katie to Sarah what Marci is to me?

"Yes and no. I think your humanness obscures what would be obvious for you to see as Lilith," Sariel said. "I'm not sure how you distributed your gifts, but what I see is destiny tied to that soul . . . that one soul."

He took my hand, guiding me to look at Katie. "Look at her. Not just a glance, with fear in your heart about what you might see, but really look. Do you see what I see?"

The noise in my mind was deafening, so first, I worked on silencing the litany of *what did you do*. As soon as my thoughts quieted, I could see within Katie, see her human soul and see the shimmer of hues embedded within it. Those tendrils emitted the same glow as the orb, the same beautiful sparkle as the sacred tree.

I did this. I tied destiny to this soul, forcing it for several millennia to live out each critical decision. How much had it endured because of me? I covered my ears as if that could somehow block the reality of what I'd done.

Here I thought I was some fucking hero, battling

demons to save Sarah from the Colosseum, but in reality, I was the villain. I was the monster.

"What's taking so long?" Astrid hissed from the doorway.

Samael was two steps behind her. But when our eyes met, he pushed past Astrid, his long strides bringing him by my side within seconds.

Dropping to the ground, he pulled me into his arms, his fingers tangling in my hair as he pressed me to his chest. "What happened? Are you hurt?"

"Everything I've done since Gadreel tricked me has been a mistake . . . a selfish, horrible mistake." Tears seeped past my closed eyelids as I spat out each word. "I'm evil."

"You have to calm down," Astrid said, kneeling beside us. "The whole family will soon be wide awake if you don't stop this. We'll end up frying their brains trying to get them to pretend they never saw a bunch of adults in their kid's bedroom."

I wrapped my arms tighter around Samael's neck, breathing him in, my mind taking a step back from its freefall. "I tied destiny to a human soul. I made that one soul responsible for humanity. Can you imagine its agony? What was I thinking?"

"You were thinking of protecting humanity from the desires of the Guardians . . . and protecting it from yourself," Samael said.

"I can fix it," I whispered in his ear, swallowing back my tears. "I'll bring it back within my own body."

"You can't in this form," he replied.

Pulling away, I looked up at him, my mind made up. "I'll leave this body as well."

He held my gaze for a moment before shaking his head. "It would still destroy you."

"I don't understand!" I cried.

"Remember when I said I watched you ripping yourself to shreds?" he asked. "I was not being metaphorical."

"What are you saying?" The room grew still.

"Even if you stepped out of your current human body, you would not be whole." He pointed at my sisters. "They are pieces of you."

I jerked away, my hands fisted by my side, my head shaking, trying to deny the obvious. The meaning of our previous conversation, where I'd noticed Samael's emphasis on the word "you" snapped into place. This was that final secret we'd almost drawn out of Samael before being interrupted—the final reveal of who Lilith was—who I was.

I ignored Samael's pained expression and stood up, wrapping my arms around my torso, trying to hold myself together. I looked at my sisters. Not a glance, as Sariel had said before, but really looked.

A sob escaped me. It was true; they were not my sisters, but pieces of me hiding behind souls within human bodies. Wrapped around those pieces was the radiant shimmer of the fates.

How many human lives have I controlled, set on a path of destruction? With each revelation, I thought I couldn't possibly get any more heinously disappointing and yet the surprises kept coming.

Looking over my shoulder at Astrid, I saw her watching me connect the dots. "Did you know?" I asked, my voice sounding flat. "Did Tarquin and James know?"

"No," she assured me. "Your sisters do look like you—the same essence within the bodies—but I thought maybe it was like how I couldn't differentiate the human souls. I only began to suspect back in Georgetown when Samael emphasized the word 'you' when answering your question about becoming corporeal. It sounded like he'd implied your sisters would not be able to manifest into a solid form outside their bodies."

I felt like a balloon drifting in the breeze, with no control over the direction it went. "Then if Tarquin didn't know, why did he object so strongly to Samael answering our questions?"

Astrid touched my shoulder gently, her blue eyes losing the usual icy appearance. "You're so strong, yet so vulnerable. While James and I see the strength, Tarquin focuses overly on your vulnerability. He fears something will happen to you, and you'll be lost forever. It eats away at him."

Tarquin had been right to be concerned, judging by my sisters' horrified expressions.

Mina kept opening and closing her mouth, reminding me of a fish out of water. When she finally spoke, her words broke my heart, "I thought it was bad enough when we were body snatchers cohabitating with souls, but now we don't even exist. What does this even mean for us?" Tears fell onto her cheeks, but she didn't wipe them away.

Harlow sat next to her, looking lost and disconnected, so unlike her bubbly enchantress self, all of her passion lost.

Getting up from the floor, I walked over to them, climbing onto the bed and wrapping them both in my arms. Our foreheads touched and our eyes closed as we sat feeling each other's essence, each other's pain.

The memories came fast, slicing into my mind like a white-hot blade: the agony of losing Sariel, of not being able to hold him one last time, the destruction I caused, the sadness in Samael's eyes, and the accusation on the Guardian's faces. The memories tumbled together as I blindly fled from them, blurring within my mind, bringing me to the brink of madness.

I felt what I felt then, the desperation bitter in my mouth. Everything I was I didn't want to be. Everything I felt, I didn't want to feel anymore. I knew I had to stop this, or I'd lose myself to the destruction, and despite what I'd done to the humans, I was still their last line of defense. If I let go, their fates and destiny would fall into the hands of Guardians . . . into the hands of Gadreel.

In my memories, Samael started appearing, finding me in my madness no matter how much I tried to hide from him. He'd want to speak to me, to force me to listen, but I couldn't . . . I couldn't bear to even look at him, afraid to see the disgust in his eyes, the same disgust I felt toward the monster I was.

And I ran . . . and ran and ran, to the corners of

the world, but there was no escape. The torment in my mind was too much, the fear I'd hurt the humans again unbearable.

So, I ripped my essence apart, peeling away the feelings I couldn't bear—my love, my self-loathing—watching them fall away and hiding them behind the souls of humans as they slept peacefully, unaware of the invasion.

But then the fates and destiny within me became too much . . . they screamed in my chest, pounded against my thoughts, clawed at my spirit. I was in shambles, fragments of me scattered within humans. I was not whole enough, not stable enough, to hold onto my own power.

Keeping the fate of the present within my core self, I relinquished the fate of the future to the part of me that held my love and passion, and the fate of the past went to the part of me that was pragmatic and critical.

Destiny, though, I tied to a soul, binding it there with a spell of instruction to join the fates when it needed help to save humanity. I owed the humans at least this, my servitude to their survival.

And then, exhausted, I too found a human body to lie in, to sleep within and not feel, only to be awakened when the path of humanity was in question.

I floated through lifetimes, feeling empty and lost —until I found Kynan. With him by my side, and the safe haven provided by my newly created immortal family, I slowly shed my self-loathing, allowing myself to forget Lilith.

Opening my eyes, I met the tired stares of my

sisters, unshed tears glistening in their eyes, and I knew they'd lived these memories with me.

"It's time we're whole again," I whispered.

They nodded, and we clung to each other for a few heartbeats, syncing together, our tears spent.

No more running, no more hiding. Like a phoenix, Lilith would rise again.

CHAPTER TWENTY-FOUR

The sun's rays peeked out from behind the trees when we finally stepped out of Katie's house. Astrid had left earlier to find Tarquin and James, who'd been patrolling the outside perimeter of the house. I watched them standing transfixed, listening to her talk, their eyes darting between me, Mina, and Harlow.

I guess Astrid had clued them in on all the big secrets, their awkwardness palpable the moment we arrived at their side. We stared at each other, unsure of what to say.

Tarquin finally broke the silence. "What now?" he asked, shoving his hands in his pockets, a lost look on his face.

I felt so sad for him. I'd trapped him by my side those many years ago, using his loyalty and love for my own gains. He'd dedicated his immortal life to serving me, tormented with guilt for my murder, seeking redemption. But I wasn't who he thought I was, and his immortal life must now appear a sham.

Shivering at my dark thoughts, I shook off the depression creeping into my mind.

Stay focused. You can fix this. Change the ending.

That last thought caused me to glance at Samael, standing on the street with our son, giving us privacy. The quote he'd reminded me of earlier now repeated itself in my mind: *You can't go back and change the beginning, but you can start where you are and change the ending.*

I met Tarquin's uncertain gaze. My chin raised, hoping I could regain his confidence in me. "We tucked in Sarah—well technically Katie—and are going to leave her for a bit." He raised his eyebrows, and I took in a deep breath, squeezing my sisters' hands as they clung to mine. "We're going to find Marci's family and give her back to them. We're going to give them all back—Mina and Harlow too. And then Lilith will return here and take destiny from Katie."

Talking about myself in the third person was bizarre. I wasn't Marci, not really, but I didn't know how to be Lilith. I prayed I'd actually figure it out soon and get through this plan.

James's stoic expression crumbled, and he scooped my sisters and me into his arms, holding us to his chest tightly. "You're doing the right thing. We're here for you. By your side, always."

To my surprise, Astrid put her arms around our shoulders, joining the group hug. "I know you feel differently about yourself right now, but to me you're always good, clever, and strong—someone I'm proud to follow."

Tarquin nodded, taking my hand in his when James and Astrid released us. "I've heard the thoughts you emit without realizing. You've been through so much and have layered a tremendous amount of guilt on yourself, but please know, I too have never been prouder to serve you, to call you my friend and my maker in this immortal life."

"Oh shit. You're all gonna make me cry," I said, a tearful smile trembling on my lips. "And I've been so completely even keeled and emotionless this entire time."

James burst out laughing, but Tarquin shook his head, his expression solemn. "I think you're entitled to your emotions," he said. "After all, it's hard work being in a meat suit."

My eyes widening, I slapped my hands over my mouth, barely muffling the peel of laughter that burst out.

"Wow, Tarquin made a joke," Astrid said, her matter-of-fact tone causing me to laugh harder.

"Yes, Astrid, I'm capable of humor when warranted. Now let's get out of here before the family wakes up and calls the police."

Composing myself, I walked over to Samael and Sariel. "How should we get to Marci's family?" I asked them. "Are we going to flash into their kitchen or something, or is it safe enough to get our cars from the motel and drive there now that we won't lead Gadreel and the rest to destiny?"

"How close are they to here?" Astrid asked.

"Pretty close," I replied. "Just one state further south."

Samael put his hand on my shoulder, and I looked up into his eyes. "What would you like to do, Lilith?" he asked.

"Drive," I whispered. I wanted to drive because I wanted more time before I had to say goodbye to Marci, goodbye to her family, and goodbye to her life.

"Down the street there's a coffee shop," Samael said, pointing in the general direction. "Sariel and I will get the cars and meet you there."

I found it a relief, as well as oddly fascinating, my usually very opinionated crew did not question this decision. They just started to walk down the street as instructed.

Hesitating to leave, my eyes latched on to the two Guardians before me, my spirit willing me to stay with them. To never let them go.

"Be careful," I said, before forcing my feet to follow the others.

The desire to look at them once more had me glancing over my shoulder, and I caught a glimpse of their pleased smiles before they both disappeared from sight.

I clutched my coffee, my knee dancing nervously as I people watched, the faux leather couch squeaking each time I adjusted my position. Now and again, I'd remember to sip the now-cold liquid.

My companions sat silently by my side, vacantly gazing off into the distance or at the floor. We were all mentally drained, our mortal flesh exhausted.

Stewing over the next steps, my anxiety pulsated throughout my body. My craving to get to my family crashed against my need to delay.

I desperately wanted to see them, wrap my arms around them. But then I'd remind myself they were not my family, not Lilith's family, but Marci's. And soon I'd be only Lilith. The thought of leaving them broke me.

The coffee shop exacerbated my mood, its vibe similar to the one I'd spent countless hours at with Cece and Farah. Those coffee dates seemed so far away now, despite the last one being only a month or so ago. It might as well have been years. I felt like I'd lived a hundred lifetimes in that span of time.

I caught sight of our cars pulling up to the sidewalk outside the coffee shop and my mouth went dry. It was time to go, and I wasn't ready.

Samael and Sariel strode into the coffee shop, their faces looking far from pleased. I put down my coffee and rubbed my sweaty palms on my pants, the worry over my readiness to proceed replaced by the fear of bad news.

"We've got a problem," Samael said, thrusting a paper under my nose.

I took it, holding the crumpled note by the tips of

my fingers as if it was toxic, my heart hammering in my ears.

Darling Lilith, I'm at the home of the lovely Marcianna's family. They've been asking about you. Come visit.

Hands shaking, I looked up at Samael. "Oh, my God. How did he know where they were?"

"Same way he knew what your best friend looked like, or where your house from the previous reality was located. He'd forced his way into your mind and into your companions' minds in Vermont, and then you allowed him back in again to show you that manipulated past of Sariel's death."

His words were said without judgment, but my brain, the queen of judgment, started kicking me for my carelessness and gullibility. I'd already lost two important people in Marci's life; I couldn't allow for anyone else to be hurt.

"We need to go!" I cried out. No one moved, their startled eyes glued to my face. "Now!"

"It's a trap," Tarquin said. "God knows how many creatures Gadreel has waiting for us. Think about this rationally . . . why would a powerful creature such as Gadreel send you an invitation to his location?"

"Because he's a master manipulator who's lost his access to your thoughts when I severed the connection," Samael answered for me, his eyes darkening. "The note not only causes psychological turmoil, but also promises to deliver Lilith to him on his timeline."

"I don't care if it's a trap! I can't just leave my family—Marci's family! If no one wants to come with me, I'll go by myself." I jumped up, ready to save the people I loved even if I had to steal a car to do so. I knew I was being dramatic, but I didn't care. I didn't want to sit here twiddling my thumbs while my human family could be in danger.

Samael caught me by the wrist, his dark eyes boring into mine. "We are always with you. But you know what needs to be done, or we won't stand a chance."

He was right, I knew it, but I thought I'd have more time. Just a little more time to grieve the loss of all I knew in this world and prepare for my new life.

"I'm not ready," I whispered, and his face softened as he pulled me into his arms. I noticed patrons of the coffee shop were looking curiously in our direction.

He held me for a few breaths before saying, "Ready or not, my love, you do not have much of a choice if you want to save Marcianna's family. Gadreel will keep escalating to gain your attention."

His hands released me, and I stood on my own as he said, "Lilith, you're such a powerful creature. Embrace it. Come back to us."

Lilith was powerful, and we were running out of time. The only way to stand a chance against this direct threat was to shed this human body and take back the pieces of me I'd severed. I needed to become Lilith, the true, complete Lilith.

My eyes went to my sisters, then to my creations, all sitting tense, their brains likely calculating what these next steps meant for them.

Though the plan had been to do exactly this, it had been on my terms, on my sisters' terms. I resented our hand being forced now. The feeling of helplessness tasted bitter in my mouth.

Stop it. Put your big girl pants on and just do it, my brain squawked.

A few seconds ago, I was going to burn down the world to get to my family, sacrifice anything to save them. But when asked to do something inevitable, I dragged my feet, overly worried about myself and my feelings.

God, I was acting pathetic. No more hiding. No more fearing being Lilith . . . being me.

"Mina. Harlow. It's time. Are you ready?" I extended my hand to them.

"Can you ever really be ready for your life to end as you know it?" Mina asked. Her teeth clenched, but her eyes were determined, unwavering in their gaze as they met mine.

Harlow left her perch on the arm of a couch and put her hand into my outstretched one. "Let's do it fast before I chicken out."

"Where should we go?" I asked, looking around for suggestions. "I don't know what will happen. So, probably in the middle of a coffee shop is not the greatest idea. Everyone's already staring at us."

"This place is as good as any," James replied. "We just need to ensure some privacy." Nodding at Astrid, the two of them took off, walking around the shop, whispering in people's ears.

One by one, the patrons left until only the owner of the shop remained. He took off his apron, handing it to Astrid and thanking her for offering to watch his business while he attended to an urgent matter.

"We don't have long," Astrid said as the door closed behind the coffee shop owner. "He's going to get home, become confused as to the urgent matter, and then race back here. So, hurry up, ladies."

I nodded, my pulse a rapid thump in my head, and knelt on the ground. How do I go about doing this? Not only was I still scared of what it would feel like losing my mortal family and the human life I'd built, but now I was even more terrified of hurting Marci's soul, possibly leaving her children orphaned.

Placing my hand on my chest, I inhaled deeply and closed my eyes, focusing inward. Whispers drifted from deep within my being, *Please, I want to go home to my children, to my parents, to my friends. I want to mourn my husband with them.*

I could see her—Marcianna—the color of her soul, beautiful and vibrant. And she was so very scared.

At first it was difficult figuring out where she ended. But then I sensed my own essence, dissecting it away bit by bit from Marci's soul, until our energies separated.

I suddenly felt painfully alone, and terrifyingly vulnerable. I wanted to cling to her once more. But I could feel how tired her soul was, how heartbroken, and I knew I needed to go now. It was time to purge Marci of this parasite.

I'm sorry for all I've done to you, I said, forcing my way from her body.

As I left, I thought I heard her soft voice in the distance say, *I forgive you.*

Opening my eyes cautiously, I gasped. I was looking at myself, my face staring back at me. But it wasn't me. I was looking at Marcianna, the true Marcianna Caruso.

It was the most surreal experience.

My head was quiet for the first time in my life. It felt unnatural and I fought back the urge to dive back into the body that had protected me for forty years.

Marci looked stunned. She tried to stand up, but her legs gave out and she crumbled to the floor. "I think I'm going to be sick," she said and covered her mouth with her hand.

Tarquin swooped in, picking her up and heading toward the kitchen, likely to get her some sustenance and hydration.

Looking down at my hands, I was surprised I looked no different. "Who do I look like?" I asked.

"You look like Marci." I nodded to Harlow's response, oddly comforted I still looked like the mortal body I'd called home.

"Who wants to go next?" I asked.

Harlow and Mina looked at each other, and then Harlow stepped forward, kneeling down to face me. "I wanna get this over with."

Gripping her by the shoulders, I pushed tendrils of my energy into her body. I called my spirit forth, surprised how willingly it came, joining my light.

Harlow's body immediately collapsed as my essence left. Astrid picked her up, adjusting her weight in her arms and followed Tarquin into the kitchen.

"Ready?" I asked Mina, and she nodded, joining me on the floor.

Taking a deep breath, she grasped my hand in hers and gave me a wan smile. It was over quickly, with James escorting her to join the other humans.

I sat immobile, eyes closed, feeling my new corporeal form hum as power coursed through it. Within me, my spirit stitched itself together, the feeling uncomfortable yet soothing, the fates of past, present, and future finally reunited.

Samael lightly touched my cheek. "How do you feel?"

I thought for a few seconds. "I feel whole," I finally said, taking his hand as I stood up.

He pressed his lips to my forehead, and I wrapped my arms around his body, pulling him in tight, my spirit crying out with happiness. I did feel whole, completely, utterly whole. But that feeling wasn't just from my broken, shattered parts healing together, it was also the peace of knowing my son was alive and well, and that my mate, the creature I'd evaded in terror for thousands of years, never gave up on me.

My fractured heart opened to Samael completely, the love buried long ago, reawakened. And I embraced it.

After all he'd been put through, he still chose to be here by my side. In his eyes, I'd left him without a word of explanation after committing a horrible atrocity and hurting his friend, after taking a weapon that could kill the immortals he'd sworn to lead. On top of it all, I'd abandoned our precious child. All these things were unforgivable, yet he'd never given up on me, his belief in me never wavering despite evolving as to the reasons behind my madness.

My spirit soared, my thoughts positive, for once. In this moment, I believed that together with our son, and with Tarquin, Astrid, and James, we could win against anything. We could protect the precious destiny of humanity.

It was time to face Gadreel. I'd do everything in my power to save Marci's family and free humanity from his rabid desire to become their ruler.

CHAPTER TWENTY-FIVE

By the time we were ready to go, it was prime breakfast hour and people were jiggling the coffee shop's doorhandle, peering in through the window, their confusion evident.

James made a sign stating the shop will be open soon and taped it to the front door as we headed toward the back exit. The fact that we'd screwed with this business bothered my conscience, and I wished I had some money on hand to leave behind to offset their morning losses.

Unfortunately, our breakneck pace these last few weeks wasn't conducive to hanging onto a wallet, and I'd even lost my damn phone. For a moment, I had a human pang of sadness thinking of the lost pictures and videos, hoping they'd been backed up on the cloud somewhere.

But these were not my pictures, they were Marci's pictures, Marci's memories, and Marci's family. Despite separating from my human host, I could still feel her thoughts and feelings, as if threads of her essence had been woven into the makeup of who I was, who I am. How long would I have to remind myself that I'm Lilith, a distinct creature from Marcianna Caruso?

With a sigh, I looked down at my empty hands, tapping into the fate of the current reality, imagining I had a few hundred-dollar bills. It was so easy now, I didn't need to close my eyes, or focus intently, there was no need to visit the orb or talk with Razma. I only had to think it needed to be, and it was, the money materializing in my hand.

Dropping the cash next to the cash register, I noticed Samael watching me, his gaze a gentle caress on my face. "Why are you looking at me like that?"

"I can't believe you're here with me. I don't want to lose you again," he replied.

I nodded, ducking my head shyly, his words causing both pleasure and worry. Though part of me wanted to dive back into the life I had with him, I didn't fully remember how to live as Lilith, how to be a wife to him, or a mother to Sariel. But I wanted to try.

As if sensing my uncertainty, he took my hand in his. "Come, let's finish this chapter and then we'll worry about the future."

I followed him out the door into the blinding sunshine, where Astrid, James, and Tarquin stood arguing—at least one thing remained constant. Sariel stood to the side, observing the conversation with a raised eyebrow, his mouth lifting at the corners as if fighting his amusement.

"You need to stay," Astrid said, poking James in the chest. "Tarquin and I are older and stronger."

"What are you fighting about?" I asked.

"They're fighting about who should stay behind with the humans. They're all hellbent on joining you in the fight," Sariel summarized

"We could just drop off Harlow and Mina," Astrid offered.

"You can't just dump them off," Tarquin said. "You have to consider the world around them has changed, and people in their lives think they're missing. We need to take care and not rush their return."

"My poor parents," Harlow cried, her hands on her cheeks. "They must be going crazy with worry!"

"We'll fix it, Harlow. Don't worry," I reassured her.

Mina shrugged. "I doubt anyone cares I'm gone."

Watching Mina's somber expression as Harlow pulled her into a hug, I wondered how much of her life would change without having parts of my spirit within her body . . . how much all these humans' lives would change. Would their personalities shift, no longer influenced by me? Would this bring them new opportunities, possibly altering their life's path?

Now was not the time to dwell on these thoughts. I'd have the rest of my immortality to stew on them. We needed to take action.

Turning to Tarquin, I said, "I think you should be the one to stay with the women. Keep them away from the encounter with Gadreel."

"What, me? Why?" He crossed his arms as James

and Astrid looked at me with surprise. "I'm not leaving you."

"Out of my progeny, you're the oldest and the strongest, well suited to protecting these humans if the demons or Guardians were to come after them." His jaw tensed, indicating he didn't want to yield. "Please," I added. "Please, I need you to do this. If anything happens to us, you need to restore them to their rightful lives and keep them safe."

"Fine," he said between clenched teeth.

He took Marci and Mina by their elbows, guiding them away, calling for Harlow to follow. I watched them leave, their fear evident in their parting glances before turning the corner.

"They're worried we may not return . . . are you?" Astrid asked.

I shrugged, though my true feelings were likely plain to Astrid. Since becoming Lilith, I'd been riding high on my hope we'd be the victors, but talking through logistics brought back my doubts and fears.

Sariel put his arm around my shoulder, pulling me into his side. "You think I'd let anyone take away my mother after I've just found her? I'm not leaving you."

His words were both burn and salve. He must've gone through such turmoil after I'd left, and I wondered if Samael in all his grief gave him the affection he deserved. Wrapping my arms around Sariel, I hugged him close, promising myself I'd do everything in my power to never leave him again.

I wiped away an errant tear as I released him, doing my best to steel my emotions. With no human soul to hide behind, I had that odd moment again of feeling exposed and vulnerable.

"Okay, let's do this," I said after taking a second to compose myself. "I propose we flash to their house, with you all staying out of sight, while I go inside. We need to have the element of surprise on our side. I'll call to you, telepathically, when I need you."

They all nodded . . . except for Samael. His eyes darkened as if ready to fight me on this. But he didn't say a word, and I decided to ignore his disapproving, growly looks.

"Can I flash, or teleport, or whatever you call what you do? Now that I'm back in my true form?"

"You should be able to. Try visualizing yourself by the dumpster over there and see if you make it," Sariel said, giving me a smile of support.

Glancing at the dumpster, I imagined myself standing beside it. Darkness enveloped me and I propelled through light, a soft swooshing sound in my ears. Within seconds, I stood by the dumpster, the smell making me wrinkle my nose, and I was thankful I didn't end up in it. The travel had felt strange but not painful, and best of all no more of that nauseating tilting sensation.

Flashing next to Samael, I grinned at him, barely containing my giddiness at my success. He smiled back, his stern expression fading as he instructed, "Now try out your wings."

My wings. I shuddered, remembering the last time I'd used them—flying full speed, desperate to save my child.

Focusing hard on my back, my brow furrowed, I felt a slight tingling on my shoulder blades, and then a tug as a cascade of feathers released from my back.

My wings enveloped me as if giving an old friend a hug after a long time away, and then stretched out into the sunshine. Unlike Samael's black as night wings, mine were white, shimmering in the sunlight, rainbows dancing within the feathers.

"Woah," Astrid said, reaching out a hand to lightly caress my wings. "Beautiful."

"See, I was right when I said you were an angel." James grinned.

I laughed, remembering that conversation at Tarquin's house, and my reaction to it.

Extending my arms to Astrid and James, I took their hands in mine and squeezed. "Let's go."

We arrived outside Marci's parents' home in the heart of a South Carolinian shoreline town. The house was a lovely colonial with a picket white fence and children's toys dotting the front lawn.

I'd weaved Marci's parents' new reality from their retirement plans, pulling together their dream of living in an inviting community by the ocean, away from the snow shoveling that comes with living in New England.

This place suited them, though I wasn't sure how everyone else felt about their new realities. Farah and her family, Marci's brother and sister-in-law, her children—I hadn't taken their feelings into account when I moved them here. Did they like it, or did they feel out of place?

"Stay here," I said to my companions. "I'm going to go to check out the inside."

Samael's hand shot out, grabbing hold of my arm before I could take a step. His narrowed eyed stare clearly broadcasted his continued disagreement with my proposal.

I sighed. "If anything happens, I'll call for help and you can come to the rescue. Okay?"

He lingered a second more, holding my arm, his fingers grazing the sensitive part of my elbow. "It'll be okay," I said, pasting on my best reassuring smile as he released my arm.

I started up the walkway to the front door, focusing all my efforts on appearing to be human. I wasn't sure how long it would take for Gadreel to notice I was the full-fledged Lilith, no longer the version hampered by a weak, mortal body, but I needed to milk the appearance of weakness for as long as I could.

I knocked tentatively on the door. There was no response, except for Dexter barking in the distance. Searching out the doorbell, I found it obscured by a climbing vine, and pressed the button, hearing the chimes ring muffled on the other side of the door.

To my surprise, little Ella opened the door and squealed. "Mommy you're home!"

She flung her thin arms around my neck as I bent to catch her mid-jump. Holding her tight, I inhaled her familiar scent, burying my face into her soft hair as tears pooled in my eyes.

Get ahold of yourself, I chastised. *You're Lilith, not Marci. She's no longer your daughter, just a child like any other.*

"Where is everyone?" I asked, settling her on my hip.

Ella showered me with kisses, refusing to stop hugging me. "We have guests," she said, wrinkling her nose with distaste. "But I don't like them. Everyone's been sitting at the table for hours and I'm bored. They didn't even touch the food grandma put out." She squeezed my neck again, whispering against my cheek, "I missed you Mommy . . . is Daddy here?"

"No baby. It's just me," I managed to croak. Ella certainly laid me bare in these few minutes.

Holding her tight, I stepped into the house. It was eerie—there was no one to greet me, only a three-year-old opening the front door. Marci's mother would've never allowed this.

My stomach clenched as I rounded the hallway, following Ella's pointing, and entered a formal dining room.

"Well, hello there," Gadreel said, a slow grin spreading. He leaned back in his chair, his arms pillowing his head as his eyes drank me in.

I took in the bizarre scene, tightening my hold on Ella. My parents, Amelia, Alex, and Farah sat at the dining room table, untouched teas and cakes in front of them, blank stares on their faces.

The three other humans at the table were not familiar to me, but the demons inside them were;

Lamia's stare bore into me from within her host. I guess she decided a new human body had been in order after our last encounter.

I turned away from the demons, my disgust growing as I met the eyes of Gadreel.

"What do you want?" I asked, hoping my face conveyed the full level of hatred I had for this asshole sitting at Marci's mother's table.

I wanted him dead. And I wished I'd been clever enough to bring the immortal-killing knife with me. I could've easily gotten the job done while we were alone, no other Guardians around to interfere.

"I want what you stole from us Guardians . . . what you stole from me," he demanded. "Return it, and no one needs to get hurt."

"I stole nothing," I spat. "I only took back what was entrusted to *me* by the One Spirit. The sacred fates and destiny belong to the humans, not to us. And I'll protect it with my last breath from the likes of you."

He slammed his fist on the table and stood up. He towered over me, his stare icy as the demon-possessed bodies cackled around us. "It should belong to me. I protected it under Samael's orders, just as I protect these damn humans. I deserve the power and control over their destiny," he snarled. "And I can arrange for your last breath."

Ella whimpered in my ear. I needed to get this frightened child out of here. I couldn't risk her getting hurt.

Hugging Ella close, my brain furiously tried to figure out what to do.

Should I call for someone to take her to safety? It would expose the others, possibly putting all of us in jeopardy by eliminating the element of surprise.

Or do we fight now before the Guardians appear? While it's still just Gadreel and the demons?

I didn't know what to do; how best to proceed. Is this why Gadreel didn't put Ella in a trance? To torture me with indecision and throw me off guard?

Before I could make a decision, Ella slumped in my arms. "What did you do?" I cried out, looking at her vulnerable unconscious form. She looked so fragile.

"She's served her purpose and is annoying me now by clinging to you," he said. "Lamia, take the child away so I don't have to look at her anymore."

Lamia slithered over to us, her pale hands reaching out for Ella. I jerked back, not wanting the creature to touch Marci's child.

"Hand her over!" Gadreel barked, and I raised my chin in defiance.

He laughed in my face. "You think you can beat me? I can destroy this precious family of yours with one thought; I have their weak minds within the palm of my hand."

Shit! He was going to hurt them if I didn't comply. I reluctantly relinquished Ella to Lamia, rage and fear ripping at my chest.

The second my hands were empty, Gadreel slammed his energy into me, scrapping at my mind, but failing to gain entry. A fleeting look of surprise touched his features before the snarling lion returned.

"No longer hiding within that slowly rotting human body, I see."

"No, I'm not." Dammit, I'd hoped I'd be zapping his ass with my power before he'd caught on to my lack of human form.

Our eyes locked, and I noticed him hesitate. Maybe I intimidated him now?

He smiled, stepping back a few steps away from me. "We could've been magical together if you'd only listened to me. Our powers combined could've ruled this world. But now we'll never find out what could've been." Lifting his arms, he called out, "She's here!"

Flashes of light suddenly blinded me. Massive wings opened to reveal Guardians within their folds.

There were ten of them, including Gadreel. I recognized Jophiel's beautiful features immediately, anger and disgust permeating through every inch of her polished skin as she sized me up.

I needed to improve my odds here. My mind frantically called for help. Within seconds, Samael and Sariel materialized by my side.

Gadreel snarled at them, lunging forward, his face inches from us. "Choose your next steps wisely, Samael."

Samael's stare was lethal. He looked like he wanted Gadreel's head on a pike, and honestly, I wanted to do anything to make that happen.

"I should kill you for what you put her through, what you put me and my son through," Samael said, his voice like gravel.

"What does he mean by that?" asked a tall, brown-haired Guardian, his grey eyes looking from Samael to Gadreel.

I recognized him. He'd been in the Vermont house when I was held captive. As Lilith, I knew him—Ramiel, Samael's second in command.

"It's nonsense. That shameless creature," Gadreel said, pointing accusingly at me. "She tried to kill me all those years ago as I protected the humans from her wrath, and now she has Samael convinced I was at fault for her insanity and thievery."

"And he'd be right," Sariel replied. "Or did you forget I was there when you reminded my mother of how the humans killed her precious son? You were manipulating her to give you the sacred fates and destiny."

"Is this true, Gadreel?" Ramiel raised a quizzical eyebrow.

"Of course not. I've only ever done what's best for the Guardians. Unlike our so-called leader, who brought this creature into our midst, causing strife and destruction." Gadreel was practically frothing at the mouth, his rage growing with each word spoken.

Some of the Guardians nodded. Jophiel's neck looked about to snap with her emphatic agreement. Others, however, stood uncertain, looking between Samael and Gadreel.

"That's a lie!" I cried out, not able to stomach Gadreel's accusation anymore. "You're the one that caused division, while manipulating me with the sole intent of gaining control of the gift bestowed upon me by the One Spirit."

Ramiel frowned. "It seems the quarrel is between Lilith and Gadreel." He steepled his fingers, bringing them to his chin. "Gadreel was wounded by a blade an immortal should never have had. And he claims he's defending humanity from a creature not fit to be in possession of the sacred fates and of destiny—a creature that uses her power to harm."

"Lilith has done nothing wrong!" Samael yelled, his eyes on fire as he glared at the Guardians surrounding us. He was acting as if he wanted to tear everyone in this room apart with his bare hands.

Sariel caught his father's gaze, and I noticed him shake his head slightly, sending a warning to tread lightly.

"Hear me out till the end, Samael. You show your bias by speaking out of turn," Ramiel chastised, his frown deepening. He turned to the other Guardians, stretching his hands out to them as he asked, "Shall I continue?"

They nodded their approval, and Ramiel smiled, making me think he relished his role in this moment.

"If I'm understanding the situation, Lilith believes she was tricked by Gadreel and her past wrongs are not her fault. She claims she's not done anything evil with the fates but is protecting the destiny for humankind." He turned to face me, pinning me with his stare. "Have I stated your position correctly, Lilith?" he asked.

I nodded tersely in reply.

Giving me a dramatic sympathetic look, he added, "I, for one, have not seen anything in the history of humanity to indicate Lilith is abusing her power or is a danger to humanity or us. But Gadreel has kept a closer eye on her over the years than any other Guardian. He has always proven to be trustworthy, so why would we doubt his word now?"

He turned his back to me, facing his enthralled audience as they waited to hear his solution to the dilemma of loyal Guardian versus random-harpy-Samael-brought-home-one-day. "Therefore, the only way to solve this dispute before it causes an even greater schism within the Guardians is for Gadreel to take what he thinks is owed to him. If he succeeds, then the fates have chosen him as their protector, and that is that. But if he fails, we shall hear no more words on this matter and allow Lilith absolution, leaving her to live in peace."

CHAPTER TWENTY-SIX

The stunned silence was shattered by Samael's roar, "That's not going to happen! I won't allow it."

Ramiel turned to look at him. "The fight is between them, Samael, not us. We only need to know the sacred fates and destiny are protected."

"A fight with her is a fight with me," Samael spat back, his hands clenched, looking like he was ready to commit murder. "Gadreel has lied about everything — the knife, what happened at the sacred tree. And he's never kept a close eye on Lilith . . . so he'd be unable to say how she's used her power. This is the closest he's ever come to her. He only twists the truth and fear-mongers."

"Is that so?" Ramiel's brows snapped together. "How would you know such a thing, Samael? When you've claimed no knowledge of Lilith's whereabouts."

Samael and Ramiel glared at each other, reminding me of two alphas on the verge of battling for the pack. A quick glance at Gadreel's smug expression confirmed my suspicion—this did not look good for Samael.

I stepped in between them, my hands on Samael's chest, my eyes begging he heed my words. "It'll be okay. I can do this."

But he shook his head, his gaze desperate. Taking a step back, he pulled me behind his large frame, shielding me from the eyes of Gadreel and Ramiel. "There doesn't need to be a fight," he continued to argue. "She was tricked by Gadreel, and if we allow this, we're showing that manipulation and traitorous actions are to be rewarded. I'll handle Gadreel. Leave Lilith out of this."

"That's your word," Jophiel said, her beautiful face twisted in righteous anger. "We always knew you'd lost all sense and reason when you found that creature in the woods." She pointed accusingly at me.

Ramiel nodded. "She's right. Though we follow you, your leadership is not a dictatorship. Gadreel's views are as valid as your own."

They didn't know me, much less trust me. Gadreel's manipulations had resulted in my isolation from the Guardians. Even when we'd lived together, we were mired in distrust—Gadreel's whispers to Samael, to me, and likely to the other Guardians resulted in Samael distrusting the Guardians when it came to my well-being and the Guardians distrusting me.

It all led to this one moment when Gadreel could justify taking everything away from me. By his earlier words, it seemed his preference might've been to have both me and my power as his own, but now he'd settle for just my power.

There was no hope of using words to reverse thousands of years' worth of lies and distortions in this one moment. I had to fight.

I can do this. Believe in me. I pushed the thought to Samael, hoping our connection was as strong as the day I left him. Samael swallowed hard and glanced over his shoulder at me before scanning the room. Some of the Guardians returned his gaze with open hostility, while others looked nervous, their eyes shifting about the room.

"She is my mate. I can't allow this," he repeated. "I should have done a better job protecting her from Gadreel all those years ago."

My heart dropped into my stomach, and I saw Sariel briefly close his eyes knowing his father's response would not be taken well.

"I'm sorry to hear that, my friend; I truly am." And to his credit, Ramiel did look remorseful as he patted Samael's shoulder. "But you leave me no choice —I'm stripping you of your leadership as you've shown you'll always put Lilith above our interests, above the greater good."

He signaled to three severe looking Guardians, and before anyone could react, they took hold of Samael and Sariel. The Guardians emitted bands of light from their palms that combined together like a rope, quickly coiling around father and son, binding them tightly.

Samael and Sariel fought to get free, their energies

pushing against the band of light. But the more they struggled, the tighter the ropes became. I watched helplessly as my mate's and my son's power drained, their energies fading as they grunted in pain and anger.

"Stop fighting," Ramiel said. "It'll only hurt more if you continue to struggle. It is necessary to neutralize your powers so the battle for the fates and destiny can proceed without any interventions from spectators. When it's over, you'll be released."

My breath came out in shallow bursts as I met Samael's agonized gaze. He'd destroy himself trying to protect me. But we were out of options. I was going to fight, and I had to win.

The French doors in the back of the room burst open, and my heart lurched as James and Astrid barreled through. Ramiel shot out a burst of light from his extended hand, hurling my friends back outside.

"Secure the house, we don't need any more of Lilith's abominations interfering where they don't belong," he proclaimed before inclining his head to Gadreel and me. "You may begin," he said, as if we were about to do a dance or some other performance.

I turned to face Gadreel, uncertain how I should proceed. He prowled toward me, his blond mane framing his face, his features twisted with gruesome happiness. He likely assumed I was unsure in my new form and weak—the perfect prey.

With a roar he charged me, and I instinctively

jumped out of the way. Losing his balance, he swayed before regaining his footing.

The rage on his face should've been terrifying, but it gave me confidence. I'd caught him off guard and wounded his pride.

I was not prey; I was as much of a predator as him. And I had as good of a chance to win. But it wasn't going to be by fighting like an animal for a blood-thirsty audience. I needed to use my power.

Energy shot out from my palms like a whip, slicing at Gadreel's skin. He screamed. He returned the favor, his power pummeling my head as he tried to force its way into my mind. The pain almost dropped me to my knees, but I resisted.

He was far more powerful than I'd given him credit for, but his power lay in his brute strength and ability to control minds. Besides altering fate, which I hesitated to do in fear he'd somehow snatch my gift away from me and win, what else did I have in my arsenal? I could only remember snippets of my talents before I went into hiding—it involved making flowers bloom and trees grow, bringing beauty and life into the natural world; not exactly something to help me in this fight.

But I did know how to flash.

Disappearing from in front of Gadreel, I popped out behind him, shooting him in the back with my power. Before he could react, I appeared in front of him, tossing a ball of energy in his face. I was surprised how quickly I could flash from one place to another.

He tried shooting his power at me, but his movements were lumbering compared to my dizzying speed. Maybe I could tire him out, but then what? This was a losing proposition for me—he could win by stealing my gifts, but what could I possibly do to him?

Zipping this way and that, I noticed Astrid and James struggling with the French doors, trying to get into the house. But that moment of distraction cost me when Gadreel's arm shot out, punching me hard in the stomach, the impact careening me head over heels onto the ground. He jumped on top of me, punching me in the face and then grabbing my head, forcing his way into my mind once more.

I tried to fight, but the way he creeped into my thoughts disoriented me. I screamed, tearing at his face with my fingernails. He slammed my head into the floor as retribution.

I needed to fight on the same level as Gadreel. He'd made a comment in my cell that we were so much alike. Did I too have the gift of controlling even the most powerful minds?

Somewhere deep inside, the knowledge my gifts rivaled that of the Guardian collective bloomed. These creatures had good reason to fear me, to desire what I had, and it went beyond my care for the fates and destiny. I had to accept all of my power as part of me and call these gifts forth.

I pushed hard against Gadreel's intrusion into my mind, shoving him back into his own head. Following him into his own thoughts, I pulsed my power within him. I imagined setting his mind on fire, burning down that putrid, evil brain that would stop at nothing, hurt anyone and everyone, to get what he wanted.

His screams rang in my ears, and he leapt off me. But he wasn't done, his foot kicking me over and over in the ribs. I held on with everything I had, pushing into his mind, imagining daggers ripping through his head; ravaging his brain until he cried for mercy was my best chance of winning.

"Get out of my head, you bitch!" he shrieked, his kicks subsiding as his hands clawed at his scalp as if they could reach inside his mind and free himself of my presence.

He fell on all fours, breathing hard. Bringing his hands to his chest, he pulled a knife out and lurched at me.

The knife pierced my shoulder, sliding in through muscle and pinning me to the floorboards. Burning pain engulfed my shoulder, and I shrieked—it was a familiar pain, one I'd felt on my side. That monster had another blade like the one I'd impaled myself on, the one that had almost killed me. Where the hell did it come from? Did he have it on him this whole time or did he just will it into existence?

Putting his foot on my chest, Gadreel took hold of the weapon, ripping the blade out of my shoulder.

Samael's roar echoed my cries as he twisted within the ropes of light. The tendrils constricted around him, choking him, until he fell to his knees, my name on his lips. I weakly crawled to him, wanting to be near him in my last moments, but I didn't get far, my body suddenly weak and limp.

Laying there, my energy seeping out around me, I glanced around the room, noting the horrified expressions on the faces of the Guardians—even Jophiel looked momentarily concerned before a mask of indifference fell over her perfect features.

No one stepped in as Gadreel slowly stalked toward me, relishing his victory, his weapon in hand, ready to strike the final blow. They'd condemned me for my actions, yet now not one Guardian said a word as a blade no immortal should possess spilled my blood.

My mind raced, tripping over possibilities of how I could still save the sacred fates from Gadreel's clutches even after he took my life. Gadreel's claim on the fates and destiny were paltry at best, which he likely recognized since he'd originally tried to win me along with my gifts.

Sariel's screams, demanding to be released, begging to be allowed to save me, sparked a hope within me. My son was connected with the fates, and maybe they'd choose him once I was gone—not Gadreel. And then he could somehow rescue Katie from destiny's grip.

Praying for it to be so, I called out to Tarquin as my power flowed from my body, hoping he'd be able to fix the messes I'd made with the humans—imploring him to make sure Marcianna, Armina, and Harlow would be able to live out their lives with their families.

Fight. Keep fighting. Tarquin's voice commanded in my head. His words were soon joined by those of Astrid and James.

Their voices gave me strength.

You must live. Fight! I've only just found you, and I can't lose my mother again.

My child, my Sariel . . . he needed me. I couldn't give up.

I wanted to live, I needed to live.

My spirit reached out, connecting to these creatures I loved, accepting all their strength and power that they freely gave me.

Lilith, look at me. Samael's voice pierced my mind, and I turned my head in his direction. He sat calm and relaxed, the bindings loosened now that he did not resist them. No one noticed him, all eyes were on me and Gadreel.

One of Samael's hands was free enough to draw something forth from his belt, and he placed it on the ground. I recognized the gleam of the knife I'd taken from Gadreel, the one I'd thought killed my child.

Still restricted in his movements, Samael shoved the blade with his heel toward my outstretched hand. I grabbed the knife and thrust it upwards just as Gadreel's weapon descended upon me.

My arm deflected his blow, earning a gash from the blade. But my knife drove into his flesh, deep into his heart.

I watched, entranced as his eyes opened wide, his mouth a perfect circle of surprise. He fell to his knees beside me, and our gazes held until he rolled onto his back, staring into space, his energy pouring out every which way.

He rasped out a word I couldn't make out, his

breath gurgling in his throat. And then he was silent, his limbs momentarily stiffening, before releasing.

Light escaped from his chest and eyes, shooting into the ether and fading from view. His corporeal form disintegrated, then floated away like dust.

His demise had been so quick that no one reacted. A shocked stillness blanketed the room.

Jophiel's anguished scream suddenly cut through the silence, and she lunged at me, other Guardians holding her back. "How did you get that knife? It is forbidden for an immortal to possess it!"

Samael's bonds released and he crawled to me, pulling me into his arms. He glared at the Guardians before replying to Jophiel, "Somehow you care about the knife that killed Gadreel but not the one that wounded Lilith? We got the damn thing from Gadreel. He was never true, hiding behind deceit. Do you see that now?"

Ramiel cleared his throat. "All is well then. It seems the correct immortal has won." Turning to me, he added, "My lady Lilith, we'd be pleased to have you as part of the Guardians once more."

"Are you kidding me?" I rasped.

Samael held me tight to his body, his hand pressing into my shoulder injury as he wove his healing magic into the wound. "You heard her . . . she means fuck off."

"As you wish. Though you're making a mistake you'll come to regret, I promise you," he replied and flashed from the room. The other Guardians followed, some looking at us with anger or disapproval, while others bowed to Samael, remorse lingering on their features as they flashed away.

Sariel wrapped his arms around me and his father, resting his head on the top of mine. "You were amazing, Mother."

"She was," Samael said. "Gadreel looked very surprised when you blasted through his defenses and wormed your way into his mind."

"I thought he knew I had this ability. When I was held in the dungeon, he told me we were alike. But is this ability even unique? I heard both you and Sariel in my thoughts." My voice was thin, sweat beading on my forehead. The healing of this damned wound was almost worse than the making of it.

"No. I think Gadreel knew you had the ability to resist his power when not made vulnerable by a mortal mind, but I don't suspect he realized you had all of his abilities." Samael frowned at my wound, his healing power doubling in output as he continued, "Communicating the way we do is something different, though. It doesn't happen by force. It only occurs when there's implicit trust between the individuals, and the channel is willingly open."

Samael paused again, this time motioning to Sariel to add his hand to my shoulder. My son's power entwined with his father's as they flowed into my wound. I could feel the healing accelerating.

"Gadreel likely thought he was the only one with the talent of controlling minds. And to be honest, I've seen you exhibit many powers the other Guardians possess, which is partly why I'd kept you away from them. I was worried what they'd think once they real-ized the extent of your gifts. However, I'd never seen you use your talent for mind manipulation until you ran away and tried to use it on me when I pursued you. Thankfully, you were too rushed and failed to wipe the memory of you from my mind." He gently touched my cheek with his free hand before adding, "You passed this gift on in a certain capacity to your progeny, and the longer they've lived, the stronger they've become in wielding it."

As if on cue, James and Astrid rammed the door down and raced to my side.

James clucked over the damage done to my new body, holding my chin and turning my face to see the result of Gadreel's fists.

Astrid though seemed satisfied with my healing progress. "You'll live," she stated. "And you're looking better by the minute. So, what are we going to do with those demons over there?" She inclined her head toward Lamia and the two other creatures standing silently in the corner of the room, as if hoping their stillness would somehow make them invisible, allowing them to slip out.

Before we could address them however, a scream pierced the room and we all looked into the hysterical eyes of Marci's mother.

CHAPTER TWENTY-SEVEN

It took some time cajoling, and a good dose of mind trickery, but we managed to calm Marci's family down. They'd woken from their trance in various states of grogginess and confusion. It didn't help that I looked like the spitting image of their mother, daughter, and friend.

While I worked my magic, the demons sat contrite, Samael raging at them. "I should destroy you all, especially you, Lamia. Creeping around, doing the bidding of Gadreel."

"You knew we were tasked with finding her." She said, lowering her eyes immediately, the creature within making itself as small as possible.

"And I instructed you to do a poor job of it. Yet lately, you've been overachieving. Did he promise you something so thrilling, so glorious you'd risk your existence to defy me?"

"No, but we needed to be convincing or else our intentions would be discovered." Lamia pouted, her eyes shifting in my direction, "And she destroyed my family."

Samael's murderous look could've wilted flowers. "As if you even cared for them. Only your pride was damaged; there wasn't a passing thought of mourning for your companions. You should know better than to lie to me. I'm aware of every poisonous thought of yours." The demons cowered from Samael, his voice causing them to quake. "If I learn of your deceit again, I will not be so kind as to forgive. My gift from the One Spirit is to care for you; my kindness is to allow you to be as vile as you need to be, and together we change humanity for the better. Stray from me again and I will end you."

Despite my thinking that these creatures were abhorrent, I blanched at the interaction, watching as they meekly professed their devotion to Samael and slithered out of the house.

Tarquin arrived within minutes of their departure. After checking that all my limbs were intact, he wrapped me up in a rib-breaking hug. "I thought we'd lost you," he choked out.

"I'm hardier than most thought, I guess." I smiled, returning his hug.

Marci cautiously entered the house, her face a myriad of emotions. "Tarquin was worried," she said when our eyes met, her voice weak. "We're so happy you're okay . . . I'm happy you're okay."

"Thank you." I replied, humbled by her words after all I'd put her through. "Your family's in the living room. They've been through a lot and Astrid's tending to their needs."

She nodded, tears pooling in her eyes as she took off to the living room. Shouts of "Mommy" echoed throughout the house.

I sank into a plush sofa as I experienced their joy. My spirit sang with happiness for them, but my heart ached at the thought of leaving the life I'd lived with Marci. That lingering regret faded quickly as memories resurfaced to remind me of other lives lived like this one, and the many humans left with grief and loss because of their relationship with me.

"Should we leave them here?" Tarquin asked. He stood over me, his voice pulling me from my dark thoughts.

I shook my head. "They never belonged here. They belong with Cece's family, with their real friends, in their real home."

He nodded. "If that's what you think is best, then let's do it."

Samael sat next to me. He hadn't let me out of his sight since the departure of the Guardians, and every now and again, he'd touch me as if assuring himself I was safe and by his side.

He caught me staring at him, and a tender smile brightened his eyes. "We should get going," he said, taking my hand in his. "Get everyone resettled and collect destiny. It's not wise to linger."

Tarquin grunted his agreement, never looking directly at Samael or me. His discomfort with our relationship was palpable, and he left briskly to collect Marci and her family.

As we waited for everyone to join us in the living room, Samael examined my shoulder for the umpteenth time, his forehead creased with displeasure.

I smoothed his lines of concern with my fingertips. "I'm much better. Don't worry."

Before I could protest, he stood up from our seat on the sofa and scooped me into his arms, crushing me to his chest. "I can't help but worry. I died a thousand deaths watching you fight with Gadreel . . . seeing him hurt you, and not being able to help you." He drew in a ragged breath, squeezing me tighter. "I wish I could bring him back, just to kill him again."

"I think it's best we keep him dead," I replied dryly. "Now put me down. I'm capable of walking."

My attempt at humor drew a chuckle from him. "You were brilliant. As much as I wanted to protect you, you don't need me to. You're powerful, strong, and brave. I was wrong to doubt you."

"Well, in your defense, it was a bit touch and go. I could barely remember what my Lilith body was capable of." Instead of soothing him with my words, he tensed, his hand clenching against my flesh.

I leaned away gently from his chest and grazed my knuckles against his cheek. "Remember, we're not looking back. We're writing a new ending."

We held each other's gaze for a few beats, and then he gently lowered me to the ground so I could stand on my own two feet. Taking my hand in his, he lifted it to his lips and kissed it tenderly. "To new endings."

Tarquin and I stood outside Marci's house, having already delivered Harlow and Mina to their homes, their realities woven with new memories, no knowledge of demons or Guardians . . . or me.

Astrid, James, and Sariel had left the house after saying their goodbyes to the Caruso family. They now sat in the car waiting for us, their laughter drifting over the night breeze.

"Will you bring Ray home to her?" Tarquin asked, his eyes glistening in the moonlight as he watched Marci through the window.

She was cuddled up on the couch, surrounded by her kids, reading stories. I'd made Ray's death only a memory, dulling the pain, but not fading it completely. Ray deserved to be mourned and remembered.

I linked my arm through Tarquin's, leaning my head on his shoulder. "I don't have such power. To force a soul back into their abandoned body is not a magic I possess."

"What about changing the past?"

"I believe I could change the fate of the past, but it would ripple across all the fates causing unimaginable consequences." I shuddered. A new fear unlocked in my mind, coupled with a determination that no one would ever use the power of the fates in such a malicious way. Not on my watch.

He nodded, and it looked like the weight of the world fell on his shoulders once again. Watching him out of the corner of my eye, my guilt picked at my conscience. Tarquin sacrificed everything for me and what he thought was my calling. He'd deserved so much more than his current lot in this world.

Forcing the words past my lips, I said, "I think it's best you leave me."

He looked at me, horrified, his mouth opening to argue, but I lifted my hand, silencing him. "Please let me finish. You've been my constant for over two thousand years, devoting your immortality to me, an immortality I forced upon you. When you told me you'd spent your years watching our child's descendants, so close, yet always at a distance, it broke my heart."

Clasping my hands to steady my nerves, I forced myself to continue, even though I didn't want to. "You were an amazing father, and it was taken from you. You deserve to find love, to have a family, to be liberated from this constant sameness. I didn't give you a choice then, but I am now. I can free you, Tarquin. Free you from immortality so you can live your life . . . so you can appreciate that sunset once again."

A tear slipped down my cheek, the idea of being without Tarquin terrifying to me. But I had to do this, give him this choice, or else I'd never forgive myself.

"I can't leave," he said firmly. "You saved me after I'd hurt so many people with that demon inside me. You gave me redemption, and a purpose."

I nodded, exhaling slowly, feeling relief for myself and sadness for Tarquin. "You don't have to decide now. But know, the offer is there." Taking him by the hand, I gently pulled him away from the house and to the car.

Out of the corner of my eye, I saw him look back at the cozy scene of Marci and her children.

I went to Katie's house alone the next night. Standing at her bedside, I watched as she slept peacefully, a teddy bear tucked under her arm. Slowly I unraveled destiny from her soul, feeling it caress the fates within me.

Touching her cheek goodbye, I weaved happy dreams for her of her family, erasing her nightmares.

"Be happy, little one," I whispered as I kissed the top of her head, extending my wings and flying into the night.

Free. I was finally free. Free of the lies. Free to be myself. With the wind whipping at my hair, my spirits lifted to the calls of the night creatures.

The moon watched me soar through the sky as the stars twinkled their approval. Admiring their sparkle, I wondered if Marci would still gaze at the night sky, enjoying the calmness of the moon, or if that was something I'd forced upon her.

I couldn't help but hope my influence in her life was not all bad. Maybe she too learned something from me as I'd learned from her—as I'd learned from all the human souls that hid me over countless years. Together we'd lived in a strange harmony, with me passively experiencing life through them; learning from their mistakes, growing in empathy and wisdom as we aged, and only taking the reins of life to guide us toward the various iterations of Kynan, or when it was time for my awakening.

Destiny fluttered around within me before settling in, its tendrils pulling the fates closer in its embrace. The whispers and images started the moment it completely entwined itself around the fates. By breaking destiny away from one soul, the possibilities became truly endless. It was no longer a binary choice of destroying Katie's family to ensure thousands didn't die.

My wings faltered in shock. There were so many lives, so many futures possible, and yet I'd been blindly forcing one. These choices were never mine to make. I was here to guide—not to be a puppeteer. And yet I had mistakenly become one in my zeal to protect humanity.

My feet touched down near the fountain at Tarquin's beautiful estate where he first informed me of my creature status, and I dragged myself up the steps of the imposing pale yellow mansion. My mind grew wearier with each scene of the future. They all warred with each other for relevance, hurting my head.

Stumbling into my room, I flopped onto the bed and stared up at the ceiling, trying to ignore the noise within me. I missed Marci's soul's incessant chatter; it was far better than the constant whispers of the fates as they searched for a suitable destiny. With each decision made in this world, something changed, the hushed tones starting again.

I'd have to remember how to tune all this out. It was enough to drive anyone mad.

A light rap on the door cut through the internal chaos. "Come in," I called out, and Samael stepped into the room. With each purposeful stride of his long legs, memories of our time together flooded back, no longer faded or fragmented, but tangible and so very strong.

Our eyes met, and liquid desire coursed through me, catching me off guard. The confusing longing of my spirit for this creature when buried deep within Marci's body was nothing compared to this insanity.

I wanted him . . . needed him . . . and yet I was unsure how to have him.

Sitting down next to me on the bed, he took my hand in his. "You look weary."

"I am," I whispered. But my weariness faded away as my eyes drank in his dark, wild beauty.

He was mine. The realization excited me . . . and scared me.

Inhaling deeply to calm my nerves, I hesitantly pulled him toward me until he lay by my side. He drew me into the crook of his arm, and I rested my head on his chest, listening to the drumming of his heart, each breath bringing with it his enticing scent.

"You don't have to do this on your own. I'm here for you. Always by your side." He stroked my hair as he spoke, his words vibrating in my ear.

Lifting myself onto my elbow, I looked down at

him, my gaze caressing his face, memorizing each line. My fingers strayed to his brow, lightly tracing it before gliding to his cheek. "We have so many memories together and yet have been apart so long that I don't know how to behave with you."

"Just be. There's no rush. We have all of immortality," he said, lifting his head, his lips brushing mine.

A sigh escaped me, and I kissed him back, my mouth moving slowly, nibbling, until he gripped my hair and deepened the kiss. We moved with more urgency, our need making us animalistic, shredding clothes in our haste.

Mouths and hands explored muscles and curves as memories and reality crashed together. We were making up for all the lost years, all the deceit and misunderstanding, all the pain we'd been through.

I cried out as he entered me, tears of joy trailing down my cheeks, and I clung to him, matching his rhythm. My power burst from within me, wrapping itself around him, entwining his essence into mine as we found our release, the fire of our powers finally burning as one flame again.

We watched the tree grow, the branches extending to the sky as the leaves shimmered in the sunlight. I'd bound the fates and destiny within its core, my power combining with that of Samael and Sariel to create a strong protective magic embedded in its bark. This was the new tree of the sacred fates and destiny. Just as before, it held the record of the past, the present, and the future, sheltering the destiny of humanity, and keeping it safe for generations to come.

Astrid and James stood a slight distance away, their faces somber. They'd been surprised when this morning Tarquin announced his decision to leave us. He'd wrestled with my proposal all night, finally making his choice to be human once more, as the sun rose.

We'd held each other tight and cried, all the while voicing our love for him, our belief that this was the best decision for him. He'd finally be able to live . . . to truly live, unfettered by the immortal world or the machinations of fates and destiny. He'd live within the embrace of humanity.

Changing his fate, I made sure he'd have access to all the money he'd accumulated over the years, wanting to make sure this lifetime would be one of his best. I removed as much of my essence as possible to make him mortal, leaving behind enough to keep his body alive. When he returns to the One Spirit after this life, he'll have no need for my power holding his damaged soul together. He'll be made whole once more, and then I'll free his soul from the traces of my essence, as Samael did for Ray's soul.

Pain rippled through my progeny as we watched recognition fade from Tarquin's eyes. He thanked us for coming to his house, his eyes polite, no longer seeing us as his family.

I lingered on the doorstep, hesitant to leave the

man who'd been my constant protector and guide for so many years.

"Thank you for hosting us," I said, doing my best to keep my voice airy. "I have a friend, Marcianna Caruso, who lives nearby. She and her family suffered a terrible loss recently. If you wouldn't mind checking in on her from time to time for me, it would ease my worry."

"Of course. A friend of yours is a friend of mine," he said, smiling, and waved to me as I walked down the steps, my heart hopeful he and Marci could heal each other.

As we left, I'd offered James and Astrid the same proposition. But they flatly refused, James looking insulted as he tucked me under his arm. "As if you could ever force me away. I'm too addicted to living forever, and occasionally kicking some evil thing's ass. And I do love being the sidekick to a lovely angel." He grinned, and I rolled my eyes, secretly pleased.

Astrid snorted. "Neither of us were any good at being human, and we didn't fit in our societies. But we're good at helping you protect them. I'm fairly certain our destinies were fulfilled when you saved us from death and gave us this purpose."

Their words replayed in my mind, and I smiled, hugging this memory close to my heart, thankful they chose to stay with me.

Turning away from the tree, I caught Samael's gaze. A smile settled on my lips as the sun's rays danced over his black hair, which he'd neatly pulled back.

I remembered his face on the night he'd stumbled upon me in the woods, the moonlight bathing my body. His hair had been wildly free then, the darkness surrounding him, making him look dangerously fascinating—deliciously so. Bewilderment and awe had shone through his eyes, like the night itself seeing daylight for the first time. That same look was there now. And I could sympathize; I felt the same way about him.

"It's better this way," I said, pointing to the tree as if convincing him but really trying to assure myself. "This way I can protect the fates and destiny, help if needed, but I don't need to control it. Humanity can choose the paths forward."

I smiled up at him. "Thank you for being here, for doing this with me."

"I've always been with you. And I always will be." Samael said, drawing me in and kissing my forehead.

I couldn't help but feel uneasy as I thought of how his situation had changed. "I'm sorry I brought such chaos into your world. I hope my actions didn't cause you to lose your Guardian family completely. Some did look like they may still be on your side."

Samael pulled me closer. "You are my family. My son's my family." His smile was sweetly lopsided as looked into my eyes. He glanced at Astrid and James, standing at a respectful distance, their arms crossed, and added, "And I guess those two immortal humans you created are now my family too."

"They'll grow on you, I promise," I laughed.

We walked together toward the car, trailed by

Astrid and James. Sariel was already inside, tuning the radio until loud rock music blared out the windows. I bobbed my head to the song, appreciating his taste in music.

As we got into the car, I wondered where we should go next, what should we do?

Part of me hoped in time I'd mend the rift within the Guardians, not for myself, but for my mate and for our son. But when I mentioned it to them, they'd shrugged, the idea not really as compelling to them as it was to me. They didn't seem bothered about being on the outs, and seemed more at peace, liberated from the constraints of being Guardians.

I decided to stop worrying and planning. What mattered most was that we'd found each other.

So, for now, we'd just be, as Samael had said. And that sounded absolutely glorious.

Before You Go!

Reviews are so important for authors, especially for indie authors. If you enjoyed this book, please leave a review!

ABOUT THE AUTHOR

Isabelle Markus is a writer of contemporary fantasy seasoned with romance and a dash of ancient lore. When not weaving stories or being a maven of science at her day job, Isabelle can be found drinking copious amounts of tea and shuttling her family around so they, too, can fulfill their dreams. To learn more about the author and her upcoming books, please visit www.isabellemarkusauthor.com